TH[illegible]M

PART ONE

BY CALVIN ELSTON

ISBN 978-1-7390821-0-9 (Paperback)
ISBN 978-1-7390821-1-6 (E-book)

Editing, cover art, and book design by PaperTrue Ltd.

Printed in United Kingdom

Published by PaperTrue Ltd.
PaperTrue, Unit 27, Old Gloucester Street, London WC1N 3AF
https://www.papertrue.com/

‘For Jessica’

‘Two possibilities exist: either we are alone in the Universe, or we are not. Both are equally terrifying.’

– **Arthur C. Clarke**

Contents

Author Profile

Calvin Elston has chosen for his writing debut a subject that is quite close to his heart—the unexplored and unknown wonders of outer space.

An electrical engineer, born in South Wales and now based in Bristol, who has also been a soldier, Calvin drew inspiration for *The Beam* from his fascination with Sci-Fi and the works of Stephen King. His struggles with depression and dyslexia fuelled his desire and ambition to become a writer

This highly engaging story about an unprecedented and inexplicable phenomenon, originating in outer space and a futuristic-technology-powered mission to outer space reflects Calvin's personal belief that anything is possible, and nothing is unachievable.

Chapter 1

Light in the dark

April 4, 2068

He stood in an empty corridor, facing a contemporary artwork by the artist Diane La Fontaine and finding himself entranced by its beauty and intricate brushstrokes. Distracted by the increasing noise of conversations coming from the room to his right, his mind began to wander: How many times had he invited the leaders of the world to one of these summits? Would this one be any different from the last? They were all set in their own political positions, unwilling to lose ground if any new policies, heaven forbid, affect their personal agendas. How could he get them to all play ball this time?

'They are ready, Mr President,' announced a chiselled-faced man wearing a fitted black suit, with a little extra space inside his jacket for his gun holster.

Then, the agent communicated through his throat implant, activated by holding his right-hand thumb and index finger firmly together: 'The eagle is on the move.'

It was clear and direct, despite his strong southern accent. The other agents confirmed his proclamation through the communication channel.

As the senior agent opened the stylishly carved heavy-set door, the president glanced at the painting one last time, turned and placed a firm hand on the agent's shoulder, saying, 'Thank you, Steve.'

Then, with a resigned breath, he walked in.

The hall, constructed to resemble an enormous oval with curving walls, was as loud as it was grand. Gentle pillars of light painted the centre of the chamber with a brilliant glow, illuminating a large mural of a blue planet, the earth. Surrounding the insignia was a crest of golden leaves with interlacing olive branches, signifying unity and inclusion.

The four-tiered hall had individual stations displaying the respective flags of different nations, hung at specific intervals from their neighbours. All of them were angled precisely towards a raised staging area, with a backdrop of a large holographic projection platform where the representatives could clearly see who was addressing them.

'Good afternoon, Mr President. This way, please.' With a radiant smile, a petite lady gestured in the direction of his table.

'Thank you, ma'am,' he said, tilting his head graciously, the New Jersey accent thick and strong.

The president shook the usher's hand, then walked towards his designated area. The directions were not entirely necessary, as he already knew where he was going to sit. After all, he and his team had spent quite a significant amount of time preparing for this occasion. Still, he didn't have the heart to cut off the helpful and friendly lady.

As he walked past several leaders, they stood up from their chairs to greet him. He was met with genuinely welcoming handshakes and smiles mostly. Some, however, would fall just short of Oscar-winning performances, given the way they gazed at him with hate and utter contempt. Yet, this did not sway his resolve. He confidently kept moving forward, occasionally stopping to greet and shake hands.

Eventually, he reached his table, but before he even had a chance to sit down, a man with a strong British accent approached him.

'Hello, Mr President. How are you this evening?'

'Ah, Dav...'

The president stopped and quickly composed himself, realising that he had been about to stray from formalities. Instead, he replied with a slight smile, 'Ah, Prime Minister. I'm feeling great this evening. Thanks for asking. '

David Lane, prime minister of the United Kingdom, realised the faux pas and quickly put the president at ease. 'It's quite loud in here. I can hardly hear myself think.'

'Well, it's a good thing we have advisors then,' the president retorted humorously. 'They can do all the thinking for us.'

Bobbing his head and laughing under his breath, the prime minister responded, 'Very good, Mr President.'

Just as they were about to engage in further conversation, a loud but harmonic ding boomed from the hall's speakers, politely reminding everyone to take their seats. Reacting to this untimely but expected interruption, the two old friends shook hands and took their designated seats at the table.

The summit was long as the usual, predictable issues were discussed – proposals to reduce the ever-growing conflicts in the Middle East, logistical suggestions for refugee relief aid and establishment of new trade routes for struggling nations. Usual disagreements also flared when matters such as new foreign policies arose. A creeping feeling of time repeating itself grew in the president's mind. It must have started to show, as the Russian President spared him a look of concern, or maybe disgust? It was difficult to decipher what Viktor Mikhailov was thinking, as his facial expressions looked as if someone had carved them out of rough-edged stone.

Time passed slowly, with delegates from all around the world selfishly making grand speeches about how their needs were greater than others, typically coated with sincerity and humility to disguise their underlying wants and needs.

The pillars of light had vanished from the centre of the chamber, replaced by the fluorescent glow of the lamps spread all along the walls of the hall. The staff, who were shifting uncomfortably, were scattered to the sides of the room, patiently waiting for any requests or requirements. However, the Secret Service looked fresh and ready to move, as if they had just begun their shift.

A clear and articulated female voice was broadcasted over the speakers. 'Ladies and gentlemen, the next address will be from the president of the United States of America, John Murry.'

Following the announcement, the president moved towards the stage.

Upon reaching the podium, he adjusted his posture with his head raised and shoulders back, adopting a neutral but hardened face, ready to address the leaders of the world. The holographic projection took less than a second to focus, then the speaker could be seen clearly in high definition by everyone at the venue.

'Ladies and gentlemen, heads of states, and my friends. We are all gathered here to make a difference with our fleeting time on earth. Our predecessors made decisions that changed the course of humanity forever. Decisions that brought us here, to this very moment. Through war and sacrifice, humanity still moves forward with determination, creativity and a limitless potential for discovery. Yet, with all the advancements in healthcare, the sciences, engineering sectors and education, we still find ourselves divided.

'Without the ability to adapt to new situations, humanity would not have been able to survive. Just as important as change is the ability to look back and learn from the mistakes of the past.

'My friends, I truly believe that the time of change is now. We need to start communicating with open minds. To share our resources with neighbouring nations when they are in need. We must share our technology and educate the young to give them the tools to expand their minds and create new ideas. Our future depends on us to unite and move from the dark, into the light—'

Suddenly, the president flinched as a blinding column of bright blue light pierced through the high windows and fell into the centre of the chamber. An uncomfortable silence filled the room as people realised that this was not part of the summit. Startled and confused, everyone appeared to have the same thought at that moment: what was happening?

For a fleeting moment, an atmosphere of frozen wonder and terror hung in the hall. Everyone watched as the light blue glow radiated over the mural of the world, in the centre in the room. Around the room, heads started to dart back and forth in desperation, trying to figure out if this was a prank, a protest trick or even a possible attack. No one moved for a while until the whispers grew louder in volume and then changed into shouts as security teams started flooding into the hall.

'Mr President,' the senior Secret Service agent called, moving quickly towards the president.

Startled as if he were being shaken from a daydream, the president whipped his head around, breaking eye contact with the light, to face Steve squarely.

'Attack?' he asked, covering the microphone with his hand. Then, seeing the urgency and the perplexed expression on Steve's face, he gathered that, that was not the case.

'Ah... well, no, sir.'

'Steve, what is it?' the president demanded, as his concern grew.

'Sir, we need to get you to a safe location first. You'll... you'll be able to see for yourself on the way there.'

Palms sweating, the president turned to see that most of the leaders were also being led out of the hall.

The Russian President looked furious as he spoke to his security detail. His hands were palms up, apparent that he was getting no more answers than anyone else. Feeling that he was under surveillance, the Russian President glanced towards the stage, worryingly wearing an expression of empathy. This made President Murry even more perplexed at the situation. What the hell was going on?

'Ok, Steve, I'm ready,' the president said after a quick exhale. Then, he moved at the pace of his agents through the large doors he had entered several hours ago. They sped down the loud and crowded corridor, passing the Diane La Fontaine painting on the wall, on his right, and flying past the woman who had previously directed him to his seat. She looked oblivious to who was occupying the same corridor space as her. She held a trembling cell phone out in front of her face with one hand, covering her mouth with the other. Tears were streaming down her blotchy red and horrified face; she looked terrified.

The president regretfully kept moving with his Secret Service, passing small groups huddled close together in front of televisions. The displays were all obstructed by shoulders pressed tightly together, with some people wrapping their arms around others in consolation.

Some seemed traumatised by what they saw, such that they began losing the energy to even stand, resulting in several collapsed people scattered along the sides of the corridor. It was as if they had undergone a life-changing devastation, and they simply could not cope. The last time President Murry had seen anything like this was when he had gone to help in a PTSD ward down in Texas.

Just before the president reached the door to exit the building, Steve held his hand up, giving the order to stop.

'Ok, Mr President. We are just about there, but I'm going to need you to do exactly as I say,' said Steve uncomfortably but firmly. 'As soon as we leave the building, I'm going to need you to keep moving towards the vehicle. I know that sounds a bit strange, but... but if the intel I'm being fed is not horse shit, then you'll wanna look up. But you can't. Whatever you do, don't look up!'

Steve had never shown such disregard for procedure, nor had he ever lost his composure, until that night.

Placing his hands on his hips in an informal yet commanding stance, the president announced his displeasure. 'Ok, Steve, but I've got to tell you. I'm starting to lose my cool.'

'Just, trust me, sir.' Steve was on the edge of unravelling himself. He lowered his head and, in all sincerity, said, 'Please?'

Still frustrated and increasingly curious, the president had no idea what the hell was happening out there. He resigned himself to the directions of not only one of his best guys, but also a man who he considered a close friend. 'I trust you, Steve, okay? I'm ready when you are.'

Steve gave the signal, and they started to move again. When they were close to the exit, the president could see the same blue glow coming from the windows, just as he had seen in the centre of the summit hall. The agents stacked up by the door, a drill they had rehearsed thousands of times before. Then, Steve gave the president a brief compassionate look, followed by a strong meaningful nod to the others.

The metal double doors flew open, hitting the walls with a thud on the outside of the building. The first two agents moved outside and began scanning the area. A few seconds later, at the all-clear signal, the rest of the party began moving.

As the president darted through the emergency access doors, his conception of the world, and the universe at large, was grounded in facts and scientific evidence, all of which changed completely within five seconds of leaving the building.

John Murry fancied himself as a strong and rational man, someone who could get the job done. A man who could find an answer to any problem, no matter how difficult the situation. However, nothing in all his years in office could have possibly prepared him for this.

His plan was to follow Steve's exact orders, and he did, for all of five seconds. Keeping his head down, the president could see everything from well-maintained lawns to buildings and even vehicles, all coated in this strange blue light, coming from... and that was when he looked up.

His fast stride turned into a stroll, until his legs suddenly weakened, and he felt like he was dragging weights. He stopped motionless, a few feet away from his armoured limousine, his head tilted, ignoring the painful strain in his neck. His gaze was frozen.

Gazing up, he expected to see the usual clusters of stars, possibly the moon or the occasional pulse of light from a satellite. Instead, the vast canvas of space was now occupied by a huge ray of blue light, so large and prominent that it lit up most of the night sky. Skyscrapers and smaller buildings suddenly looked eerie against the blue background.

While he stood there, trying to comprehend what he was seeing, or at least come to terms with it, a single tear ran down his face. Steve stood to the right of the president. His lips were moving, but the words were somehow lost in this surreal moment. It was only when he grabbed the president by the upper arm, bringing him face to face and staring gravely at him, that the words started to gain volume.

'Mr President!!!' Steve bellowed, as the sound flooded back into John Murry's ears. 'Mr President!! We gotta keep moving!!'

Brought back from the edge of a complete informational overload, the president of the United States of America stood bewildered and horrified. Then, wiping his eyes, he looked at his old friend and quietly mouthed, 'God help us.'

Chapter 2

Truth

The world was stunned. The entirety of planet earth was encapsulated in a permanent state of light. The sun provided the warm comforting radiance throughout the day, then the chilling blue dawn would rise, covering the land at night. Religious groups were thrown into a frenzy, seeking refuge in their places of worship and believing that this was a foreshadowing of an apocalyptic prophecy.

Tensions reached a boiling point across the globe with sceptical leaders pointing fingers at their rivals, insinuating that the beam was some sort of a weapon. Tactical military positioning increased around religious landmarks and historical sites, in response to growing civil unrest. China and Russia declared martial law, effectively closing all borders to repel mass migration.

As a sign of unity, an agreement was reached by all nations to send their best and most remarkable minds in the fields of physics, astrology and even theoretical physics. They exhausted every available resource to try to establish whether the laws of the universe applied to this light source. Information from the scientists was eventually passed up the chain to the various governments, who claimed that the beam was a natural occurrence and that there was no need for concern; however, the collected data was still being processed.

A year had passed since the first appearance of the beam. All the while, there was massive public outcry, demanding transparency. Thus, a global committee was assembled for a live broadcast to publicly release the findings. The event was held at the Grand Hotel Heiligendamm, on the Mecklenburg Baltic coast of Germany. With its tall and narrow architecture, the main pearl white building stood strong and proud against the backdrop of the glistening Baltic Sea. Horizontal shadows cast by the midday sun gave the windows somewhat of an ominous and overbearing character.

Inside the busy press hall of the elegant building, journalists were deep in conversation, swapping stories and theories, speculating on what the scientists would reveal. Among them was Dillon Chambers, a successful news reporter from the BBC, squeezing past the others and moving towards his seat. He was renowned for his no-nonsense approach in his dealings with officials. Dillon was also one of the few people chosen to be part of the question panel at the event.

Why must they insist on squeezing us all into such small rooms, he thought. He set his small tan leather briefcase down and took a seat directly opposite the committee table. Trying in vain to get comfortable, he tried edging his chair closer to his desk, cringing when he heard the feet of his chair squeal against the floor, signalling that he had scuffed and tore the expensive carpet underneath.

'Perfect!' He angrily sighed to himself, shaking his head. 'Just... perfect.'

With another heavy sigh, he leaned to the side to inspect the damage, creaking the arm of his chair in the process. Seeing the damaged spot at the base of the leg, he couldn't help but remember the last conversation he had had with his wife the previous morning.

He had been standing in front of a large mirror, in the second-floor bedroom of his small Manchester home, trying on an outfit that he was possibly going to wear for the live press broadcast.

'I don't know what you're looking at, but if I can't see my trouser button, then I'm definitely overweight.'

Sandra Chambers was sitting at her small white desk, glancing over the questions that her husband had noted for the press conference, as usual. Sandra was a petite woman, her pale skin contrasting against her jet-black hair, which was tied into a high set bun. She turned in her seat, pushing her rouge-rimmed glasses above the bridge of her button nose.

'Well, I think you look lovely,' she said with a well-educated look, inspecting him with a slight smile at the corner of her mouth. 'Like a young Trevor McDonald!'

Readjusting herself, she marked one of the prompt cards with a pencil, brushing a strand of hair that had escaped her bun behind her ear.

Dillon knew she was lying, of course. After all, they had been married for over a decade, and they both had this way of always complimenting each other, regardless of their actual appearance.

'Thanks, love,' he returned sarcastically, raising an eyebrow. 'Well, at least, when I burst a couple of buttons on TV, the world will say, "Oooh, did you see that guy's stomach fall out all over the desk? But it's ok. His wife said he looked lovely."'

Her head sprang up as if it were a coiled spring, and she turned around to give him a look that only a wife could; the type of look that a lioness would give, if you were to reach for her food.

'Sarcasm is the lowest form of humour, Dillon, did you know that?'

At that moment, he couldn't help but imagine his future if he continued on his current path. A gravestone sprung to mind, inscribed with the words 'Here lies Dillon Chambers, rude husband to his wife'. So, he decided to withdraw and submit to the stronger foe.

'Sorry, love!' He backtracked, holding his arms open, earnestly. 'I'm just a bit nervous.'

I am also the size of a beached whale, Dillon thought, but stopped himself from opening up that line of discussion again.

'I'm done,' Sandra declared, moving the conversation forward. She tapped the cards on the desk, gathering them together, but stopped, placing her index finger down on one of the cards.

'They're good. I had to tweak only one a little bit, but... the question on card three?' she asked, apprehensively, 'How reliable is the source?'

He turned and let go of his belt, which was desperately holding on to the last notch in the leather, and placed his hands on his hips. He noticed that she seemed slightly apprehensive.

'Top brass,' he claimed, straight to the point but in an upbeat manner, hoping to alleviate the tension building in her. However, this attempt was short lived when doubts of authenticity started working their way to his own mind.

Suddenly, his tone changed. 'I'm still deciding if I should use it or not. Hell, I'm not even sure how on earth I'm going to approach it,' he admitted in a frustrated undertone.

Sandra placed the cards down on her lap and took a breath before looking up at her conflicted husband. She sat back against the chair for a moment, weighing the risk of revealing the information he had against the potential backlash and mistrust this bombshell would bring.

'Let's just hope it doesn't come to that,' she said, standing up and brushing the creases out of her skirt.

She carefully set down the cards on the desk and walked over to him, placing her hands on his wide chest, and gave him a warm reassuring smile.

'I love you,' she said softly, calmingly. Then she gently kissed him on his lips.

'You ain't gonna find answers down there,' a voice said with a slight Southern drawl.

Dillon was instantly shaken out of his stupor and snapped back to the richly decorated interior of the Grand Hotel Heiligendamm. He abruptly sat upright in his seat and looked in the direction of the voice. Chad Bradshaw stood tall and handsome, with his hand resting on the seat beside Dillon's, his CNN lanyard dangling against his lavishly expensive suit. The man wore an obnoxious smile, displaying his perfect white teeth, akin to a Cheshire Cat.

'Well, well,' Dillon said, reluctantly donning a polite smile. 'I thought you were still on the outskirts of Russia.'

'Not anymore,' Chad replied, taking a seat while making sure his American flag on his suit pocket was in the correct orientation. 'Got pulled from the peace negotiations to cover this job.'

‘What a shame,’ Dillon mumbled to himself.

‘What?’ asked Chad, sorting his table-top and composing himself in his seat.

Thinking on his feet and gesturing around the room by twirling his finger, Dillon quickly replied, ‘I said, what a shame about the noise.’

Looking around at the various reporters, camera operators and technicians, Chad pursed his lips as a sign of indifference.

‘Yeah,’ he began, raising his voice in a mocking tone and emphasising his accent, ‘it’s like a damn Saloon in here, just without the bourbon and prostitutes.’ Laughing at his own joke, he slapped Dillon on the shoulder.

You would be the first to get strung up in the wild west, Dillon thought.

Luckily, he was spared the compulsion to respond to Chad’s statement, when the selected members of the science community began filtering into the front of the room. Dillon always felt unnerved when the room went silent, only to be filled with a rapid succession of camera shutters and flashing lights.

Dr Harold Schwimmer sat down at the centre of the panel for the world press conference. The Swedish forty-seven-year-old looked dishevelled. His stressed and weathered face gave him the appearance of a man in his mid-sixties. The enormous responsibility of leading the collective team researching the beam had taken its toll. That also meant that Dr Schwimmer was the face of the team and bore the scrutiny of 'the court of public opinion'.

He organised his paperwork, which he had brought to the table, while waiting for the other members of his team to settle in. With a glance over his shoulder, he leaned back and gave a nod, indicating to an assistant patiently waiting in the wing that he was ready. He began by tapping his microphone and angling the neck up in the direction of his mouth.

'Good afternoon and welcome to everyone here today, and to the good people watching around the world. We, and the scientific community, are working around the clock to ascertain as much information related to the energy source as possible. I would also like to take this opportunity to thank my colleagues and the world leaders for their quick response during this historical time. Be under no illusion! This energy source is unprecedented, breaking every known law of science. Hence, ascertaining any data has proven difficult. So, we ask for your patience during these confusing times. And remember, this energy source is the most significant occurrence in earth's history. The floor is now open to questions, starting with... Chad Bradshaw, CNN.'

'Thank you, Doctor Schwimmer,' Chad said, leaning closer to his microphone. 'Doctor Schwimmer, what effects has the beam had on our planet's ecosystems? Is It true that the beam has increased the growth rate of certain plant life in areas of the world? We have had several reports sent to our research teams at CNN that show evidence of uncontrollable growth, threatening the foundations of urban infrastructures.'

Leaning closer to the microphone, with a look like a hunter going in for the kill, Chad continued.

'And finally, Dr Schwimmer, is there a direct link between the beam and the increased suicide rates, medically diagnosed as the new "blue depression"?'

Leaning back in his chair, Chad looked confident and satisfied with the questions he had presented, turning his head to give Dillon a brief but egotistical wink.

Smug bastard, Dillon thought, he does this every time.

'Thank you, Mr Bradshaw,' Dr Schwimmer responded. 'As for the first question, our ongoing studies surrounding the effects the energy source has had on the ecosystem have proven thus far that it has had no direct effect on creatures of the planet.' Taking a sip of water, he continued, 'It has also been proven, yet not fully understood, that most animals that normally respond to visual stimuli are unable to detect the presence of the energy source at all.'

Murmurs throughout the room started to grow.

'Regarding your second question, our current investigations have found substantial evidence to corroborate your researchers' findings. Specifically, the ones focussing on enhanced growth in plant life, due to the light from the energy source. You will usually find in most cases that plants and vegetation with increased exposure to light over a prolonged length of time tend to react negatively. In previous test conditions, the research yielded predictable results: the plants eventually die because of lack of moisture.'

Selecting one of the sheets of papers in front of him, referring to the notes he had made prior to the event, Dr Schwimmer proceeded.

'However, there have been several confirmed reports that plants and vegetation have been reacting, shall we say... uncharacteristically. Thriving in all environments in an incredibly positive way, with continued exposure to the light source. Unexpectedly, some of the most significant cases are being seen in the harshest areas of the world. For instance, there has been one case in Iceland, where roots were able to push through dense layers of ice, creating small fields covered in sunflowers. You must understand that sunflowers are not local to this specific area. Not only is this unprecedented behaviour for that region, but the speed of growth is also a question that we are still working towards answering.'

Turning his head towards the phytology scientist sitting at the end of the panel table, Dr Schwimmer received an agreeable nod.

All around the room, journalists were taking notes and whispering to their colleagues. Some were fiddling with earpieces, specifically designed to translate the event into the language of their native tongue.

'And finally, Mr Bradshaw,' Dr Schwimmer began, raising his eyebrow with an irrelevant pitch to his voice, 'we are here today to focus on the science data, gathered by the world's scientific community. The mental condition of the human psyche is not something we can comment on at this time.'

Furious with the last answer, Chad began: 'Dr Schwimmer, surely you must recognise that the—'

'Thank you for your questions, Mr Bradshaw,' Dr Schwimmer interrupted him, voice raised, stifling Chad to the point of a meltdown.

Dillon was just as shocked by the response as Chad. Why did he shut down Chad so quickly? Dillon thought about Chad. He is an obnoxious dick, no questioning that, but at least give him the dignity of a respectful answer.

'Next, we have a Dillon Chambers from the BBC News,' Dr Schwimmer said confidently, taking a final sip from his water, then looking over to his assistant and shaking his glass for a refill.

Dillon took a second to look over his questions. Cards one and two were informative but nothing ground-breaking, nothing that had not already been leaked or discovered independently.

'Mr Chambers?' Dr Schwimmer prompted impatiently.

For a fleeting moment, the room went quiet in anticipation for the next question, even the camera flashes became more staggered. Dillon collected himself. He was about to speak when he turned to card three and was stunned. Above the question was a small doodle of a beam of light, ending with a heart. Inside the heart, eloquently written with a pencil, was just one word: 'Truth'.

'Mr Chambers,' insisted Dr Schwimmer, his assistant filling his glass with water. 'If you don't have any questions then...'

'Actually...' Dillon began, smiling to himself. He briefly looked at Chad, who had a bewildered expression on his face, which turned quickly into one of curiosity when Dillon returned the wink that he had previously given him.

'Actually, yes, Dr Schwimmer. I do have a question.'

Confident and spurred on by the disrespect the good doctor had shown, he went for it.

'Dr Schwimmer, would you consider yourself and your board of expert advisors as truthful and honourable representatives?'

Taken aback by the question, the board turned to each other, frantically whispering and trying to decipher the question. The bobble-heads eventually stopped moving and turned in the direction of Dr Schwimmer.

'I am sorry, Mr Chambers, would you mind asking your question again?'

'Sure. Let me rephrase. Doctor, do you consider yourself a good and honest man?' asked Dillon.

'What sort of question is that?' Dr Schwimmer asked incredulously.

'Isn't it true that several weeks ago, a probe was sent directly into the beam and the data recovered was shared around the world by you and your respectful team?'

The scientists shuffled in their seats, one slightly loosening his tie, followed closely by another taking a substantial gulp of water. Most of them avoided eye contact.

Come on, bite you son of a bitch, Dillon thought, ready to spring the trap and resisting every urge to just blurt it all out.

With a shaky voice and sweat running down his face, the doctor leaned closer to the microphone. 'The results were... released to all nations ahead of this press conference to... well... as a sign of unity.'

Dr Schwimmer proceeded to tie the noose around his neck by shuffling through his paperwork with haste. 'Ladies and gentlemen, I believe we can leave it here for today...'

Dillon felt a sense of disappointment when he listened to the doctor's attempt to close the conference. As much as he disliked Dr Schwimmer's deception, he genuinely thought that this was a perfect opportunity to get him to admit the truth...

'Guess I'll have to help you unburden yourself then,' Dillon told himself and then decided to push through. 'Excuse me...' Dillon said to no avail.

He tried again, this time, his voice commanding the room, causing everyone to quieten down.

'Excuse me, Doctor. What would be your response, as well as your esteemed colleagues', about the fact that the probe did not collect any useful data at all? Furthermore, what would be your personal response to the fact that all the detailed information shared with the world, since the beginning, has been nothing more than pure fabricated lies?'

Every single eye in the room was now fixed on Dr Schwimmer. A needle could drop in the room and sound like a hammer on an anvil. Even the camera operators leaned out slightly, awaiting the response. Chad Bradshaw, whose eyes were now so wide that you could barely see his eyelids, turned to Dillon and mouthed the words, 'What the hell?'

'We.... ah... I mean, I.... ah...' Dr Schwimmer stuttered, desperately looking around the room for a lifeline. In a final attempt to gain any semblance of control, he grabbed a hold of the microphone and said hesitantly, 'No comment.'

Following that, the room erupted with question after question from the press. They hounded Doctor

Schwimmer for more information. All he could do from that point on was repeat that he had no comment. With no success, the press pushed harder, no longer waiting their turn. The room was now a rowdy crowd of angry people, all demanding an explanation.

Reading the room and with the help of security, Doctor Schwimmer and the scientific team began to retreat, backing out from their entrance. As they exited, bright flashes from the photographers lit up the room like a violent lightning storm.

Whilst everyone else in the room was on their feet, yelling out accusations, Dillon sat quietly with a bittersweet taste in his mouth. He had a strong feeling in the pit of his stomach that the aftermath would be devastating. Chad placed his hand on Dillon's shoulder and leaned in close to be coherent in a loud room. 'Cat's outta the bag now, my friend.' He continued to pat him on the shoulder, before turning to leave.

Dillon sat there whilst the technicians packed away their gear, unintentionally frozen to the spot. All the other reporters had left the room, phones glued to their ears, trying to get the scoop out first. By now, the news would have already spread globally. He mostly thought about the tedious emails that he would inevitably have to trawl through or the inevitable meetings with board members of the BBC, praising him for cracking the story wide open. Just thinking about it made him nauseous.

Picking up the card that would undoubtedly cause more chaos in the world, he once again was drawn to his wife's doodle. Reaching into his leather briefcase, he pulled out his phone, ignoring the bombardment of messages and emails, and dialled the last number he had called.

'Hey, baby,' his wife answered after two rings. He welcomed the sound of her voice. It sounded calm, soothing and thoughtful.

'Hi, love,' he exhaled. 'Well, I went with card number three.'

At the moment he finished his last word, two buttons on his shirt flew off across the room, one landing in front of the table just opposite him and one hitting the back of a technician.

'Sorry!' Dillan apologised, raising his hand at the man, who looked quite displeased.

'What was that?' Mrs Chambers asked.

Looking down at his stomach, Dillon noticed that his dark belly button was on display. 'Oh! That would be my shirt buttons popping off. One almost killed a bloke.'

Giving into the situation, he began to smile. 'I told you I am becoming overweight.'

Chapter 3

Momentum

Daylight was fading over the city of Boston, Massachusetts. A blanket of shadow was creeping up the walls of the Boston Public library, emphasising the city's tall colonial architecture in all its glory. Yachts moored in the dock of Back Bay were creating parallel silhouettes, bobbing up and down. Just as the sun was dwindling to the last of itself in the west, the rise of the ominous blue light began from the east.

Meanwhile, roughly four miles west of Boston, stood the world-renowned University of Harvard's John A Paulson School of Engineering and Applied Sciences, where Professor Andrew J Thomas sat deep in thought, holding a steaming white porcelain cup of tea. Placed centre stage and in the front row of his lecture room, he had an optimised view of the blackboard before him. With the class empty of students, the room was the perfect type of quiet for the professor's thought process.

It had been three years since he was given the most sought-after position of tenure, which had proven to be quite controversial at the time. It had been highly unusual as very few professors get the privilege of tenure, much less at the tender age of twenty-seven.

Andrew was known throughout the university as a somewhat unorthodox tutor. Often, he would encourage his students to approach a problem from radical angles that were generally frowned upon. This alternative method of problem solving was also one of Andrew's biggest character flaws. In fact, one such case had occurred just over a year ago.

A student had claimed to have come up with a method to store a vast amount of energy within readily accessible lithium batteries, using a new technique that essentially extended the life of the energy contained with the battery indefinitely.

This can't be right, can it? Andrew had pondered the proposal while looking over it.

'And you've done the math?' he had asked, sceptically.

'Yes, sir, and verified by several witnesses shown right there,' the student had replied, pointing at the multiple signatures at the bottom of the page.

Holding the paper in one hand, he stroked his chin with the other. Andrew raised his head to meet the tall young man's apprehensive gaze, raised his eyebrows and smiled. 'Well, Jamie, you never cease to amaze me.'

Jamie Sidis was the most gifted and promising student Andrew had ever had the privilege of teaching. Jamie was very tall at 6'10, weighing 230 pounds and built more like a professional athlete rather than a science student. He was incredibly quiet and always sat at the back of the class, because if he sat any closer, no one would be able to see past him; it was like trying to watch a movie while sitting behind a skyscraper.

Jamie intrigued the professor. He absorbed everything the professor taught them and passed every test with zero mistakes. He could also speak several languages from French and Spanish to Russian and Chinese. He always carried with him a plethora of textbooks, varying from biology and sociology to the endless depths of applied physics. Sometimes, the kid's intelligence made the professors feel like their own knowledge was somewhat lacking.

'So?' Jamie asked, impatiently.

Andrew could see how important this was to Jamie, as the kid was nervously tapping his thumb and forefinger together, down at his side.

'Sorry, Jamie,' Andrew replied with a well-rehearsed poker face. 'Unfortunately, the timing is bad, and I'm afraid I can't recommend this to the board.'

Jamie lowered his head, causing streaks of his unkempt fair hair to drop onto his forehead. Then, Professor Thomas burst into laughter.

'I'm busting your balls, kid,' he boomed, tapping Jamie on the shoulder. 'Of course, I'll put this forward. It's an awesome idea.'

Relieved as someone finding out they didn't have cancer, Jamie relaxed and exhaled. 'Jesus Christ, Professor.'

'Hey, I'm from Boston. What can I say?' Andrew chuckled. 'Look, leave this with me, and I'll get back to you.'

Agreeing with a smile, he threw his tan bag strap over his shoulder and turned to leave.

'Hey?' the professor suddenly yelled, stopping Jamie in his tracks and making him look back.

'You did well, kid,' he said, giving Jamie a thumbs up and a wink.

Jamie smirked confidently, holding his head high as he continued to leave the room.

Andrew knew that this would be a historical and momentous technological advancement and, if proven successful, would warrant a definite nomination for a Nobel Prize. Thus, putting his reputation on the line for Jamie, the professor was granted funding for the project.

A short time later, a fully equipped development facility was constructed on campus. As the hype surrounding the project spread, excited shareholders donated over half a million dollars for expenses.

When it came to the initial stages of Jamie's revolutionary idea, everything was on track and going to plan. Results were analysed and interpreted, and the first energy readings proved very promising. The concept seemed to be fundamentally sound. Morale was high within the group with frequent interactions through high fives and the occasional fist pumps. However, by the mid-stages, some of the tests started to show a few worrying results that did not match the projections laid out by Jamie.

'Jamie?' Andrew called him over one day, concern growing in his voice. 'Are you sure you got the math right?'

Jamie, who was arched over a workbench, soldering cables to a small circuit board, didn't even raise his head to look at the professor.

'Yep, you saw the signatures, right? So, back off.'

Andrew stood there with a look of confusion. Jamie had never been that blunt with him before, but considering the amount of pressure that everyone was under, the professor let it go. Plus, Jamie was right; his mathematical equations had been verified by three others. Then, why did something feel wrong?

The aim of the final stage was to test the largest containment for energy. The building of a storage unit was purposed to be used as a makeshift capacitor. Being roughly the size of a pickup truck, it was huge. Cylindrical in shape, the huge capacitor stood in the centre of the test area, encaged with a metal support structure firmly bolted into the floor. Various cables, some of diameters about the size of an Olympic medal, were trailing out from the base and travelled up the side of the walls.

Confident and hopeful in the trust he had placed in his student, the professor gave the nod for the test to begin.

'Go ahead,' said the professor, smiling and full of pride. 'You've earned this.'

Jamie stood by the main control panel, nervously tapping his thumb and forefinger again. He looked even more dishevelled than usual, with a clammy complexion, and was visibly sweating.

'Jamie?' Andrew asked again, concerned that the pressure was getting too much for Jamie.

The assistants in the control room began to look back and forth between Jamie and the professor, feeling a sense of uncertainty.

'Look, Jamie, if you don't want to proceed, then we can go to Vegas for the weekend and spend the rest of the money?'

'No!' Jamie interrupted, ignoring Andrew's attempt to alleviate the uncomfortable atmosphere. He then turned, uncharacteristically glaring at the professor, hair forking over his eyes, and giving him a sinister look. 'Always the comedian,' he spat, then spun around and powered up the machine.

The mechanical hum of the transformers suddenly changed into a pulsating buzz. The control board with multiple dials and indicators were all lit up by green LEDs. Jamie stood there, hands behind his back and wearing a presumptuous smile. In front of him, the assistants had stopped typing commands into their computers and were waiting eagerly. The specially designed equipment, which had cost the department hundreds of thousands of dollars, powered up and allowed current to flow into the capacitor.

3.05 seconds.

That was all it took for complete and utter disaster to ensue. The storage cells rapidly filled to full capacity and catastrophically ruptured. Then the equipment, which was also in place as a precautionary safety feature, completely failed and could not isolate the growth of power. The capacitor exploded with such ferocity that it punched a hole through the side of the testing facility's wall, covering the cars in the parking lot with harmful dust and debris. Car alarms created a symphony of destruction, set off by projectile bricks smashing into the sides of the vehicles.

Few windows on the side of the building were left unscathed by the sheer force of the incident. Shattered glass spread everywhere and covered the road. Even the roof, which had a solid and sturdy support structure, was left devastated, resembling a contorted dirty hand. The professor stood in the control booth, ears ringing with random distorted sounds. He slowly lowered his hands, which he had raised to instinctively cover his face. He was dazed and bewildered by the destruction, which was just a couple of feet away, as he stood behind the reinforced glass. Beside him were the assistants, all with the same horrified expressions.

Trying to regain some control of the situation, he quickly began to look around to make sure everyone was ok, and to his relief, everyone was shaken but unharmed. He thanked the Lord that the university had insisted on the use of reinforced glass, which he later discovered was the kind used in missile silos. The blast had not penetrated the window, but it was extremely loud as it had rattled everything in the control booth, akin to the aftermath of an earthquake.

However, Andrew was suddenly repulsed by what he saw. His most promising student, whose research would have been a huge step forward in the realm of power storage, was cowering behind a female member of the team. Jamie must have grabbed her and positioned her in front him, directly in the path of the blast. Jamie remained there for a while, squatting behind the terrified girl, grabbing her by the hips with his vice-like hands.

At this, the only question repeatedly going through the professor's mind was, what the fuck had just happened?

Many weeks later, after the dust had settled and the inquest was complete, the evidence gathered by the forensic teams was condemning, to say the least.

Andrew remembered sitting in an office, feeling like a child in the principal's office, as the long and extensive list of projected costs were read out to him in thorough detail: the structural damages to building and the test facility amounted to over three-quarters of a million dollars. Damages to vehicles, the road and sidewalks cost near one hundred thousand dollars. Alongside them, there were lawsuits from pedestrians injured outside the building. One claimant was awarded over one-and-a-half million dollars in damages for an amputated leg, severed due to a propelled metal object that hit her whilst she was walking her now-deceased dog.

The professor was surprised they didn't ask for their parking tickets to be paid too, he regretfully remembered thinking to himself.

Costs aside, the forensic team with the support of forensic scientists, also dove into the specifics of the project. The team were meticulously thorough and managed to collect all the contributing evidence that could be factored into what had caused the catastrophe. As the project leader, the professor was investigated regarding all the decisions he had made, leading up to the accident. He found himself, time and time again, against the ropes, defending himself and his actions. The investigation into Professor Andrew J Thomas was finally dropped when the investigators discovered that he had followed every step in the process correctly. Worrying results arose only when the focus was diverted towards the student, Jamie Sidis.

The professor was later told that following the explosion, Jamie had fled the facility, returned to his accommodation to collect a few things and vanished. Considering his size and the fact that CCTV cameras were everywhere in the facility, it was impressive as it was disturbing.

The more the forensic team dug into the student, the quicker the truth unfolded. Discrepancies were found in nearly every aspect of the student's workings; his equations and testing records, along with his witness statements, were all revealed to be nothing but forgeries. Furthermore, his quest for knowledge had led him down some dark and disturbing paths: links to extremist organisations and evidence of weapons construction were found hidden in his apartment.

By the end of the investigation, the professor was deemed not guilty of any wrongful decisions made throughout the project, but his ability to place trust in people and his reputation were forever tainted.

'Andy?' a woman called out. 'Annndy?' The second time she called him was slower and more playful.

Andrew woke from his lethargic daydream in the lecture room, still holding his ceramic mug of his favourite brand of earl grey tea, cold in his left hand. He was resting his head in the palm of his right hand, staring at the enormous blackboard at the front of the lecture room. His favourite mug, given to him by a former student, had 'Professor X' written on the side.

The woman called louder and sharper, 'Casper?'

Startled, the professor jumped in his seat, spilling some tea on his black suit pants. Over by the large rustic doorway stood a young frowning lady, in the mid-stages of her pregnancy. She had long hazel hair, which reached the top of her shoulders, slightly covering her pink woollen cardigan. The twenty-seven-year-old had a kind, caring face dotted by a few subtle freckles.

'Janine, I wish you wouldn't call me that.'

The students called him Casper as a nickname, especially when discussing the professor behind his back. The nickname had appeared a few years prior when someone revealed that the professor's middle name was Jasper. Then, naturally, it had changed and evolved into the same name as that of the friendly ghost. Though, the professor did not see the connection.

'I know you don't, but I think it's cute,' Janine said, walking across the room.

She slowly sat down in the seat next to the professor, using the armrests to support her descent. To regain some semblance of elegance, she immediately tucked in her skirt at the back and smoothed out the creases in her lap. Then she curiously followed the professor's gaze to see what had him so entranced.

The blackboard, which had a polished mahogany finish, spanned the entire length of the raised platform, end to end. The schematics on the face of the board looked like a mural of complex mathematical equations, alongside several engine concepts. Janine had seen this ongoing puzzle many times before, so she turned back from it to face Andrew.

'Any luck tonight?' she asked hopefully but expecting disappointment.

'Nope. Still not right.' He turned his face to her, suddenly realising how rude he had been. 'Shit! I am so sorry. You, ok?'

He handed her a tissue, which he had kept in his chequered red and orange shirt. She dabbed her forehead.

'Thanks. I'm telling you. Give me a room full of hungover students over a pregnancy any day.'

Smiling, the professor turned his attention back to the blackboard. 'Well, feel free to take one of my classes if you want. Don't think I'm getting through to them anyway.'

Janine's eyes narrowed as she looked at him, concern reflecting in her voice. 'Why? What happened?'

'Ah, nothing. The Dean is just on my ass again.' Placing his cup down, he stood up and walked to his table. 'I mean, how can I get complete focus from my kids when the world's going to shit?'

As he said this, he pointed to the newspaper, resting on the edge of his table. The front-page headline read: 'Dr Schwimmer found dead, suspected suicide just months after conspiracy unearthed.'

He picked up several sheets of paper and compared them to what was written on the board. Frustrated, he dropped two of them back onto a pile on the table labelled 'Wrong Again'. Once, just once, I'd like to put one in the right pile, he pleaded with himself.

'Maybe you should take a break? Take me away for a few days? Hell, when are we gonna go to that Italian place again?' She threw her hands up.

Stunned, the professor turned to face her, arms dropping to his sides and a boyish smirk appearing on his face.

'Umm, well, look at what happened the last time we had meatballs,' he said, nodding in the direction of her baby bump.

Rubbing her bump, she raised her eyebrows and gave him a teasing look.

'I'm just saying, you need time away from this. You seem to forget that mamma needs attention too.

'And some loving,' she added with a giggle.

Playfully, the professor stood up straight with his chest inflated and fists on his hips, mimicking a prised stallion.

'That date was, hands down, the best night of your life, baby,' he said playfully. He then slowly looked down and saw the wet patch on his pants. 'I think I spilt my drink that night too.'

Collecting himself, the professor relaxed, placing all the sheets of paper back on the table and continued.

'I don't know. Maybe my heart's not in teaching anymore. Maybe I'm just wasting my time here. I know I'm close to solving this... but it also feels like it's out of reach.'

His shoulders slumped, and his voice became barely audible. 'Maybe I am wrong. What if it's all just a goddamn waste of time.'

A silence descended in the lecture hall, then Janine slowly rose to her feet, leaving the tissue on the foldout table, next to Andrew's cup.

'Well, sometimes, a break is a good thing. I'm heading for a bite to eat. You're welcome to join me.'

The question hung for a moment. Dejected and getting no reply, she resigned herself to the notion that maybe she was wasting her time too. Dusting herself off, she began to leave.

While the professor stood there, contemplating his life choices, and Janine was gathering herself, thin strips of blue light entered the room through the wooden venetian blinds.

With a final attempt to break him out of his fixation, Janine turned with desperation in her eyes. 'Umm, night then?'

Still no response.

But this time, something wasn't right. He stood there, hunched over with his gaze rapidly moving between the paperwork on his desk and the blackboard. The blue lines of light were streaking across his work. He took two large steps away from the desk and slowly moved his hand in front of him, pointing at a crucial section at the board.

Moving towards him cautiously and genuinely concerned over his quick shift in persona, Janine placed a hand on his back. 'Andy, what's wrong? Andy?'

'It works! Holy shit! It actually works!'

His eyes were fixed on the board, now filling with tears. He turned his head towards Janine, urged her to look at the board and began to clarify, 'It's the light... the light has shown me what I've been missing.'

As he moved to his desk to make the notes as fast as he could, Janine kept standing there with her arms crossed, staring at his work. She started to see what was happening. The light filtering through the blinds was perfectly falling on sections of the board, highlighting all the fundamental aspects required to finally complete his cryptic engineering puzzle.

Janine froze, her eyes widening. 'I can't believe it.'

Turning back to her and holding her hands in his as a single tear ran down his cheek, he said, 'Janine, endless energy. This... well, this is going to change everything... This is going to change the world...'

Chapter 4

Fit for Duty

The San Antonio light was pouring in through the large, untarnished windows of the first-floor bedroom of the apartment. Flooding the minimalistic space with an ambient white glow, it made the room seem grander than a standard home on Wilson Boulevard. Decorated with simple and modern light fixtures, the materials coordinated with the white acrylic bedside draws, with handles painted metallic silver. Even though the room appeared bare and empty, it felt warm; it felt cosy; it felt like all the pain and suffering in the outside world had melted away at the front door.

Michael Quade lay on the king size bed, staring up at his beautiful wife, leaving his weathered combat boots on the floor. Abby's immaculate long, blond hair was carefully draped over her left shoulder. She smiled back down at him, biting the side of her glossy lip. She had a look of anticipation, emphasised by her raised eyebrows and wide entrancing blue eyes. Beguiled by her beauty, he just watched her while resting his head on her modest baby bump. She twitched.

'Oh... did you feel that?' she quickly whispered, grabbing his arm and watched him adoringly, as his head jolted away from her stomach.

'Feel it? Shit, I thought he was gonna kick a field goal!' he said, starting to rest his head back down carefully.

'Ow!' he said playfully, rubbing his arm after she had slapped him.

'No cursing,' she said, feigning a serious face. 'Besides, how'd you know it's a boy?'

'I dun know. I just... know,' he said shrugging, before stubbornly continuing, 'And he'll be breaking hearts before you know it.'

Frowning at him, she slapped him again.

'No, he will not,' Abby said firmly, shaking her head. 'If it's a boy, he's gonna be brought up right, respectful and romantic... just like his daddy-bear.'

Dwelling on the fact that she just gave him a compliment, he decided to roll with it. 'Hell yeah, I'm romantic. I even leave the toilet seat down for ya.'

She cringed slightly at the terrible joke, trying to forget the mental image. So, she tried to change the conversation. 'Do you remember when we first met?'

'Yeah, baby, I do,' he said, playing with one of the buttons on her light blue dress. 'I was crashing at a friend's place when I was on leave, and I heard the playhouse was showing a rerun of...umm... Jaws, I think?'

'And I was out with ma girls,' she added, gently fist bumping the air and bobbing her head, as if what she was really saying was 'out with my girls to PARTY!'.

'Yep, and as I was getting out of the cab by the cinema, you were standing there under the lights, on the sidewalk, waiting to jump in.'

He found himself playing with her hand while reminiscing, interlocking his fingers with hers.

'And then?' she asked, her voice levelling out as she remembered the moment fondly.

'Well... then I saw you and thought daaaamn. You know, I almost didn't have the courage to say anything, but I thank God I did. I think I was like, "hey beautiful, wanna come to the pictures with me?"'

'What you actually said was...,' Abby corrected, trying to impersonate him, '"Umm, excuse me, ma'am... do you like fish?"'

They both began to laugh at the most bizarre pickup line ever.

'I dun sound like that,' Michael said, raising his eyebrows at her. 'Do you like fish? Yep, not my best moment. But I sure didn't sound like that.'

'Na, it was perfect. A bit weird, but perfect. I mean I saw you get outta that cab, tall, dark and handsome, with your eyes. God your eyes... just like that of a big old husky dog, and I was like... damn it, he's gonna walk straight past me.'

Stroking his head, she continued, 'But then, you asked if I liked fish?' She laughed again, his eyes rolling. 'It sounds crazy, but I knew right there and then that I would spend the rest of my life with you. The shark movie was ok too, I suppose.'

'I love you, Hunnie-bunny,' he said, kissing the back of her hand.

'I love you too, daddy-bear,' she returned, softly.

Michael closed his eyes, and a moment later, he woke up underneath the duvet covers, curtains drawn, with blue light peeping through the sides. Getting up, he made the bed to military precision, taking great care to have every corner the same as the other. Then he moved into the ensuite bathroom, where he brushed his teeth and shaved. He stared blankly at the gaunt reflection looking back at him, hardly recognising himself. He quickly got dressed, picked up something small from his bedside draw, put it in his pants pocket and headed downstairs.

As he went past the open living room door, his movement triggered the sensors to make the TV spring to life; CNN was set as the default selection. More riots? He thought, the world is going to hell in a handbasket anyway, so why the fuck not.

He took the last protein bar from the barren food cupboard in the kitchen, then proceeded to the hallway, where a painting of Pink Floyd was hung on the wall. Moving it aside revealed a large safe installed in the wall, with a security keycode lock. He opened it quickly, as he had done a hundred times before, and inside it, amongst some cash, medals and paperwork, sat a small tin box. He took out the box, along with a small rag covered in patches of black marks, and moved into the living room.

Michael took a seat in his comfortable, faded leather armchair. Moments later, he had finished his snack and had already thrown away the half-eaten contents into the empty wicker bin, next to the fireplace. His mind started to wander, the TV a muffed murmur in the background. The sound of a neighbour's car door slamming outside brought him back to reality, with a literal jolt.

He opened the scuffed tin box and laid the contents on the table in front of him, pausing only to look up at the pictures above the varnished fireplace. Deflated, he looked back down at the table, where his Glock 20 service pistol sat.

He went about disassembling the weapon, which took a matter of seconds due to muscle memory from years of experience. Spending several minutes cleaning up the small parts, he ensured no carbon was built up in the mechanical assembly. Meanwhile, the TV displayed a live report from some guy taking cover from projectiles in the so called 'warzone' of the streets of LA.

'Same shit every day,' he said aloud to an empty room.

After reassembling the weapon and testing it, each test ending with an audible metallic snap, he was content with its functionality. He placed the rag back in the box, then carefully positioned the container next to a neatly piled parade uniform.

As he got up from the armchair and walked over to the fireplace, he froze before the dated picture of Abby and himself. He was holding her and kissing her on the cheek. She looked happy, so happy. Kissing two of his fingers and placing them on the picture, he held them there for a short while. His bottom lip began to shake as his eyes started to well up.

He lowered his hand into his pocket and pulled out a nine-millimetre round. Placing it into the chamber of the pistol, he cocked his weapon, then raised and placed it in his mouth.

As his finger slowly squeezed the trigger, his cell phone decided to awkwardly vibrate on the table, followed by a very loud rendition of 'Run to the Hills' by Iron Maiden.

Please... Please, just let me go, he pleaded in his mind.

But the phone kept ringing...

And ringing...

And ringing.

Releasing the trigger, he pulled the pistol from his mouth with a quick and deliberate movement. Turning, he barked, 'God damn it!'

He quickly snatched his phone from the table. 'What?' he asked hoarsely, then cleared his dry throat.

'Mickey?' A deep gravelly voice responded through the phone. 'Mickey, it's Doug.'

'Admiral?' Michael shook his head in surprise. 'Admiral... ah... Doug, why are you calling me? I haven't heard from you since...' He trailed off, turning his head to the fireplace.

'I know. It's been a while,' the admiral said regretfully, in a heavy voice. 'Michael... I apologise for not coming to see you recently, but well... something's come up. Something big.'

Michael was lost for words. Why now? He asked himself. Of all the goddamn times to call, why now?

'Mickey, I need you to come in,' the admiral stated, straight to the point, close to sounding like an order.

'Admiral,' Michael said, resisting the temptation to snap back at his old boss. 'With all due respect, Doug, I resigned from my post, and for good reason.'

'I know why you left, son... I know. Look, I can't say too much over the phone, and you of all people know why. All I can say is, I know you, I know what you're capable of, and I need the best and *that is you.*' The Admiral emphasised the last part passionately.

Michael found himself with his mouth open, yet unable to speak. Instead, he just looked down at the weapon in his hand, realising he had completely forgotten that he was still holding it.

'Ok, just listen,' the admiral continued, the determination evident in his voice, 'What if I get someone to pick you up in thirty minutes? And what if I were to tell you that you won't have to go back for a very, very long time. You know... Ah shit, maybe it'll do you some good?'

'Doug, I...' Michael began saying, then hesitated when he remembered his old life. Flashes of uncomfortable flights, hauling baggage around and, oh yeah, the constant battles in war zones. 'I've done my time, Doug. I think I've been to more places than even the Bible has reached. I care to wager... I've served my country enough.'

'Goddamn man...' Doug barked down the phone, some of which was distorted, then quickly regained his composure. 'Fine. You've always got to make it difficult. Screw it. What if I said, you wouldn't have to return to EARTH for a very long time?'

Taking a second to digest what he had just heard, Michael thought, wait, what? Hold up a second... what did he just say? What the hell does he mean by 'won't have to return back to earth'?

While figuring out the rather vague code word for earth, he found himself looking at the picture of his wife again. Everything he touched and everywhere he went reminded him of her. Then, as if prompted by some deep inner voice, he started to entertain the idea. It was as if a part of his subconsciousness demanded him to do something now, to break his endless circle of sorrow.

It dawned on him that he had been fighting his entire life. He had fought to protect his mom at an early age from his abusive, hands on, 'I'm too pissed to stand' stepdad. Michael had persevered even when he was air-dropped all over the world, usually in some asshole of nowhere. Those missions were usually off the books and dealt with all the unseen evils of humanity. He had never run from a fight, but his old life had left its scars. He knew that if he didn't do something, he was going to lose the fight. Then, stealing himself and taking a deep breath, he flicked the weapon's safety catch on with his thumb. Exhaling and gripping the phone tighter in his hand, he simply responded with two words that he hoped would give him purpose. 'I'm in.'

'Great stuff,' Doug responded, relieved. 'Mickey, trust me, this is exactly what you need. Do what you need to do. Pack the usual long-haul kit, and I'll sort the rest.'

'Thirty minutes?' Michael confirmed.

'Affirmative, Captain. It'll be good to see you, son.'

Doug promptly hung up the phone.

By the time the dusty black saloon with military plates turned up, Michael had already packed two large olive-green rucksacks labelled Quade. M. He also carried one weathered black backpack, thrown over his shoulder, straps taped up with a dark grey fabric.

He opened the front door and saw the driver standing at attention, waiting rigidly on the white porch. Giving a quick salute to put the man at ease, he handed the driver one of the green rucksacks. Just as he was about to leave the property with the rest of his luggage, he stopped and dropped his bags. Then, he signalled to the driver, who had jumped back behind the wheel, to wait just a second.

He briskly walked into the living room and headed straight up to the fireplace. He picked up the picture of his wife, then safely stowed it into his rucksack by the front door. Heaving the backpack over his shoulder, he picked up the rucksack and left his home for the very last time.

With the bags in the car, he took a second to look back. The apartment had so many memories. Every room in there would take him for a walk down nostalgia avenue. This was his home, but somehow, he knew that he would never kick his boots off in this place, ever again.

After what seemed like an excruciatingly long journey, between catching a red eye to another long drive, Michael was finally approaching the location where he had planned to meet up with Admiral Douglas Taylor.

The car turned off Route 95, heading north past the Creech air force base in Nevada. Apparently, landing at that base was classified as unsecure, which only made him even more curious about what the Admiral said to him over the call.

Could Doug have been talking about a new type of jet? Maybe a low orbiting space station or something? Aghh, it just didn't make a blind bit of sense. Michael was skilled at many things, but being a pilot wasn't one of them.

Looking out of the car window, he could see a barren wasteland: dust, rocks and a couple of staggered Joshua trees, as far as the eye could see. He remembered that the government used to test nukes out here somewhere, then shuffled in his seat at the thought that his balls could be cooking like a bag of popcorn. In fact, the only thing missing in this stereotypical scenario would be a rolling ball of tumble... oh wait, there it was, a ball of tumbleweed.

The car made a final turn off road, when they passed a rusty old sign saying 'munitions disposal area, do not pass', with a fading depiction of an explosion within a flaky black triangle. The direction that they were heading was fenced off with what looked like prison style barbed wire.

Heading down the dusty road, with more potholes than the moon had craters, it looked like the path was leading directly into the centre of some sort of rock formation. They passed an inconspicuous silver post with three yellow stripes, which prompted the driver to slow down.

'You lost, son?' Michael asked the driver, glancing around for landmarks.

'No, sir,' the driver promptly responded, looking at a compass fitted to the dashboard of the car.

A few minutes later, the car was still heading in the direction of the rocky mountain, in the middle of nowhere. As they got closer, Michael noticed that the road sloped down underneath the ground. Support structures and lighting underneath the rock formation were camouflaged from the elements outside.

Michael was impressed. The thought that creating such a base must have been a logistical nightmare struck him. It was completely under the radar. If this area were to be seen by any aircraft or satellite images, it would just look like another rocky mountain. Even the route they had just followed seemed random.

The vehicle came to a halt at the front of a guard post manned by multiple soldiers wearing full desert gear, carrying modified weapons. They had an aura about them that seemed to say, if you make a wrong move, we will put you down. Lowering the window, the driver flashed a badge from inside his suit jacket.

Without saying a single word, the security guard raised some sort of scanning device and hovered it over the driver's identification. After a beep and a moment of pause for confirmation, the guard took several steps back.

Waiting for the barrier to open, Michael was interested by what he saw on either side of the car. He could see two large, fully automated and mechanically driven tubes, moving horizontally beside the car. The loud clunky cylinders were scanning the entire car, probably for foreign devices and such. That's new, he thought.

The scanning tubes finished their business and crawled back to their starting positions, noise dissipating as they wound down. The lead guard, who was leaning into the control box for confirmation, straightened up and moved towards the barrier. With a push of a button on his strange wrist strap, the metal bar rose in the air, leaning to one side. The driver released the parking brake and slowly creeped forward, giving Michael little time to see what device it was.

As the vehicle moved along at snail's pace, a set of huge blast doors began to open. Michael also noticed three remote-controlled .50 cal turrets, just out of view of the security stop. This implied that if you were crazy enough to break into this place and managed to get past the first hurdle, the second hurdle would be a little more... challenging.

They slowed down again and came to a halt in an underground car lot. The underground facility was massive, as if the entire mountain had been perfectly hollowed out. Bright bars of luminescent lighting, as far as the eye could see, and the blemish-free paint and directional lines gave Michael the impression that the facility was well funded and maintained. It also looked like they had a subway station. When was that built, he wondered.

'You're expected in the conference building, sir,' the driver said, pointing at the first of several buildings.

'And my luggage?' Michael asked, peering out the window.

'I'll take care of that, sir,' he replied in his monotone voice. Then quickly looking at his watch, he repeated, 'They're expecting you, sir.'

'Gotcha.' With a stern slap on his shoulder, Michael got out of the car and headed over to a set of double doors.

He entered a modern, long prefab building with a plaque on the front labelled 'Conference Rooms 1 – 9'. The inside was more like the interior of an office block, with freshly decorated white modular rooms.

'Captain Quade?' asked a pleasant receptionist, who sat behind a desk.

'Yep,' he replied, with hand on his head. This just keeps on getting weirder, he thought.

Smiling politely through her bright red lipstick, the dark-haired woman nodded, then picked up the desk phone and keyed in a direct extension number. 'He's here, sir.'

Michael swore that he could hear the admiral's distinctive grainy voice over the handset. 'Yes, sir,' she replied, placing the phone down with a click. 'Go right along in, room two, second on the right.'

She directed him with perfectly rehearsed movements, and as she did so, he noticed that she was wearing a wedding band. He wondered what she must say to her husband when leaving her home in the mornings. 'Bye, honey, I'm off to work down... the... post office?'

Just as he approached the room, the door flew open, shaking the plastic tiles in the corridor above.

'Good to see you, Mickey.' The big burly Admiral greeted him with his booming voice, hand stretching out and grabbing Michael's.

Shaking his hand felt like he was greeting a grizzly bear.

'Doug,' he said plainly, grasping his old friend's shoulder. 'What the hell is going on here?'

The grin the admiral gave Michael bunched up his greying thick moustache. The creases that appeared on his forehead and at the sides of his eyes gave him the look of a sheriff in an old wild west movie.

'Come in, Mickey. I want you to meet someone,' Doug said, turning and walking into the conference room.

I forgot how tall he was, thought Michael, arching his head up to look at the back of the admiral's head. As they moved inside, Michael hesitated for a split second, discreetly sniffing the air. He recognised that all too familiar scent. The old bastard is smoking again, he thought, disappointed. Took him years to get off that shit.

'Captain Quade, I'd like you to meet Professor Andrew Thomas.' The Admiral introduced him before taking a seat at the head of a black sturdy table.

Closing the door behind him, Michael turned to see a nervous middle-aged man, with white streaks running alongside his head, holding out a sweaty hand.

'Umm, nice to meet you, Captain,' Andrew hesitantly said, trying his best to demonstrate a firm handshake.

Tuning his head to the side, without losing eye contact with the strange little professor, Michael responded, slightly bewildered. 'Likewise.... Admiral, am I going to be kept in the dark or...?'

'Take a seat, Mickey,' Doug said solemnly, 'We've got a lot to cover.'

The professor backed away, discreetly wiping his clammy hand on his beige trousers, then sat down next to where a mug was steaming on the table. Michael proceeded to walk around the table, taking a seat opposite the professor.

'Right,' Doug said, leaning forward, clasping his hands together gravely. 'I'll just come out and say it. Mickey, a long time ago, the man sitting opposite you came up with a new source of energy and—'

'Actually, it was there all along,' Andrew interrupted him. 'I just figured out how to use it.'

Michael incredulously looked over at the professor and watched as he dunked a teabag into his mug. Then, he mockingly said, 'You know... the British take the teabag out of the cup.'

'And they also drive on the opposite side of the road,' Andrew replied coolly. 'But I'm not planning on doing that any time soon either.'

Smirking, Michael began opening his mouth. He was about to continue what would have been an interesting back and forth, when he realised the admiral's eyes were burning holes into the side of his head.

'Sorry, Doug.' Michael apologised, awkwardly scratching his head, where the furious glare had made contact.

'As I was saying, the professor discovered how to USE this energy source. The discovery was utilised in several engineering fields, advancing our technological capabilities tenfold.'

Michael pursed his lips and nodded at the professor. He was reciprocated with a toasting gesture with his raised mug.

'Furthermore,' Doug continued, 'the advancements in the past couple of years have enabled us with the opportunity to travel outside of our normal zones of space travel.'

'Outside our normal zones? Space travel?' asked Michael incredulously. 'As in, to boldly go and all that jazz?'

Ignoring the delivery of the question, the admiral sat back in his chair. 'Well, that's where you come in, Mickey. I need someone to lead the expedition, and I can't think of anyone more perfect for the job.'

Michael let out a half-laugh, then turned to the professor, who calmly carried on drinking from his mug labelled 'Professor X'. He turned back to the admiral only to discover his face hadn't changed at all. Holy shit... he's serious, Michael thought.

'Expedition? Doug, I thought you wrangled me a spot on the ISS. I didn't think you wanted me to go find Spock or something!'

'Well, considering you just referenced Star Trek twice,' Andrew interjected, 'I'm sure you would have done fine at the international space station.'

Michael gave the professor a sly look, who responded by giving him the middle finger. That made

Michael smile. He knew right then that they were gonna get along just fine. Michael turned back to the admiral to wait for further information.

'Jesus Christ, it's like I'm dealing with two kindergarteners!' Doug said, raising his hands in the air. 'Michael, you ARE perfect for the job, even if you don't believe it. You have set records in the past that will never be touched. You forget that I was there that day on the firing range, when you beat all the top snipers... with no scope.'

The admiral continued, leaning forward intently.

'I want you to lead, not for your efficient weapon skills, but because of your ability to control any situation. There are men alive today because YOU kept your cool, because YOU got them out of the shit.'

Suddenly, Michael found himself back in his home, with a pistol cocked in his mouth. He thought about what Doug had just said. 'Ability to control any situation.' He's definitely got the wrong guy.

'Doug, that might have been the case in the past, but... ah, I just don't think I...'

Within a heartbeat and a direct tone, suggesting that the words have been prepared for a long time, Doug responded, 'That's just bullshit, and you know it. What happened to Abby wasn't your fault, and she sure as hell wouldn't have put up with this self-loathing crap. Now, I'm offering you a chance to do something special, and if you don't want to do it for yourself, do it for her.'

Torn between furious rage and unyielding sadness, all Michael could do was sit in his chair, mouth trying to open, but the Admiral's words had hit him like a slap in the face.

'Ahem, umm...' Andrew cleared his throat, finally letting out a breath that he had been holding. 'Also, *my* discovery... that wasn't all me.'

'Ah, here we go,' Doug said, shifting uncomfortably in his chair.

Andrew continued, looking directly at Michael, 'I'm just saying.... The beam helped me.'

The professor explained the details of what had happened that night in Boston. Going into details about the strange and inexplicable moment, when the blue light from the beam highlighted his work, essentially connecting the dots for him.

Michael studied the professor for a while, one half of him struggling to believe what he was hearing, and the other half definitely not believing. Coincidence, he told himself. It was just a lucky trick of light.

'And that's how I ended up here, with a grumpy old admiral who looks like a beaten-down Tom Selleck, and a guy with freaky eyes, who, I may also add, is dressed like a 1980's assassin.' The professor stopped, content with his story.

Michael turned his head towards the admiral, who quickly downed glasses of some sort of brown translucent liquid, probably bourbon. Given the speed at which it disappeared, you'd swear he hadn't had a drink in years.

Locking eyes with Doug, Michael jerked his head in the professor's direction, smiling mischievously. 'Well... now I can see why you're back on the pipe.'

For a brief second, the admiral had a look about him, as if someone had just announced his deepest darkest secret. Then, just as soon as the burn of the bourbon hit the back of his throat, he burst out laughing. Like the chuff and wheeze of an old-fashioned locomotive, the sound was so palpable that both Michael and Andrew couldn't help but join in.

With a throw away 'son of bitch', the admiral picked up a remote off the table and spun in his seat, switching on the huge monitor fixed to the wall. 'Ok, let's begin.'

Over the following months, Michael was updated on some of the advancements that had been made in the past couple of years. He was most impressed with the massive ship that he was going to be commanding. It was assembled in orbit using resources from countries all around the globe, through synchronised launch schedules.

The ship was retrofitted with the latest and most advanced propulsion systems, as were all the smaller transport shuttles, all of which were specifically designed and tested to move at phenomenal speeds; the fitted engines were named T-Drives.

T-Drives, short for Thomas Drives, were such an advancement in technology that Andrew compared it to giving a caveman an electric car.

Despite his eccentricities, Michael got to know Andrew pretty well. They even spent some time kicking it back over a couple of beers or two... or ten. To Michael's delight, the trendy professor actually had a great, albeit dark sense of humour. In fact, this supposed genius of a professor was the main culprit behind both of them being banned from the rec-room. This happened when Andrew had one too many cocktails one night and, to everyone‘s surprise, ran around the bar area with a pool cue between his legs, annoying the bartender by repeatedly shouting, 'WHITE BALLS, CORNER POCKET.'

Although it sucked for them to not be able to relax at the bar, it was worth seeing the look on the Admiral‘s face. No one did ever find that pool cue.

The rest of the time on the Nevada base was divided up between combat training, navigation and shuttle instruction. There were certain aspects of the course that Michael excelled at, and there were others, such as space navigation, which were better suited to Andrew's intelligence.

The whole objective of the training was to ensure that the crew consisted of multi-skilled members. In the unlikely situation that someone was injured or, say, sucked into the dark and endless vacuum of space, someone else would be able to do their job.

Michael was happy in the knowledge that all the training the crew had gone through had them prepared for any situation.

Well, he thought while waiting at the transport shuttle door, we will just have to see.

Chapter 5

No Risk, No Reward

The transportation shuttle jolted to one side, causing the pilot to relay a perfectly timed message to the passengers.

'Ladies and gentlemen, we might be experiencing some slight turbulence. Nothing to worry about.'

'Turbulence?' Andrew spat with venom in his voice. 'Jesus Christ! That felt more like being hit with a giant fly swatter...'

Michael sat smiling opposite him and drank from his chilled bottle of water labelled Crystal Spring. According to the tagline, it was supposedly the clearest and best tasting water in America. Michael, however, thought it tasted like the crap that comes out of a kitchen tap.

He stared at the roll-down monitor connected to the harness into which he was strapped. Scrolling through the pages on the screen and studying the manifest one more time, he ensured that he was putting faces to the names. This routine had become more of a habit than a chore. In the months leading up to this flight, he had repeated the same memorising activity countless times.

He sat there, recalling the first time he was shown the test facility, where all the advanced equipment and amazing technology were being developed in the Nevada mountains. Some of it belonged in the imagination of some crazy scientist, and that had helped alleviate some of his doubts about the mission. The fact that they already had these ships fully functional, in such a short span of time, was amazing. However, he was still more surprised to discover that most of the crew had already boarded.

The transport shuttle shook and vibrated again, only for a much shorter interval this time.

'Goddamn it!' The professor shouted, eyes locked in anger, in the direction of the small grey speaker above the entrance. 'Why didn't they engage the main drive as soon as we left?'

'Safety reasons, dude,' Michael replied nonchalantly.

'Safety? It's perfectly safe after take-off, and they know it. Stupid assholes.'

'Andy?' Michael said, in a calm distant voice, peering briefly over the top of the monitor. 'Relax, man.'

Turning his head away from that little box, but not before giving it one final scornful pass, Andrew shuffled in his seat and checked his harness. He also couldn't help but vigorously scratch behind his right ear.

Michael remembered that the T-drive had two steps. The first was a basic propulsion, but without the horrible side effects of being strapped to a rocket. The second enabled the insane speed to travel through space. The eccentric and outright wacky scientists had discovered an accidental advantage of the T-drive. They were able to manipulate localised artificial gravity for the first time in history. So, no more bobbing about in space.

Michael looked up again and sighed. 'Stop playing with it.'

'What?' Andrew shot back, quickly dropping his arm.

'Your implant?' He tapped behind his own ear. 'If you break it, then you have no coms... wait, what the hell am I saying. Have at it!'

Andrew swiped his interactive wrist strap, selected the direct call to Michael option and whispered, 'I'm in your head, Michael.'

Michael gave him a smile and returned to his work.

Andrew ended the call and resisted the urge to scratch his communication implant again. To distract himself, he started to investigate his surroundings.

Glancing down the gangway, he could see two other people on the captain's side, leaving five seats spare. They wore blue bands on their arms, identifying themselves as computer technicians. The fear on their faces intensified as they saw Professor Andrew Thomas feeling unsafe in a ship that he had helped design.

On his side of the gangway, he could see four others. Three of them were wearing green armbands with an embroidered tree at the centre – he knew that meant they would be reporting to the agricultural and logistics quarters. The other seat on Andrew's side was occupied by an Asian woman, wearing a white band with a red cross surrounding a small blue planet earth in the centre.

The strange thing about this woman was neither her feet dangling a couple of centimetres off the floor nor her stockings, which had a fat rabbit holding an umbrella over its head printed on them. It was the way she kept frowning over the rim of her glasses at the captain. That was the look of someone holding a coin over a coin-slot, trying to figure out the timing to select to win the most money.

To break her unsettling focus on Michael, Andrew tried coughing at an increasing volume. Instead, he found himself becoming the focus of everyone else, except her. The two people holding on for dear life, just a moment ago, now carried a look of disgust.

Mind ya business, he thought, as he returned a stern glare.

'Can I help you with something, Miss Tang?' Michael asked nonchalantly, keeping his focus on the monitor.

Unfazed and still as fixated on him, she pushed her glasses further up the bridge of her small nose.

'Are they products of genetic inheritance or mutations?' she asked, expression unchanged.

The professor locked eyes with Michael, shrugged his shoulders and gave her a dumbfounded look. Swiping one last time, trying to imprint the last page of the crew members into his brain, Michael turned off the device. He then rolled it up and secured it back to the harness, tightening a strap around it.

'Professor, this is Dr Jiao Tang,' he said, gesturing in her direction. 'She's our chief medical officer.'

Not even acknowledging Andrew, she remained fixed on Michael.

'And if you're referring to my eyes, Miss Tang...,' Michael continued, crossing his arms and resting them on the harness handles, 'they were blue, up to about the age of thirteen. Then, they began to turn grey, and no... before you ask, my folks did not have them, just lucky old me. Does that answer all your questions?'

'I just... I just find them fascinating,' Tang replied, lowering her head, looking like a small child who had been told to be quiet at church. 'It could be a melanin deficiency,' she whispered to herself.

'It's fine, Miss Tang,' Michael said encouragingly. 'Lots have tried to figure it out, and lots have arrived at that disappointing same conclusion.'

At this, she raised her head with a cute and grateful smile, emphasised due to a little beauty spot at the crease of her mouth. Immediately, the communication speaker began to buzz.

'Ladies and gentlemen,' the crackling little box announced, 'we have reached our maximum thrust altitude and will be engaging our T-Drive system to push through the lower orbit all the way to the high orbit. Starting in t-minus three minutes. Thank you.'

A subtle beeping began above the passenger's seats, signalling the next stage in the process. Just as soon as the pilot disconnected from the receiver, a digital clock began counting backwards on an LED display.

'Ok,' Michael commanded, slowly gazing all around and grabbing the crew's attention, 'Just as you've practised, hundreds of times before, remember, the pods you're sitting in are designed to handle all the G-forces. So y'all just need to sit there and look pretty.' As he finished, his head stopped in the direction of the professor, who was rebelliously flipping him the bird.

Cheeky bastard, he thought, squinting and trying to hold back a laugh.

Popping open a storage box by pressing a release catch on his armrest, Michael placed the bottle of water into the slot. Once he finished pinning it down with a metallic mesh, he closed the box with the knowledge it was secure.

Just as the digital display reached 60 seconds, the engines of the transport ship began to clang and clunk as the mechanical components of the exterior of the shuttle prepared for extreme speeds.

A second audible sound came from above the crew's sitting area, followed by a hydraulic sounding release of air. Michael had later discovered that the equilibrium pods were originally designed for the protection of high-speed freight containers and transportation devices. However, the technology wasn't quite there yet: unsustainable power issues had resulted in objects imploding during transport.

Luckily, due to the professor's discovery, the concern regarding sustaining the energy consumption of the technical systems had pretty much disappeared. This resulted in a technological boom of novel devices and breakthrough applications, including the newly redesigned and fully functional equilibrium pods. Michael remembered something about the inside of atoms controlling the movement of exterior atoms, or something like that, it was all a bit of a haze after that.

The pods, resembling transparent halfpipes, began to slide down the walls automatically. All the other equipment aboard the ship, outside the pods, were designed in such a way that extreme forces would have no effect on the components inside.

Activating the individual pods was only a safety measure, in case the shuttles' main containment pod, which covered the entire ship, should fail. In that situation, standing outside of the pods during a T-Drive thrust would be a terrible idea – a person would be exposed to forces that would essentially crush them in seconds; hence, the complete focus on pod safety prior to a thrust or a skim, as people referred to it on the main ship.

As the pods reached halfway, out of pure habit, Michael glanced around at the other crew members to ensure they were in the correct seating positions: knees together, arms at ninety degrees and head back on the headrest, controlling their breathing. He was relieved to see that they all remembered, so he relaxed.

Their pods closed with several clicks in unison, ending with a quick wheezing sound as the oxygen equalisers made an airtight seal. Controlling the release of his breath, Michael took in a half-breath, as taught by his tutors at the base. It was a method he was well accustomed to, having used various types of respirators during his years of military service. The air was good, so he relaxed his breathing pattern.

Ten seconds on the clock.

As he waited, his mind drifted to the time he and his wife Abby had an appointment at the hospital. They were waiting for the distorted image on the monitor hooked up to the sonogram machine to clear. He remembered holding her soft delicate hand in anticipation of seeing their developing baby, Abby's skin turning to gooseflesh as the nurse spread the gel over her baby bump. She was so beautiful.

He forced himself away from the memory. Even though the memories were becoming less frequent as the time passed, they occasionally slipped into the forefront of his conscience, pushing him towards the lonely void of depression.

Three... two... one...

As the smaller T-Drives engaged, switching from the normal propulsion system, the front of the shuttle began glowing. The transport shuttle started moving forward, slowly at first, then gaining momentum with frightening speed.

The aerodynamic construction of the shuttle lent it the appearance of a submarine with narrow and smooth features, except for the large silver panel a couple of feet ahead of the bow. The trail of white light left an afterglow, streaming from the craft, making it look like an angelic arrow flying through the darkness of space.

In the cockpit, the ship's pilot and co-pilot were both buckled down inside modified piloting pods, surrounded by holographic instruments and control panels. As the ship was propelled forward at top speed, a small object was increasing in size at the horizon. The pilots confirmed the instructions to each other over their headsets and adjusted the course and speed accordingly.

A few more seconds passed and the T-Drive wound down, reverting to the standard propulsion system. The mechanical systems on the exterior of the shuttle clunked as they returned to their initial positions. Then, with a beep, the pods equalised the pressure, and with a couple of clicks, the safety locks were released. When the pod covers retreated fully, the pilot addressed the passengers.

'Ladies and gentlemen, we will be beginning our docking sequence shortly. Please remain seated. And for those who have not travelled off world before... welcome to space.'

Michael shuffled in his seat and looked over at Andrew—who, for some reason, was sitting there with his eyes closed.

'Andy?' Michael enquired, with no response. 'Hey, Andy?' A little more assertive the second time.

'Whaa... what is it?' Andrew said groggily, rattling his head as if he had been startled out of a deep sleep.

'Andrew J Thomas, did you pass out?' Michael mocked him in a fatherly tone as if Andrew were a child.

Frowning at the captain with contempt in his eyes, the professor hastily replied, 'No, I did not PASS out. I was just... resting my eyes.'

'Do you, or members of your family, have a history of narcolepsy?' Doctor Tang asked, leaning forward, eyes wide and waiting for a response.

'No... I do not have...' He stopped midway. Getting frustrated with a woman he had met only a while ago was not a good start, Andrew thought. Deciding not to bite, he turned his head back to the captain. 'Soo, what's the plan when we dock?'

Dejected, Doctor Tang sank back into her seat and withdrew into her quiet self. 'It could be a case of syncope,' she muttered to herself.

'Well, if you had paid attention to the mission brief, you would have known about the orientation post docking,' Michael said, with a hint of impatience.

'See this big brain of mine?' Andrew said, pointing at his head. 'Well, it's so full of information that I decide to switch it off and let others learn something, occasionally.'

'Is that science speak for "you didn't listen to the critical mission briefing"?'

Taking Andrew's silence as confirmation, Michael continued, 'Well, as everyone else on this shuttle knows, you will be shown to your designated areas.

Then, there will be the safety tour, which includes all the emergency bulkhead control panels.'

Gesturing towards the ship's medical officer, Michael continued, 'Miss Tang will be reporting to the portside of the ship, alongside the living quarters and logistics.'

Directing towards the crew wearing green bands, he said, 'The starboard side is almost completely dedicated to the tree people.'

Noticing the confused and offended expressions on their faces, he raised his hands in an apologetic fashion. 'Sorry guys, I mean no offence. Without y'all, we would run outta air... and I like air.'

It dawned on him that he had no Idea what they did, other than produce oxygen for the entire ship. He made a mental note to find out more about them.

'Thanks, boss,' Andrew butted in, relieving the captain from the looks of contempt he was getting. 'I think I remember something about the engineering sector being at the centre of the ship?'

'Umm... yeah, just a few decks under the tech labs.'

Michael found it difficult to remember the layout of the ship. With over one hundred decks, massive storage facilities, labs for research and development rooms, the ship was the marvel of engineering creation. He was still slightly confused as to why the ship looked like a squid–shark hybrid.

He supposed it had something to do with the two gargantuan collection plates fixed to the front and the fin-like deposition exhausts mounted as the protruding tails.

Once again, the grey box came to life, issuing a slightly distorted voice. 'Ladies and gentlemen, this is your pilot speaking. We have now boarded. Please remain seated until the docking bay has pressurised. Thank you.'

'Well,' Andrew said, looking at Michael, 'It's a bit too late to change our minds now.'

Michael was still shaking his head as the rear door began to open. He released the safety lock on the harness, then pushed the frame upwards to the roof of the shuttle. He was able to stand up and stretch, cracking his back in places that he didn't think had bones. He also soon realised that the fabricated gravity in the ship was slightly lighter than earth's. That will take some getting used to, he thought.

'Andy...,' Michael began, with a playful smile and heaving the professor up onto his feet, 'Nope, no turning back now, my friend. Welcome to your new home: The ALETHEIA.'

Chapter 6

Last Arrivals

Leaving the shuttle with his luggage, Michael was greeted by a parade of uniformed officers, stood to attention and saluting.

Dropping his rucksack down on the deck of the docking area, he returned the age-old gesture, with a respectful salute back. Then he cleared his throat and addressed the officers.

'Stand at ease, everyone.'

He continued, clapping his hands together, 'Ok, first, even though this will not be my first official address, I'd like to get one thing crystal clear...'

Some of the relaxed officers, standing with their hands behind them, began to twitch, with eyes darting back and forth; they were expecting the captain to be a hard ass.

'... That will be the very last time you all salute me, understood?' he added, looking around at the surprise and confusion on his officers' faces, 'Understood?'

'Sir, yes, sir!' they all replied in unison and with vigour.

'Good. Command structure will remain the same, as will all the other basic procedures. I just hate the idea of saluting a superior on a goddamn spaceship.'

A couple of shoulders hitched up at that remark, followed by a few back-of-the-throat giggles.

'Second, as far as I am aware, this is going to be a long and unpredictable journey. So, to help us keep our focus on the mission and retain moral, we have a grand total of 63 working families on board. I will make it a personal goal to get around the ship and meet each and every one of you. Until then, please carry on with your normal routines and stand by for further instructions. Remember, this mission is to explore the origin of the beam, so we will all remain focused on the end goal. But that doesn't mean we can't all enjoy the ride. So, what do you say? Shall we get the show on the road?'

'Sir, yes, sir!' they chorused.

'I'm sorry. I can't hear you,' Michael yelled in a baiting tone.

'Sir, yes, sir!' they screamed.

Comfortable in the knowledge that the message had gotten across, Michael brought his heels together and, stiffening his back, dismissed them. 'Good. Company dismissed.'

Moments later, the officers disbursed and slowly filtered out of the docking bay. Michael was then approached by a female lieutenant in her late twenties, wearing a black uniform with a red security band on her arm.

'Welcome, Captain. I hope the fight wasn't too bumpy.' She handed him a rolled-up tablet. 'Sorry, sir... my name is...'

'Gemma Saunders, second in command of the security on the ship,' he finished. 'You grew up in California, graduated top of your close quarters combat class, very efficient with firearms... and recently dyed your hair black.'

The last comment forced a smile to break through the cold disciplined exterior that the lieutenant was trying to portray.

'Very good, sir. I'm impressed that you can read,' she said, smirking. Moving to his side, she stood poised and ready to move on his command.

Raising an eyebrow and feeling a glint of satisfaction with the sarcasm in her response, he picked up his rucksack and began to walk towards the exit.

'Shit... gimme just two secs,' he said quickly, turning back towards the shuttle that sat perfectly between two black and yellow guiding lines.

The rest of the crew, including the thorough, if not eccentric, Doctor Tang, had already left with their chaperons. The professor had decided to hang back to speak to the captain.

'You know, that's the first time I've seen you speak to people in an official manner,' Andrew commented.

'Yep. Better get used to it,' Michael stated, with a touch of regret in his voice. 'I've got a feeling that I won't have much time to kick back from now on. You know where you're going?'

'I'm good. Besides, if I do get lost, I'll just grab someone and tell them you ordered them to escort me.' Adjusting the strap on his shoulder, Andrew set off, waving his hand above his head. 'Catch you later, boss!'

Turning his back on Lieutenant Saunders, who was patiently waiting at the side, Michael nodded and began to walk alongside her.

Walking through the surprisingly spacious hallways of the ship, he was happy to see that everyone was diligently going about their business. Most of the function testing and critical safety checks had been conducted in the previous weeks, in preparation for departure.

He found himself still getting used to how light his foot placements were aboard the ship and was distracted more so by how normal everything looked. Carpet? Plastic walls? This place was better decorated than some of the apartments he had lived in.

'Sir?' Lieutenant Saunders called out, stopping just short of a sturdy double door entrance.

'Yep,' he responded, completely distracted by the stylish light fitting running alongside the carpet.

'Sir, I...'

She struggled to find the words, then steeled herself.

'Sir, if you have access to all my information, do you know about my physical history?'

Turning his gaze from the floor, Michael looked directly at her intense hazel eyes. 'And what part would that be? Oh, the sexual transition thing?... Is that what you mean?'

Shocked by his candour, but still keeping her composure, she said, 'Yes, sir. You see, in the past—'

'Is it going to be a problem?' He interrupted her.

'Umm, no, sir. Not for me.'

'Can you kick most of the crew's asses if they are out of place?' he asked nonchalantly, pressing the release button on the double doors.

'Yes, sir,' she replied confidently, smiling as she relaxed a little.

The doors opened to a large horizontal tunnel, cylindrical in shape. Michael began to walk through, then turned back to face Lieutenant Saunders.

'Well, if it's not a problem, and you can do your job effectively, then it's not even an issue, is it?'

Gratefully nodding, she fixed her gaze in the direction of the tunnel and followed the captain.

A couple of feet into the room stood two fixed panels attached to handrails, reaching into the far distance. As the two stepped between them, the floor began to move forward at a brisk pace. Just like airports, that's cool, Michael thought.

'Watch your step, sir. With the lighter gravity, it's easy to misjudge the moving floor,' she said, holding her hand out at a distance, behind his back.

Noticing he was stable, but entranced by the viewing holes leading to the outside of the ship, she realised she had completely forgotten the feeling she had the first time she had gone through this tunnel. This was the first time that Michael was able to see the earth from aboard the Aletheia.

The view was as breath-taking as it was unbelievable. He could see that the earth was divided between the radiant glow of the sun on one side and bathed in the ominous glow of the beam on the other. Silently appreciating the sight through the windows, he was awestruck that this was even possible in his lifetime.

'Sir, we'll be getting off soon,' the lieutenant announced, reluctant to break Michael's moment of tranquillity.

Pulling himself away from the wonder that was home, Michael began to walk forward with controlled caution as he got off the moving sidewalk. He felt his knees buckle ever so slightly, as the momentum of the floor mixed with the lighter gravity of the ship made for an unsteady combination. By the time he proceeded forward through the double doors at the end of the room, he had managed to steady himself.

'How many transfer rooms do we have on the ship?' Michael asked, praying that she answered 'only this one'.

Taking a second to think about the question, she nodded and replied, 'Two per deck, and four, including this one, are in the neck of the ship.'

The Aletheia was huge, Michael thought whilst nodding.

Finally, after traversing the maze of the officers' quarters, rec rooms and restroom facilities, they reached the captain's quarters alongside the ship's bridge.

'Well, this is my stop,' Michael announced, placing his hand on the palm reader of his room. 'Inform the head of security that I expect an update within the hour.'

'I'll pass it on, sir. He had some technical issues with his accommodation and had to get the techs to help him out,' she informed him.

'That's fine. Thank you, Lieutenant,' he said, reaching out to shake her hand.

Bracing herself and covering a salute with a firm nod, Lieutenant Gemma Saunders spun on her heels and walked away.

The first thing Michael noticed as he entered the room was the emergency equilibrium pod, which was taking up a large amount of the far wall. He remembered being told that every quarter had one fitted in, according to the number of people occupying that room.

Dropping his rucksack on the bed, he immediately unzipped the top compartment and pulled out the picture of him and his wife. He then walked over to his desk, cupping the photograph in his hands, and gently placed it down against a docking station on his desk, facing towards his chair.

He unpacked his gear into the usual drawers, narrow cupboards and overhead storage containers. Then, he quickly changed out of his clothes and took a quick shower. It wasn't bad, considering only roughly ten to fifteen feet separated him and the vacuum of space.

After drying himself off, casually ignoring the multiple scars etched all over his body, he donned his old official uniform. He wore his formal but casual dark navy-blue uniform, complete with a set of comfortable combat pants and a fitted short-sleeve shirt, which hung over the top of his pearly white t-shirt. Four silver bars, accompanied by a star, were displayed on both of his shoulders, and a golden spread eagle was sewn into a small patch on his chest.

After another glance out the room's viewing port, he turned and left his quarters.

While he was walking down the hallway towards the bridge, he disturbingly felt the hairs on the back of his neck stand up. The kind of feeling that has been a constant evolutionary response to the suspicion that someone or something was behind him. Quickly spinning around, with his survival instinct kicking into overdrive, he became even more unnerved to discover that the hallway was quiet and empty.

Something's wrong, he thought, running his hand over his neck. Squinting, he stood there for a moment, staring at the vacant space. Still suspicious, but wanting to get the ship moving, he decided to suppress the weird feeling and just put it down to pre-command jitters.

The sensors recognised his approach, and the huge doors swiftly opened.

'Tupoy ublyudok!' a man roared in a strong and distinctive Russian accent. Michael knew enough of the complicated language to decipher the words: 'Stupid bastard'.

Before Michael even had a chance to address the outburst of what sounded like a giant having caught the smell of an Englishman, someone decided to announce his arrival.

'Captain on deck!' yelled a young, pale-faced man. Describing him as a man was a slight oversight, as he looked no older than sixteen, imitating a soldier that he had just seen on his parents' TV.

All officers sitting at non-critical stations were suddenly on their feet and saluting. Goddamn it, Michael thought. Reluctant on the inside, he formally braced himself and responded, 'Thank you! Carry on.'

With the officers returning to their seats, he took a second to look around at the bridge – the place that would be his to command for the remainder of the mission.

The room was large and arrow-shaped, with all the designated stations facing outwards towards the bow. The captain's seat was close to fifteen feet back from the others. This was because in the centre of the room was a huge holographic projection of the Aletheia and the flight path.

The ship's AI utilised the super advanced long-range sensors and was in a constant state of searching, updating and adapting. Some whiz-kid had created a helmet to coordinate the pilot's brainwaves with the ship's navigational computer. Michael didn't know how it worked, but he knew it stopped the ship from heading straight into the path of a random asteroid, which was a good thing.

All along both sides of the bridge were large circles, resembling manhole covers, containing emergency pods. The pods all across the ship were also designed to be used as temporary jettison capsules.

While taking in the layout of the sophisticated and downright impressive bridge, Michael remembered that during the quick show of respect a little while ago, one person had not turned around.

'You must be my chief of security,' Michael said, walking over to the big Russian.

As he approached the man, he suddenly wished that he were three foot taller. The guy was ginormous. What was he six, seven feet? Trying to label him would be a toss-up between a professional NFL line-backer or an ox on steroids. With broad muscular shoulders, the Russian was as wide as he was tall. His bulk made the dark uniform look like it was sprayed straight on to his vein-popping arms.

'It is a pleasure to meet you, Captain,' the Russian said in his deep booming voice, thrusting his arm out at a speed that made Michael think for a split-second that he was going to slice him in half.

'I am Lieutenant Commander Roman Sokolov. Head of this ship's security.'

Michael shook his hand, and it instantly revealed to him the calibre of the giant who stood before him. Admiral Taylor had once told him that you could tell a lot about a man from his handshake, and he was right. Roman's grip was firm and controlled. His calloused palm hinted at hard labour. What Michael especially picked up on was something that few people looked for: the area between the thumb and index finger was indented with hardened skin, likely caused by years of rifle wielding.

All these deductions indicated to Michael that the man before him was a strong, calculating and, more importantly, an extremely dangerous man.

'Yeah, it's a pleasure to meet you too,' Michael said, releasing his hand and keeping eye contact with the beast. 'What's got your panties in a twist?'

Roman gave him a look of confusion as he translated the question in his head from English into Russian.

'Ha.' He laughed abruptly, sounding more like a bag of falling gavel. 'For some reason, the reader for hand will not work.'

Roman's gaze slowly turned towards the scrawny little technical assistant, who was visibly sweating with fear. He was slightly cowering behind a tablet he held in his hands. No doubt, it was a result of what must have been an uncomfortable conversation with the big guy.

'What's wrong?' Michael asked the poor man, trying to mediate between them.

Holding the tablet tight and leaning it towards the captain, the man sounded nervous as he replied, 'Sir, the...a... the palm reader does not recognise the handprint. I fixed the lock on his quarters... but... but...'

'That's fine.' Michael interrupted him, mostly to stop the man from bursting into tears. 'What's your name, son?'

'John... Jonathan Daniels, sir,' he replied, wiping his forehead.

'Well, John Jonathan Daniels, is there any way of resetting the reader?'

'Yes, sir. As I was telling the chief...' he flicked his eyes to Roman, then quickly back to the captain. 'I just needed your authorisation for the security terminal, sir.'

Michael decided that the quicker this was resolved, the quicker they could get the show on the road. Besides, Roman loomed there like a dark cloud, ready to pour down with rain.

'No problem. What do you need?'

Sighing, Tech Assistant Daniels held out his tablet towards the captain, which displayed a digital outline of a hand. 'Just here, sir.'

When Michael placed his hand on the reader, the device instantly recognised the captain's unique handprint and authorised the reset feature for the security access.

'See,' Michael said looking at Roman, 'No problem.'

The smaller man turned to Roman and begrudgingly held out the reader. With a ping, the palm reader accepted the imprint.

'No problem,' Roman said contemptuously, looking at the small man.

'Will there be anything else, sir?' the assistant asked, moving out of the giant's shadow.

'Nope, that's all, Jonathan. Thank you for your help,' Michael said, giving the kid a reassuring slap on the back.

Turning and heading towards the exit, Tech Assistant Daniels left the room at such speed, you would swear he was attempting a world record in power walking.

Michael turned and walked over to his chair, leaving Roman to his business. The captain's chair looked quite simple in design. It had a curved metal back, supported from the floor to the ceiling. The arms were stepped in sections, like the padded sections in a massage chair. It was only when he sat in the temperature-controlled, gel-padded seat that the technology was truly revealed.

Sitting back in his chair, he motioned his arm up towards the ceiling, which brought up an interactive projection, in turn. Through here, he could see everything about the ship, from life support and water levels to navigation to deck and ship exterior pressure gauges. After he selected the communication function, the ship's intercom burst into life, causing everyone to stop what they were doing and pay attention.

'To the crew of the Aletheia, this is your captain speaking.' Looking around at the officers on the bridge, Michael took a deep breath. 'Let's get this show on the road!'

Chapter 7

Au Revoir Mon Amour

A woman had entered the bridge and was waiting patiently by the side of Michael's chair.

She spoke in a prim English accent.

'My apologies, Captain. There was a confusion regarding the location of certain storage units, down in the logistics sector.'

'You must be my second-in-command,' Michael stated, more for himself, then turning to look at her. He was stunned as if he had seen a ghost.

'Commander Elizabeth Jenkins, sir,' she affirmed, distantly gazing into his eyes.

Normally, Michael would be uncomfortable when people became entranced by his damn eye colour, but this time, it was hugely different. She looked like... Abby?

Tall and slim with a healthy complexion, she wore the same dark navy-blue officer's uniform as he did, except she had worn it with a touch of elegance. Her combat pants were better fitted to her, showing off her hour-glass curves. Though her toned features were that of an Olympic swimmer, she looked soft and delicate. The shirt she wore had three glistening silver bars with a star close by, lying flat on her shoulders. She also had a perfectly pressed, silver oak leaf on her chest.

Michael could not get over how her face was an exact replica of Abby's. It was as if the universe was taunting him. The striking similarity was evident in the way her high cheek bones gave her a wonderful, uplifting smile, and her blue eyes had the same bright and soul piercing glint, entrancing and breath-taking. He held onto the one and only difference, her hair was dark brown instead of blond, neatly tied up in a bun.

In his mind, he was lauding whatever god that had decided to keep kicking him while he was down. Of all the women in the world that mission control could have chosen, the chances of having a second-in-command who looked just like his wife was downright gut-wrenchingly hilarious.

'Captain?' she prompted him, breaking his moment of contemplation.

'Sorry about that, Commander Jenkins. Has the problem been sorted?' he asked, collecting his trail of thoughts.

'Yes, sir.' Commander Jenkins informally responded, 'The bloody fools couldn't tell the difference between the numbers six and nine. But it has been resolved.'

'Good. I'll be going for a walk before departure.'

He turned towards the holographic display. 'I want you and Roman to come with me.'

Selecting a function on the interactive panel, he moved his left arm downward, resulting in the projection to disappear. He then stood up and looked over at his chief of security, who was hunched over his data terminal. We will need to get a bigger chair for that guy, Michael thought, amusing himself.

'Roman?' He called out, resulting in the big guy thrusting himself upwards and turning on his heels.

'Yes, Captain,' he replied in a voice so deep that it made the kid in the pilot seat flinch slightly.

'Let's go for a walk,' Michael declared, turning towards the exit and walking out with intent, both his second-in-command and his chief of security following close behind.

After some time, walking the corridors of the Aletheia, Michael could not help but laugh at the vast contrast between his two escorts. On his left-hand side, he had a scar-faced battle-torn giant: a muscled Russian who demanded obedience through fear. Then, on his right side was a beautiful, calm and an intelligent woman: a woman who led by respect earned though years of perseverance.

Commander Jenkins moved forward and pressed the release button on the huge double-doors labelled

'Engineering'. All of them noticed that to the right of the word 'Engineering' was an additional and discrete hand-drawn spanner and two nuts – a not-so subtle and poor interpretation of the male genitalia. Immediately, she spun her head over towards Roman, giving him a look akin to a teacher disappointed with childish classroom profanity. Without uttering a word, Roman trailed the position of where she had just looked, frowning with disgust; he released a low snarl. On the other, Michael saw it and sniggered to himself.

Just as the double-doors opened, a blast of music flooded the corridor, where the leaders of the ship stood wincing slightly.

'And if I catch you fooking around with the capacitors one more fooking time...' a man spat loudly in a southern English accent.

Michael knew the song to be an incredibly old rock track called Thunderstruck, by AC/DC. Good taste, he thought as he walked into the large room.

The room was shaped like an open box, all built centring the ship's three massive engines. Two of the engines were the latest and most advanced ion propulsion systems. The other and most impressive looking one had been designed by Professor Thomas. If Michael had to describe it, he would say that three rings surrounded what looked like a spinning ice-cream cone, with a collection chamber situated at the end, pulsating with light.

'Fooking hell... Chris, turn the music down,' the man shouted from the other side of the machines.

As the music died down to a distorted background muffle, Michael spotted a big thick beard through the moving parts of the device. Hilariously, it looked like it was floating by itself for a while, until the man came into view.

'Isn't she the sexiest girl you've ever seen?' the man bellowed proudly, attempting to clean his hands with a dirty rag.

Remembering the manifest, Michael knew that he was talking to the ship's chief engineer, Robert Humphries, also known as 'Big Bob'. The title of Big Bob was well deserved, as the man who had an English West Country accent also looked like a Viking. Middle-aged with a shaved head, he had a face that had the same texture of a slice of worn-out leather. Tribal tattoos covered his neck and travelled down both his arms, ending at the tops of his hands. He did not look like nor was he as big as Roman, but his physique leaned more towards that of a powerlifter than an engineer's.

'Good to meet you at last,' Michael said, walking over and shaking Bob's still greasy hand.

'Same mate. Andy's told me a lot about you,' Bob said, noticing in his peripheral vision an assistant creeping towards a box labelled capacitors. 'Don't you fooking dare.'

The assistant froze, then walked away with his head lowered.

'This is our chief of security, Lieutenant Commander Sokolov.' Michael gestured to his left, then turned slightly to his right. 'And this is my second-in-command, Commander Jenkins.'

'Bloody ell!' The dirt-stained man gasped, moving closer to Elizabeth. 'I think I was wrong. The T-Drive is the *second* sexiest lady on the ship.'

Rolling her eyes, Elizabeth met his pathetic gaze and sternly asked, 'Are you aware that you have graffiti on the outside of your door?'

Bob's eyes turned suddenly from a playful gaze to thunderously furious. 'Graffiti??! On MY fooking door??!'

He spun around and, like a werewolf searching for its next target, fixed his gaze on the assistant who had turned down his radio. 'Youuu...'

The assistant he was addressing was called Chris, his name aptly sprayed across the back of his chair. He had his back turned and head down, but he knew that he had been discovered. His station was covered in models, topless girls, stickers and doodles. However, he turned and attempted to play innocent. 'Yes, Bob?'

'Don't you give me that shit! Get out there and clean it off, you dirty little bastard!' Bob yelled while pointing at him.

Laughing internally at the situation, Michael turned to gauge the reaction of his escorts. Elizabeth looked disgusted by the sheer amount of profanity that poured of Bob's hairy mouth. Roman..., well he just stood there assimilating every device in the room with no regard for what the people were discussing.

'Bob?' Michael said, pulling the big guy's focus once again.

'Sorry about that, boss. These little fookers don't know how good they've got it sometimes.' Scratching the back of his head, he asked, 'What brings you down here then?'

Michael found it funny when he was referred to as boss by the non-enlisted crew members. It just felt a bit weird, but he allowed it; after all, what else would they call him? Top dog? Chief? Nope, boss would do just fine.

'I thought I'd come down here to see if you are all set for our first skim?' he said, looking around the room, still in awe of the advanced technology scattered around the place.

Cringing at the term skim, Bob reached under his aging beard to rub his chin. 'Now's a good a time as any. Just make sure everyone's wound the windows up, ok?'

Laughing, Michael reached out his hand once again. 'Yep, give me sixty minutes, and we are a go.'

Nodding and returning the handshake, Bob returned to his work... well, yelling at the crew to turn the music back up. He did, however, turn one final time to smile and wink at Commander Jenkins, in turn, receiving an eyeroll, a huff and an intentional turn of the head.

The shortest reigning criminal mastermind, aka Irish Chris, was still scrubbing the graffiti off the engineering room sign, as the three of them left. Something told Michael that this wasn't gonna be the last time Chris would be punished for his... side-projects.

When they finally reached the bridge, Roman's second-in-command, Lieutenant Saunders, was waiting with a rolled-up tablet by her side.

'Lieutenant,' Michael greeted, stopping a couple of feet away from her. 'Do you need something?'

Keeping her eyes on the captain and turning to Roman, she clarified 'Actually, sir, would it be ok if I run over a few things with Lieutenant Commander Sokolov?'

Roman stepped forward, eclipsing the light to the side of his captain, and asked in his bellowing voice, 'Do you require any further assistance, Captain?'

'Nope, just be ready for departure in...' Michael looked at his wristwatch and noticed that he also had a notification from mission control. '...departure in twenty minutes.'

Roman needed no further sign of dismissal and began to walk away with Lieutenant Saunders. As they did, Michael noticed that she passed Roman the tablet and leaned over to point something out with her finger. He gave her a scornful glare with his scarred face, which told Michael that Roman was not impressed by the interruption. Christ, he's tall, Michael thought again.

As he glanced back at Commander Jenkins, she noted his wrist strap, which had an incoming call and pre-empted his next command. She said, 'You should take that, sir; I'll wait on the bridge for you.'

Then, without waiting for approval, she entered the bridge and immediately began giving orders.

Michael entered his quarters and took a seat behind his desk. When he swiped at his watch, a projection appeared standing vertically in the centre of two glowing lights on the desk.

After a few moments, a familiar weathered and wrinkled face appeared. 'Mickey?' The admiral spoke in his distinctively grainy and hoarse voice.

'Admiral,' Michael responded, happy to see a familiar face.

'How's the preparations going, son?'

'All set to hit the road, I guess.'

He was smiling at how ridiculous Doug's moustache looked in the projection.

'I bet. Look, this will be the last transmission you'll receive for a while so...' The Admiral cleared his throat and shifted in his seat. 'So..., ah shit! I'm no good at this. Look, just remember that you are there for a reason. Don't take no shit from anyone, and have some goddamn faith in yourself.'

Looking away from the projection, Michael thought about the number of times that Doug had been there for him; a hell of a lot more than his dead-beat father had ever been. He remembered the number of times Doug had personally broken international laws, just to pull him out of bad situations. He had even sat by Michael's bed in the hospital after a mission had gone sideways. Michael wished that he could just tell Doug how grateful he was to have him as a mentor.

'Doug, I...' Michael found himself choked, trying to speak to the man who he viewed as a father. He continued, eyes welling and trying to cover his sadness with humour, 'I think I left the gas on.'

Doug flashed a smile that caused his eyes to crinkle, showing amazingly both concern and pride. He chuckled. 'Well, I'll get someone right on that. In the meantime, try not to break our new ship. I don't think the insurance will bail us out.'

They both sat for a while, letting out bittersweet laughs. Then, and for the first time in many, many years, Michael sat up straight in his chair, determined and confident. Raising his hand to his forehead, he presented his mentor, his idol and his father the most respectful salute that he could muster.

'Thank you, sir.'

With a look of disbelief quickly followed by a disciplined focus, the admiral stiffened and returned the salute. Giving a firm encouraging nod and a final farewell to his protégé, he added, 'Good luck, son.'

The communication link ended, and the projection disappeared, leaving Michael alone in his cold and empty quarters. The uncomfortable feeling in his stomach, along with the lump in his throat, left Michael numb. Nevertheless, moments later, he collected himself and took a quick glance in the mirror, allowed himself a deep sniff, and rubbed his nose with the back of his hand. He left his quarters in the direction of the bridge.

'Ten-hut!' the pilot shouted again.

That's going to get really old, Michael thought, taking his seat.

The rest of the crew took the hint and carried on with what they were doing, except for the young pilot who stood in attention, avidly awaiting instructions.

'Ensign, let's get the ship ready for departure.'

As soon as Michael uttered those words, the kid began to shake with excitement.

'Sir, yes, sir!' he responded, taking a seat and spinning to face the control panel.

Moving his arm to bring the interface projection with it, Michael engaged the ship's intercom function.

'Ladies and gentlemen of the Aletheia, this is your captain speaking. As we begin the departure procedure, I would advise that everyone remain seated. This is not as a precaution. The Aletheia has the same technology as the equilibrium pods, built into every single inch of the wall of the ship. I just want y'all to remain seated to enjoy the ride.'

With that, Michael disengaged the intercom system and studied the information in front of him. Happy that he had green lights from all sectors, he turned to where the pilot was sitting and smiled.

'Well, Ensign, let's go for a ride.'

Quickly, turning to give the captain a beaming smile and displaying a perfect set of white teeth, the kid responded, 'Aye, Captain!'

He placed his hands on his station's controls, and the lights of the ship became brighter, a feature fully factored into the design of the ship's electrics when the T-Drive was being spun.

With nervous apprehension, compensated by well-rehearsed movements, the pilot engaged the ship's main drive. The Aletheia began to creep forward, leaving the small and lonely Earth far behind.

Chapter 8

Proven Route

As the ship began to move, Michael still had an uncontrollable feeling of unease. He knew that the technology had been previously tested, time and time again. He kept his faith in the professor, reassuring himself that Andrew was a very smart guy.

He remembered a time when both he and the professor were sitting in the rec-room at the Nevada base, discussing Andrew's discovery. The professor was working on his usual notes, occasionally lifting his head to take a sip of his beer.

The usual suspects were drinking at the bar, and the atmosphere was energised with the mission drawing closer. The guys were laughing and cracking jokes while placing bets at the pool table. There was also the occasional thudding of a dart on the board, from the other side of the room.

Michael, who had already collected an assortment of emptied bottles on the table, leaned in closer to the professor to view his work.

'Soo... is it like... light speed?' he asked, his words beginning to slur. The alcohol was going down way too easy.

Stopping mid-scribe, Andy sat up and faced his inebriated friend. He tried to hold back a laugh, respecting the major difference of intelligence. The problem with that was that Andy ended up red-faced with puffed cheeks.

Just as Michael was about to ask why that was a stupid question, Andy exploded in a fit of laughter, slapping the table with his one hand and holding his side with the other. A few curious heads turned towards the rocking professor to figure out what was happening.

'I'm sorry,' Andrew wheezed, holding his hand up in the air. 'I'm sorry, dude. No, it's very different to light speed... umm look...'

Andrew leaned over the centre of the table, knocking over one of the empty bottles in the process. He grabbed the salt container out of a silver condiments basket and began to create a thick line in between the beer drenched coasters.

'Ok, so, imagine my finger as the Aletheia.' He started to explain, placing his finger next to the line of salt.

'Now, if I pushed my finger over the table, without the salt, there would be no resistance. Well, except for the table, but ignore that. A quick and easy journey, right?'

He then moved his finger so that it was in line with the line of salt.

'Now, the salt represents space. More importantly, the area between two points in space.' Pushing his finger though the salt, he continued, 'A lot more resistance means a slower journey.'

He looked up to see if Michael was following, who took a big gulp of his drink and nodded, intently observing the demonstration.

'The new engine bypasses the resistance completely.'

He pushed his finger through the same path he had just made, then poured the salt just behind. 'You see? The engine creates a kind of field that displaces the quarks... or space from one area and replaces them in another.'

'So... with absolutely no resistance, a ship can move as fast as the speed of light?' Michael asked earnestly.

'Absolutely correct... and absolutely incorrect at the same time. The speed of light isn't actually that fast, when it comes to distances in space. It takes just over eight minutes for light to reach Earth from the sun, and that's roughly one-hundred and fifty million kilometres away. Look, all you need to know is that even at, as low as, ten percent of the engine's full capacity, the ship with be able to travel entire solar systems in one skim.'

Returning the salt container to the basket and sweeping the demonstration salt off the table, Andy dusted his hands and took a sip of his drink.

Michael snapped out of the memory and found himself back on the bridge. The silence was palpable, leaving the crew literally on the edge of their seats. The nervous expectation of what was about to happen resulted in increased heartbeats and anxious sweats all over the ship.

Breathing deeply, Michael regained his composure and looked out at the spectacle, just ahead of the bow. The ship moved into a parallel position, alongside the beam. Then, when the pilot was ready with the pre-loaded co-ordinates, the ship's T-Drive was engaged.

He could see that just ahead of the bow, the once picturesque canvas of space began to warp and move. It felt like the ship was being enveloped by a sort of translucent gel, contorting the stars ahead and forcing them to blur. A low hum filling the dead silence of the bridge was interrupted by a deep intake of breath from Commander Jenkins. She sat a few feet away to the left of Michael, gripping the armrests of her chair, leaning forward expectantly.

The stars ahead that were stretched started twirling, creating a white lined doodle on the dark canvas of space. Then, within a split second, the picture snapped back into place with the deformed image becoming a crystal-clear view.

Holy shit, Michael thought. It actually worked....

Darting his eyes to catch the readings on his terminal, he relaxed to see that all systems were green. He briskly turned on the intercom. 'Ladies and gentlemen of the Aletheia, welcome to a new solar system.'

The ship erupted in celebratory cheer and screams of joy, with crew members explosively jumping out of their seats to embrace the closest person. As they shared the moment with friends, family and loved ones, the ship was ecstatic with delight.

Switching off the intercom and getting straight to work, Michael turned to his second-in-command. 'Commander?'

He noticed that still squeezing her armrests and facing forward, she was exhaling a controlled breath with her eyes closed.

'Commander...' he said with a smile and a reassuring tone. She opened her eyes and turned to face him. 'We're ok.'

Slowly nodding, then controlling herself with difficulty, she returned the smile. 'Yes, sir.'

The bridge crew collected themselves and began to gather as much information as they could about the new system. Fourteen new planets were discovered, with a fierce looking rouge dwarf star at the centre. Huge gas planets accompanied by moons, some akin to the earth's, had been hit by meteorites or asteroids. There were even planets with landmass, full of untouched vegetation and life. Under any normal situation, the crew would have metaphorically dropped anchor and studied the system in great depth. However, the mission was to follow the beam, straight to its origin, and reveal the truth of the light.

As soon as the ship was ready, the objective was to skim slightly further by steadily increasing the output power of the T-Drive. The engine had used only seven percent of its full potential to leave the earth's solar system, but caution with the new technology was critical for mission safety.

Michael decided that what they had just been through was a huge step forward for humanity. So, he wanted to let the crew digest their first skim, then continue forwards in twenty-four hours.

Turning to Commander Jenkins, who was already looking at him expectantly, he declared, 'Commander, I have decided that the Aletheia will resume skimming in exactly twenty-four hours. Have the crew gather as much data as they can.'

'Yes, Captain.'

She turned and relayed the order to the officers on the bridge, clearly and precisely, as protocol required.

Closing his digital interface, Michael stood up and addressed the bridge. 'Well done, guys, very smooth. Commander, you've got the bridge.'

Then he turned towards the exit and left the bridge, heading in the direction of the engineering room.

Damn it, he thought, smiling to himself, remembering a side-bet he had on whether the ship would blow up; he realised he owed Andy some money.

Meanwhile, in 'engineering', the rumbles of the T-Drive were alleviating, being overseen by Big Bob and the professor.

'Shit the bed, Andy. I love it!' Bob said, ecstatically looking at the spinning engines. 'Of all the engines I've worked on, this one turns me on the most.'

Leaning back in a chair near a console, listing results and statistics, the professor laughed. 'I'd leave you two alone, but I think she'd rip your dick off.'

Robert Humphries looked like he was brought up as a Nordic warrior, with the rite of passage being through war and blood. Years of working on large and powerful engines contributed to his size. After a long and tiresome, thirty-five-year-long career, Big-Bob was the most sought-after man for largescale power projects. So, the professor knew that when a man of Bob's dedicated spirit towards engines said he loved an engine, that was a huge compliment.

'Chris, you weedy little shit, where are you?'

Irish Chris popped his head up from behind a terminal, with the tools still in his hands. He had grease stains on his uniform and was covered in dirty black marks, streaking across his face.

'There you are,' Bob said, fixing eyes on his target. 'Go and get the blue box.'

Chris relaxed his shoulders, realising that he wasn't going to get roasted for something he did wrong. Then, he walked over to a metal cabinet labelled in bold red writing, EMERGENCY FIRE EXTINGUISHER. With a suspicious glance over his shoulder, he proceeded to unlock the release catch and open the door.

Inside and placed covertly underneath a large rag, sat a smooth sky-blue utility box. Withdrawing the box, with the faint rattle of glass clinking inside, Chris held it tightly as he moved towards Bob.

'I like to keep this for special occasions,' Bob whispered, though with a mischievous grin. However, just as he cracked the lid on the box and reached inside, the large double doors leading to the rest of the ship opened.

'I hope there's a glass for me?' Michael said, crossing the room.

'Two fingers.' The professor laughed, holding two shot glasses. 'You gotta drive tomorrow.'

Wheezing in amusement, he poured the Scottish branded liquor lavishly into four glasses and uncharacteristically handed one to Chris, much to Chris's amazement.

Michael held up his glass in a toasting gesture. 'Well, I didn't believe it would work, but I was proven wrong. So, to the nutty professor!'

The others joyfully raised their glasses, repeating the toast through wide grins.

'And to a hundred bucks that our captain owes me, for not blowing us all up,' Andrew added, gleefully.

Shaking his head and reluctantly lifting his arm, Michael joined the others and slammed the shot back.

'Right,' Andrew said roughly, as the whiskey hit the back of his throat, 'Seeing as we've got some time before the next skim, I think it's about time that you met the wife.'

Glancing at his watch, after passing their glasses back to Chris, Michael looked at the professor with a cheeky smile and an outstretched hand. 'If she asks me about my eyes in under a minute, how about we call it quits on the bet?'

Grabbing his hand in a stronger handshake then when they had first met, Andrew amended the deal. 'If she doesn't... it's two-hundred?'

Lost in the meaningless deal, involving money that couldn't be retrieved or spent, Chris scurried away with the blue box.

'Deal.' Michael firmly accepted, then turned to Bob. 'You good here?'

'Yes, boss. She'll be all good and ready for the next skim.'

'Sweet.' Dropping his hand on his friend's shoulder, Michael continued, 'Ok, Andy, let's go meet the real brains in the Thomas household'

Then, with a winking nod and a thumbs up, Michael and the professor left engineering and headed towards the transport tunnel. Stepping onto the moving sidewalk, they could not help but gaze out of the windows at the alien solar system.

'Look at that,' Michael said, pointing at the distant green planet the size of Saturn. 'Could you have ever imagined that you'd see something like that?'

'Nope. Not in my lifetime,' Andrew replied, leaning on the safety rail.

'Ain't that the truth. Well, it's all down to you and your big brain, you know.'

Watching the changing colours on the giant green planet, Andrew let out a deep breath, lost in contemplation.

'Remember when I told you that the beam helped me solve my riddle?'

Michael joined him by leaning sideways, resting on his elbow, curiously looking at his friend.

'Yeah... you said the light came through the windows... and lit up parts of the blackboard.'

'Well...' Andrew began, then shuffled uncomfortably. 'Well... this is going to sound crazy, but it highlighted something else. Something I can't figure out yet. It displayed some words randomly: Abort, hold off thee?'

'What? What the hell does that mean?' Michael asked, waiting for some sort of explanation.

'Haven't a goddamn clue. But I'll tell you one thing.' Andrew turned his head, voice unsettlingly serious. 'I've never been a religious man, but sometimes... just sometimes, reason and probability fall just short of faith. And I have a feeling those words are just as important as the ability to travel like this.'

Turning his head back to the wonders of the foreign space, Michael tried to decipher the strange code. 'Abort, hold off thee?... Could it be just a coincidence?'

'Mickey, come on. You are standing on a ship in the middle of a different solar system, and you think we weren't meant to be here?'

'I don't believe in fate or any of that shit, you of all people should know that.'

Noticing that he had struck a nerve by mentioning a higher power, Andrew tapped Michael on the arm.

'Shit, sorry! Look, all I'm saying is, I was given an extra puzzle to solve, which I intend to crack before we get to the source of the beam.'

'No dude, my bad. I just get pissed-off talking about faith. And, to be honest, I owe you a lot. So, if there's anything you need to crack it, just ask.'

Accepting each other's opinions on the matter, they both stood there in a comfortable silence, lost in thought.

Reaching the end of the moving sidewalk, they stepped off. After navigating through the corridors of the ship, they finally arrived at the professor's quarters. Andy leaned in and pressed his hand onto the palm reader, resulting in the door opening to a large room.

The spacious family accommodation had the usual homely amenities, except for a kitchen stove. All cooking facilities were in the dining areas as a safety precaution. Fire on a spaceship was probably a bad idea, he thought.

Surprisingly, the room had a large window filled with the ever-present and looming beam. Not that Michael was jealous or anything, but he did wonder why, as the captain of the spaceship, he had a relatively smaller window.

Michael turned his eyes back to the room as Andrew entered it and stood by a large and exceptionally comfy-looking couch.

'Captain, I'd like you to finally meet my wife, Janine.'

Janine stood up with excitement, holding a small child. Andrew gently tickled the kid's neckline. 'And, this is our little monster, Billy.'

Instantly recognising his father, Billy slurred something in baby speak and reached out his chubby little arms towards him.

'It's about time,' Janine said, carefully passing over the excited ball of energy. 'I was beginning to think my husband was having an affair.'

Just as Andy was about to roll his eyes at the comment, Billy clawed at his face and chuckled, the way babies naturally did. Andy responded to the little guy by lifting him in the air and repeatedly blowing raspberries on his belly.

Embracing Michael with a warm and welcoming hug, Janine regarded him with a smile. 'It's nice to finally meet you. Come and take a seat.'

They sat down facing each other on the grey sofa, with the large pillows supporting them – it felt like he was sitting on a cloud.

'Ahhg... pee-eww! You stink, kid.' Andy's face was contorted as he started to look for the diaper-bag. 'Umm honey? Where's the...'

'By the changing table, in the box by the restroom.'

'Gotcha. I'm gonna deal with this little situation and be right back,' Andy said walking away, bouncing his playful and talkative son.

'So?' Janine asked, after looking over her shoulder at her sometimes-forgetful husband. 'How are you holding up?'

It was a question that Michael hadn't had time to consider yet, with how busy it had been since the moment he had left the earth.

'I'm good. It's a bit overwhelming, but yeah, I'm ok.'

'Oh my god...,' she said, tilting her head, squinting and raising the volume of her voice, 'Oh my god, Andy! Have you seen his eyes?'

Looking back, Michael saw that the professor was, at that very moment, trying to hold his breath while wiping his baby's tushy. Michael could not help but laugh when Andy shot his wife a red-faced, puffed-cheek look of betrayal. He signalled at Michael with his head, as if to say you have won.

Chapter 9

Blue Dawn

A cup of Earl Grey sat on a small metal side table, with wisps of steam billowing from it. Andy positioned it so that Billy's little arms couldn't reach and grab it.

'So, wait a sec... you can't honestly expect me to believe that?' Janine said sceptically.

Leaning forward to pass Billy another small toy building block, Andy chuckled. 'It's true. He's just a year younger than me.' He was referring to Michael, who sat relaxed on the sofa, his feet resting on a footstool. Smiling, Michael rested his arm across the back, facing the married couple.

'But you look like you're in your late twenties?' Janine said incredulously. 'Well, whatever moisturiser your using, I want a tub.'

'Moisturiser?' He chuckled. 'The only cream I've ever put on my face was more of the camouflage kind.'

Tilting her head in the direction of Andy, she playfully raised her eyebrow. 'But you look so young, and well... he looks...'

'Hey!' Andy interrupted her, looking at Janine with a frown.

'What? It's true,' she said playfully.

'I know it is, but Mickey doesn't need to know that.'

Laughing at the lovers' tiff, Michael donned a look of pride and slowly turned his head side to side, as if presenting himself for an inspection, just to wind his friend up even more.

'Andy, it's ok. It's obvious that Janine wants to trade you in for a younger model.'

Janine accidentally made a small raspberry sound, then burst into laughter. Andy feigned a scornful look and waved his fist. Billy, however, decided to crawl away from his father and position himself right next to Michael's boots.

'I'm flattered, but I'm sure you already have a beautiful woman with you,' she said, regaining control of herself.

Scratching his head uncomfortably, Andy gave an intentional cough to silence his inquisitive wife.

'What?' she said, confused.

'It's ok,' Michael said, raising his hand towards Andy. 'I don't mind if she knows.'

Turning her head back to Michael, Janine looked both apologetic and curious at the same time.

Michael prepared himself by taking a deep breath and shuffling in his seat. Knowing that this wasn't going to be comfortable story, he became serious as he released a long breath.

'Ok... so, ten years ago, my wife Abby and I decided to take a vacation. I had just left the military, and we thought that it was time that we did something on our clock, for a change. Her parents were originally from Wales, so we rented a nice little cabin on a reserve called the Brecon Beacons.'

'That sounds lovely,' Janine said softly.

'Oh, it was. Stunning mountain terrain, reaching high up into the sky. It had a reservoir of clear fresh water, fed from the hills. I am telling you: you could have just drunk straight from it; it was that fresh. There was even a little bridge with a tall white café in the centre. We went there a few times on the first couple of days.'

Andrew, who was sitting in the far chair, smiled as he took a sip of his warm drink, solemnly imagining the scenario.

'Thinking about it now, that was the place where she decided to tell me that we were going to have a son...' Michael paused for a while, picturing that moment in his mind.

Janine put a hand on top of his, deducing that the story was causing him pain as he continued.

'We had been so determined to not find out, but she just couldn't help herself. Anyway, I was crazy happy because I had guessed it from the start. I just couldn't wait to see the little guy.'

Turning his head briefly in the direction of their son Billy, who was playing with his bootlaces, Michael smiled then looked at Andy, confused.

'I thought you had two kids?'

'We do,' Andy replied, clapping his hands together, trying to distract Billy from chewing on Michael's laces. 'Ian... I think you've met him already. He's your pilot.'

'But that would make him...'

'Sixteen.' Janine finished his thought, then continued with restrained pride, 'But you put him against any other pilot on the ship, and he'll blow em outta the water.'

'I bet,' he replied cautiously. 'Don't worry! I'll keep an eye on him.'

Michael remembered the kid who called everyone to attention when he walked onto the bridge. The same kid who was so excited to depart, that if he had a tail, it would have been wagging. Impressed with the capabilities of the kid, Michael decided that he would take him under his wing on the bridge.

'Thank you.' She patted his hand in appreciation. 'So, that place you mentioned, by the reservoir, it sounds beautiful.'

'Sorry. Yeah, it was a pretty nice area. I don't know if it was due to the huge ferns and pine trees that were around the place, but the air... the air was just... awesome. Anyway, we decided to go into the capital on the third day, and we got there around about three in the afternoon. The place even had a castle if you can believe it, right in the centre of the city.'

'A castle?' Janine muttered, looking at her husband with contempt. 'I remember when someone else said he was going to take me to a castle.'

Trying his best not to lock eyes with his sneering wife, Andy concealed his face by raising his mug to his face. Ignoring the still ridiculously hot tea, he gulped down the rest, causing a flourish of heat down his chest. Thinking that a tactical retreat was a good idea, he abruptly stood up. 'Drinks anyone? No? Ok then.' He moved towards the kitchen area.

'Anyway,' Michael continued, 'a little distance away was a swanky little opera house, covered in slate and varnished wood. The place was packed full of people. Didn't have a clue what they were saying though, couldn't understand the language. They did speak in English when we talked to them, so that was cool, I guess.'

'Ahh, I just remembered... that's where Merlin the wizard came from, in the King Arthur stories,' Janine said with her eyes wide.

'Umm, I think so? ... Where was I... Oh yeah, we were drinking some sodas, just opposite it in a little restaurant called Horizons. Which was right next door to a couple of water fountains. It's weird the stuff you remember.... Anyway, a couple of kids were running in and out, doing their best not to get hit by the water. It was hilarious, Abby couldn't stop laughing.'

That happy moment appeared like a flash in his mind, just like a picture. He could see Abby's beautiful lips, spread into a wide laugh. Her hair flung over her shoulders, golden blond and straightened to perfection. He recalled her laugh being so infectious that he didn't care that one kid got hit by a jet of water. He laughed because she was happy, because she was safe....

'Then, it happened,' he said, his voice cold and emotionless.

'I still don't know if one of the shots was for me, but... I guess I'll never find out now. I just remember the look on her face as the round passed through her, hitting the guy in the suit behind her. She looked at me, and her smile dropped... she... she was scared... then she fell from her chair. I took cover beside her when they started open firing on innocent people.'

Janine was tightly holding the back of his hand as he began squeezing the back of the sofa.

'It's not like the movies, you know? Abby looked awake in her eyes, and when I was holding her head in my hand, she still had colour in her face, but I've seen enough wounds in my time to know... it was too late. It's hard to explain, but you get a feel of death... ah, never mind. I... I knew I couldn't save her. She smiled at me though...'

Janine's eyes began to well up, as she pursed her lips at that image.

'Then,' Michael continued, determined to get to the end, 'just as she was leaving me, she looked over my shoulder and smiled. I know she said something, but with the people panicking and the shots being fired, I... I didn't catch it. And she was gone.'

With a sympathetic tut, Janine gave his hand an extra squeeze. 'Oh, Michael, I'm so sorry!'

The tears had started to stream down her face. Anticipating this reaction, Andy had returned with another mug of tea, passing a tissue to Janine as he crossed her.

'Oh, Michael, that must have been awful,' she said, her voice choked with emotions.

Even little Billy, who was content with crawling around the table until that moment, had now stopped. He was looking at his mom, trying to understand why she was crying.

'Bastards,' Andy said, with complete sincerity.

Normally, Janine would have grilled him for cursing in front of the baby. However, she thought, considering what she had just found out and what she felt about those assholes herself, she couldn't agree more with her husband. She found that she had a renewed admiration for Andrew, as this was a huge secret to keep, even from her. He probably knew the effect that this story would have on her and didn't want to see her upset. She made a mental note to cuddle him in bed for a little bit longer that night.

Shifting his gaze from Janine and with his eyes becoming distant, Michael continued.

'I managed to take down four of them that day. Two, with their own weapons, as they were open firing on anything that moved. The other two, I caught up with in a vehicle I commandeered from an old man. Poor bastard had been hit in the head by a stray round. Let's just say, I returned the favour for that guy.'

In a moment of clarity, Michael realised where he was and who was present here. He omitted the part where he managed to get one of the guys into a headlock and, with one quick movement, swooped under the terrorist's blue bandanna, savagely fish-hooking the pleading guy's face and leaving him with an open bloody tear that reached around to his ear.

He also didn't tell them about how he threw a steak knife, which he kept with him from the restaurant, into the eye of the driver of the car he was chasing. The flying blade hit its target, as the driver was looking out the window, eyes wide full of fear. The car swerved into oncoming traffic and collided with another vehicle. The driver's head hit the steering wheel with such force that the knife punched through the back of his head.

Yep, that would not be a good bedtime story for Billy.

'Anyway...,' he said, looking back at the married couple, 'I managed to persuade one of them to tell me who they were working for. They were part of that bullshit terrorist group called Blue Dawn.'

Janine turned towards Andy so fast that she cricked neck and looked at him with a face that seemed to signal as if the missing factor of an equation had finally been revealed. She turned back to Michael, wide-eyed.

'The first Blue Dawn massacre,' she said with a whisper. 'I remember watching a news section about them. They were a couple of religious group fanatics that thought that the beam was their sign to cleanse the world, remember, baby?' With the last bit, she tapped Andy's arm, prompting him to take a better grip of his mug.

'Yes, honey, I remember.'

Then Andrew curiously looked at Michael. 'How come you didn't tell me about Blue Dawn?'

'I know you, and I know you would have wanted to look into it further. But trust me. I have contacts who have contacts in places that aren't even on maps anymore. All I found out was that May 5th, 2073, the day my wife and son died, was Blue Dawn's first major hit.'

Leaning forward and listening intently, Andy looked troubled; he was deep in thought. Michael couldn't figure out if he looked like he had seen a ghost or if he was already trying to put the puzzle together.

'My sources,' Michael continued undeterred, 'tell me that about eight years before they hit the UK, the group went dark. Due to a kind of restructuring or new management, so to speak. They became organised and incredibly well-funded.'

'Yes, yes!' Janine jumped in. 'They managed to steal millions of crypto currencies by accessing accounts, extracting a portion of the balance and disguising the lost funds. No one knew it was happening until one company went bankrupt, but they couldn't close the account because of the fake balance remaining in it. But by that time, Blue Dawn had already diverted the funds completely.'

Michael nodded. He was all too aware of how Blue Dawn carefully left no trace. He had depleted a small fortune of resources and money to try and find them. He had even used all his old CIA contacts, the one who didn't exactly exist but owed Michael a favour. Whoever the leader of Blue Dawn was, they were good.

'I did find out who the bastard who fired that the first shot... the shot that took her away from me. It was the leader of Blue Dawn himself. The goddamn ghost that I chased for years. I wish I got him before we left.'

'Hey,' Janine spoke up, consoling him. 'I'm a big believer in karma, and after all the evil things they have done, I honestly believe that they will get what's coming to them.'

Placing his hand her on top of hers, he nodded with a hopeful yet realistic smile. Noticing that Andy was still staring straight ahead and deep in thought, Michael opened his mouth, about to say something. However, he was interrupted when his wrist strap vibrated.

'Sorry,' he said, bringing his watch up in front of him. Then, swiping the illuminated screen, he connected the call.

'Sorry for the intrusion, Captain,' Commander Jenkins said respectfully.

'It's fine, Commander. What is it?'

'Well...,' she began saying, but the connection went silent suddenly.

'Commander?' Concern grew in his voice.

'...Sir, I think you need to get back here as soon as possible. We've found something on the ship's sensors.'

'On my way.' He swiped again and ended the call. 'Sorry, guys. Duty calls.'

'That sounded ominous,' Andy said, finally back in the room.

'Yep, but when does it ever get easy for us?' Michael replied, swinging his feet onto the floor, ready to stand.

'Please, come back any time, Michael. You will always have a home with us,' Janine said sweetly, tightly cupping his hand before releasing it.

'Thank you, Janine.' He began to stand up. 'That means a— Ahhhh!'

Both Andy and Janine looked at him with immediate concern as he hunched over in pain. Sliding his hand down his right leg and leaning on his other one for stability, Michael rummaged in his boot, only to pry out a bright yellow children's building block.

'Really?' Michael said, smiling and holding up the small brick towards Billy. 'Booby-trapping my boot already?'

Billy responded by kicking his legs out and clapping his hands together, muttering something like 'Dad-da umm da'.

Laughing, Michael reached down and gently rubbed Billy's head. 'Oh, so your dad put ya up to it.'

Janine covered her mouth, trying to stifle her laugh. Andy, who had also joined her in laughing, had his free hand up pleading innocence. 'Don't look at me.'

'Well, whatever you're teaching him, keep it up,' Michael said, dropping the brick on the table. 'I'm beginning to like this kid.'

He turned towards the door as Andy and Janine rose from their seats and followed.

'Thanks, guys,' he said, turning to face them. 'It's been... well, you know.'

'You're welcome,' Andy said, easing his friend's awkwardness by slapping him on the shoulder.

After one final embrace from Janine, Michael turned back towards the exit and left in the direction of the bridge, feeling slightly unburdened.

Walking back over to the sofa, Janine stopped, realising that her husband was still by the door.

'You ok, baby?' she asked, concerned as he had the same distant look from before.

Andy snapped out of his trance and forced a half-smile. 'Yeah, honey, I'm fine. It's just...'

'Just what?'

'Well, it's just that thing he said, about Blue Dawn... I can't explain it, but it just feels wrong.'

'I know,' Janine said, moving closer to him and rubbing his arm. 'What happened to him was awful and...'

'It's not that. When Michael told me about losing his wife, he said it was a couple of years ago, by some...'

He looked over her shoulders and back at her, before whispering, '...asshole terrorists.'

'And?' she asked impatiently, waiting for him to get to the point.

'And now that I know what attack it was, it's just become a whole lot weirder.'

Before Janine had a chance to ask why, he continued.

'You see. I remember that attack because the guy in the suit who got shot, who Michael talked about, was called Alexander Hoffer. Do you remember? He was the lead investigator on that Jamie Sidis project. You know the one that exploded everywhere? Well, what was weird about him being shot dead is that a day later, Alexander Hoffer video-called me, but didn't say a word and his screen was blank.'

'I don't know. It was so long ago, baby. But I think I remember you talking to someone,' she said, baffled at the revelation.

'Yep,' he nodded. He stopped and turned to her, his face dire. 'I reported it to the cops. They said they would investigate it and told me not to dwell on it because it could simply have been an accident. But... after everything that has happened and what happened to Mikey... it just makes me really want to know... who the hell was on the other side of that call.'

Chapter 10

Milestone

By the time Michael had reached the bridge, the double doors were open with a couple of tech guys walking out. They looked captivated by the data they had on their tablets, having no idea who had just walked past them.

Not giving Ian Thomas, the ship's young and enthusiastic pilot, a chance to call the room to attention, Michael briskly walked straight over to Commander Jenkins. She was leaning over the ship's navigation terminal, accompanied by the ship's technical communications expert, Shabir Ali. Shabir was in his late twenties, donning a pair of thick brown glasses with flecks of red.

'Commander?' Michael expectantly asked, prompting Elizabeth to flinch.

'Captain! Sorry, I didn't even know you were behind me,' she said, straightening up. 'You need to see this. Shabir, show the captain what you've found.'

Shabir Ali turned to face the captain.

'Captain, how do you do?' Shabir asked in a thick Indian accent.

'What have you got for me, Shabir?' Straight to the point, Michael wanted to know what had the bridge in a borderline frenzy.

'Ok. So, we were collecting data from the nearby planets, using our detection beacons and laser scanning technology, practically pinging at all frequencies, shortwave and longwave. We wanted to establish—'

'Shabir,' Michael interrupted him, impatiently rotating his finger.

Raising his eyebrows and nervously blinking, Shabir turned sideways and pointed at an image on the monitor. 'Well, we... ah... we found this, sir.'

Moving closer to the terminal, to his amazement, Michael saw what all the fuss was about. The image on the screen displayed what appeared to be a formation of buildings surrounded by roads. Michael wondered in awe how that was possible.

'Optical illusion?' Commander Jenkins asked, 'Or lighting, maybe?'

'Nope,' interjected Michael, pointing at the roads leading away from the buildings. 'Nature doesn't work in straight lines. How did you find it?'

'Umm... well, here's where it gets stranger,' Shabir said, pulling at his shirt collar uncomfortably. 'From the very first appearance of the beam, scientists were able to get a sort of package frequency, like a whole bunch of frequencies together. But no one knew what to do with it or even had a clue about what it was. So, one of my secondary objectives was to keep an eye on it, to see if it changed throughout the journey. Well...'

It seemed like the entire bridge had gone quiet, discreetly turning their heads to listen. Even Roman, who normally had no time for what people had to say, had uncharacteristically turned his chair to listen.

'What I didn't expect...,' Shabir continued, 'not in a million years was to find the same strange signal, coming from that planet, right there.'

'What are the conditions down there?'

'Nitrogen, oxygen and argon levels all look good. Surface-suits will be needed though. The gravity is a little heavy down there.'

Michael stood, arms crossed, trying to figure out how this was even possible. He turned his head towards Commander Jenkins.

'I think we need to take a closer look.'

Nodding, she turned to address the bridge. She raised her voice to be heard clearly. 'In light of the new information, we will need to gather a reconnaissance party. This will be an in-and-out job, so put out the call and prepare to depart within the hour. Dress order, surface-suits and essentials only.'

As she turned back to her captain, the bridge erupted with sounds and movements. Officers switched on their communication devices in their ears, informing the relevant departments of the upcoming expedition. Even Roman put a call through to Lieutenant Saunders, instructing her to prep a team for additional support.

'Was there anything you wanted to add?' Commander Jenkins asked, mirroring Michael by crossing her arms.

'Nope, couldn't have said it better myself.' Then, he turned and slapped Shabir Ali on his back, saying, 'Good job, kid.'

'Sir?' The young ensign Thomas called out.

Michael walked over to him, resting his hand on his shoulder. 'What's up?'

'Sir, would you like me to adjust our course and get us closer to the planet?'

'Sounds good to me.'

Patting the kid on the shoulder, Michael shifted his weight as he began to turn.

'Ah, sir?' Ensign Thomas hesitantly asked, stopping Michael from leaving.

'Yep?'

'Sorry, sir, do you need me... to pilot down to the surface?'

Looking at the kid's face, Michael could see that the kid was clearly uncomfortable with the idea. So, shaking his head slightly and giving him a smile, Michael eased his tension.

'Nah. You sit this one out. Besides, I've heard that no one else can pilot the Aletheia as well as you.'

Commander Jenkins approached the captain along with Roman. Their cold looks and body mannerisms gave Michael a feeling that they had an issue about something.

'Keep an eye on the ship for me, kid,' Michael said quietly. He then turned to face his second-in-command and head of ship security.

'Captain, would you mind settling a disagreement for me,' Commander Jenkins politely asked, face beginning to strain. Something was bothering her.

'Shoot.'

'For some reason, Lieutenant Commander Sokolov seems to deem it acceptable to bring all his security to the planet. I personally think it is unnecessary, considering the only dangers I foresee would be from vegetation.'

With his arms crossed and looking at her from the corner of his eyes, Roman waited until she had finished. He then presented his side.

'Captain, it is my responsibility to ensure the discipline on ship. It is also my responsibility to see to the safety of the crew. I feel that since the location is an unknown area, there might be unknown dangers.'

Weighing both arguments, Michael realised that Elizabeth had a good point; it was just a couple of buildings and plants after all. Roman, on the other hand, was also right; they had no idea what they were walking into. Michael decided to find some middle ground.

'Ok, here's what we're gonna do. Roman, you and two additional members of security will escort the party. Commander, I understand where you stand on this, but Roman has a good point. We don't know what's down there, and I don't want us to be blindsided by something on our first daytrip. Understood?'

Reluctantly, both agreed, with Roman immediately turning to make a call. Elizabeth hung back to speak with the captain.

'So, I take it, you're coming with us?' she asked in a disapproving tone.

'Yep. Hell, I'm gonna be the first person to set foot on that planet.'

'I've got a feeling that I won't be able to talk you out of it. So, I'll see to the preparations.'

Michael could tell that she was still not happy. It was obvious not just from the tone of her voice, which was still quite composed, but also from the stare that could melt paint off a wall.

Well, I'm not gonna back down, Michael thought, keeping eye contact but subconsciously backing away.

'Will there be anything else?' she asked, maintaining the eye contact.

'No, Commander, you've been great.'

What the hell was that, he thought. 'You've been great?' The words that came out his mouth sounded like a child's feeble attempt to say sorry for pulling someone's hair.

With a smirk of satisfaction, she turned and saw to her business. Unsure if he had won that encounter, Michael quickly checked his watch and proceeded to leave the bridge.

After a short while, Michael had changed into the gear needed for the surface, then headed straight to the docking bay. He was met by an ensemble of crew members, specialising in different fields of research: archaeologists and cryptographers accompanied by a couple of botanists and wildlife experts.

Approaching the doors to the bay, Michael could feel the presence of someone standing close to him, just out of eyeshot. Turning his head slightly, he relaxed when he figured out the person was none other than the ship's chief medical officer, Doctor Jiao Tang.

'Hey, Doc, you scared the bejesus outta me.'

Keeping her head down and facing the doors, she pursed her lips. 'I doubt that very much, Mr Quade.'

Fidgeting with the pouches on her suit, she seemed concerned that her buttons weren't tightly done. 'And besides, I've seen all of your medical records, and your heart rate has never been elevated to reflect fear.'

The doors opened, and with a roll of his eyes, he began to move forward. Then, surprisingly, Doctor Tang grabbed him by the arm.

'Ah... Doc? We need to go this way,' he said, wondering why she was making sure they were out of ear shot.

'I needed to ask you something,' she said, satisfied that they were alone. 'Did you give the order?'

Not having a clue as to what order she was talking about and not having the time for her eccentrics, he decided to be blunt. 'What order?'

Awkwardly, she raised her head but dared not look him in the eye. 'Disposal of the back-up blood banks?'

Beginning to feel like he was out of the loop, he could feel frustration creeping down the corridor of his mind. 'Wha... what blood banks?'

'Before we left the earth, remember, everyone gave blood a few times? Well, that was for emergency situations, such as vital blood transfusions. But our cold storage is automated and has a biohazard disposal feature.'

Still confused but curious about what had happened to the blood he gave, Michael gave her his undivided attention.

'Fifty-nine samples were destroyed, which can be done by only authorised personnel. I just wanted to know if you know anything about it.'

'But what would be the point?' he asked, frowning and trying to figure out why someone would get rid of blood.

'That is why I need to find out who gave the order. The medical bay is under my direction, and no one else's.'

'Ok...,' he began saying, gesturing her to calm down. 'Look, first things first. We go down to this planet and have a look around. Then, when we get back, I promise that we will get to the bottom of this.'

Still unhappy with the situation, Doctor Tang reluctantly accepted his terms with a short, sharp nod. Then, she began to walk through the docking bay doors, followed by a concerned Michael.

Everyone who were selected to go on the side-mission stood close to their shuttles in squads. There were no more than two dozen crew members, not including the bridge crew, Lieutenant Commander Sokolov, and Michael himself.

Standing on the raised platform and overseeing the transport ships, Michael waited until all eyes were on him before he cleared his throat and addressed them.

'Ok, guys. You have all been briefed on the land formation down there, so we need to find out as much as we can in the shortest amount of time. Take as many pictures, recordings and samples as you can. But be careful. The gravity is heavier on the surface. Even though we are all wearing these suits, we are still vulnerable to environmental elements. So, take your time and stick to your training. Apart from that, let's enjoy our first steps on a planet untouched by people from the earth. Stay safe, and see y'all down there.'

Then, the crew began to board their ships, with apprehensive excitement in their eyes. Roman, Lieutenant Gemma Saunders and one other security personnel remained behind to monitor the boarding of the crew.

Michael approached the team and couldn't help thinking that they resembled a bunch of sheepdogs, herding the flock into their pens.

'Captain,' Lieutenant Saunders said, then quickly turned back to watch the crew continue to board.

'Hey,' Michael replied, looking at the ever-diligent lieutenant. 'How are we looking? Any issues?'

She was about to answer but was cut off by Roman's deep and dominating voice. 'Everything is under control, Captain; you should take your seat.'

Michael didn't take kindly to the way Roman was telling him what to do, so he locked eyes with the big guy and smiled. 'Actually, I'm gonna stay right here, until you have boarded.'

The emphasis on *you* was not lost on Roman. Although he showed no signs of change, Michael could tell that he didn't receive the counter-order well. The left side of the big guy's mouth twitched before he turned and signalled his team to follow.

I won that one, you big tree, Michael thought. Then he walked into his designated shuttle and took a seat at the front of the ship, next to the pilot. The shuttle door closed behind him with a hiss, creating an airtight seal.

The dull grey surface suits were made from a flexible material and were adaptive to the people wearing them, but they were not very comfortable when sitting down. After several adjustments, including the straps that were cutting off the most important area of circulation between his legs, Michael opened a com channel to the other ships.

'Ok, guys, let's go!'

After sending their confirmations back to the lead ship, the shuttle engines started to ramp up while waiting for the docks to vent. Amber lights flashing adjacent to the huge dock doors switched to red as a safety feature, to warn the ships that the door was opening. Releasing the ship's securing clamps, the shuttle began to slowly move forward, then picked up speed when the pilot engaged the stronger propulsion system.

Just as the shuttles were approaching atmospheric entry, a call came through from the engineering section. 'Captain? Hello... Hello? Is this fooking thing on?'

'This is Captain Quade.' Michael quickly jumped in, realising it was Rob Humphries on the line. 'What is it, Bob?'

A moment went by where it was just radio silence, probably caused by the entry disturbance. Then, with his thick west-country British accent, the voice of the Aletheia's chief engineer reappeared. 'Yeah, there's a little delay from my end, so I thought I'd play you guys a record... you know, to help you relax...'

Michael did become a bit suspicious, especially when he heard the big guy laugh at the end of that transmission, but as a rock fan himself, he was curious as to what record he had chosen.

'And here it is. Enjoy!' Big Bob said, switching to the music he had carefully selected.

As soon as the music began to play, Michael smiled; he could tell within the first few chords what the song was: The Bangles' cover of Hazy Shade of Winter. Michael immediately switched to all channels, broadcasting the song as they descended onto the planet.

Soon, the shuttles broke through the atmosphere and began circling the area that they deemed safe as the landing spot. Even with the force stabilisers engaged, they encountered more resistance than expected, making the ride less enjoyable for some. Good thing the professor stayed behind, Michael thought, or he'd be reaching for the nearest trash-can by now.

Just as they approached the ground, the air became calmer. The pilots showed their skills by landing the shuttles routinely, as if they had been doing this their whole lives. When the shuttles hovered above the ground, the downward winds made circular dust spots, which looked like small whirlpools of dirt. Plants began to sway back and forth, waving and twisting for the first time in an exceptionally long while.

The shuttle's landing gear reached out in preparation to handle the weight of the ship. The fleet that left the sealed compartments were carefully located at four weight bearing points, at every corner. Then with a crunch, the shuttles landed on the open field, a small way off from the building formation.

After everyone had done their final checks of their equipment and all the surface-suits were switched on, the lead shuttle's exit door slowly opened. Two lines of crew members stood, facing the door and awaiting

Michael's word to disembark. Michael stood ready, wearing his modified and combat-ready helmet. Then, with a quick adjustment of his rifle, down by his side, he was ready.

With a deep breath and a profound sense of wonder, Michael stepped out of the shuttle, into a new world.

Chapter 11

A Bridge too Far

It was a strange feeling for Michael, standing on a ground that felt like the earth's, but, at the same time, so different. The instant realisation hit him that if it weren't for the suits they were wearing, he would have already been feeling the effects of the intense pull of gravity. He also knew that just under a centimetre of fabric separated him and the environment around him. He made a mental note to be careful.

Turing to face the shuttles, he realised that the crew had already assembled themselves into their assigned groups. All of them were expectantly looking at their captain, awaiting orders to proceed.

Roman had ordered his security team to spread out and ensure that the environment held no hidden surprises. Scanning the horizon and checking the ground for surfaces that looked suspicious, they were remarkably effective at providing the scientists comfort and making them anxious at the same time.

However, Michael almost burst into a right fit of laughter when he saw Roman in full view. What he found particularly hilarious was just how the chief of security looked in his surface suit. Whoever had measured him up must have had a bad day or something. The guy, being the size of a bull, was wearing the suit like he was ready to try out for a bobsleigh team.

Giggles from a couple of blushing female scientists emphasised how revealing the suit really was. The snug fitting accentuated Roman's body, especially around the sensitive areas.

Subduing his amusement and realising the genuine potential for Roman to get into trouble, Michael caught his attention by spreading his fingers on top of his own helmet, giving Roman a clear sign to approach immediately. A moment later, the man stood looming over the captain, eyes still darting back and forth, ever vigilant of the surroundings.

'Yes, Captain?'

'Roman,' Michael said, clutching the straps on his chest and letting his elbows hang. 'I couldn't help but notice that your... your suit is not correctly fitted.'

What he really wanted to say was 'hey, would you mind putting your dick away? You're making us all look bad'. However, he thought maybe a more diplomatic approach would be more prudent.

'I apologise, Captain,' Roman said, looking down at his body, then back at Michael. 'My measurements were taken by a little mouse of a man. He measured wrong, I think.'

'Never mind about that,' Michael said with haste. 'How are you feeling? I mean, can you carry on down here?' He was referring to the difference in gravity and the effect it would have if the suit were to malfunction.

'Yes, Captain, I have checked that the suit has not been compromised.'

Roman slipped his weapon round to his back and raised his arms to the side, flexing his impressive muscles. The suit held under the strain and showed no signs of tearing.

'Ok,' Michael said, relaxing. Then, he reached into his utility pouch and handed Roman a large bandana. 'But, for safety reasons, put this around your waist.'

Tilting his head in the direction of the red-faced scientists, Michael wanted to be discrete in the concealment of the big guy's junk. After a moment of confusion, Roman figured out the source of the distraction. He proceeded to nonchalantly tie the cloth around his waist.

Michael turned towards the rest of the crew, resentment evident on some of the women's faces for blocking their view of Roman's package.

'Ok, let's move out.'

Michael turned and headed in the direction of the ruins, followed by the expedition party.

The planet was beautiful in its simplicity, its land flat and undisturbed as far as the eye could see.

Under an unsettling red glow, the land was a mixture of strange green plant life, with thick blades of tall grass shivering in the smallest of wind currents. In between the patches of the intertwined plant life lay blankets of yellow dusty mounds of earth, resembling miniature sand dunes. Lean and weathered trees were sporadically spread throughout the patches of grass, including along the rubble road that the crew walked on.

'Doctor Smith?' Michael yelled towards the party.

Recalling the manifest, Michael knew that if he had any questions regarding land formations or the geography of a planet, Doctor Ryan Smith was the man to ask. With over three decades of experience and multiple published papers on the formations of landmasses and geological theory, Dr Smith was respected and well-established in his field.

'Yes... Yes, Captain.'

The doctor shuffled towards the captain with haste. Given that the party was still on the move, this caused the man to breathe heavily.

'Thank you, Doctor. Would you mind walking with me for a while?'

The exhausted doctor was fifty-four years old. He had spent most of his life sitting behind a desk. As a result, he had the fitness level of someone much older.

'Not...' He tried to catch his breath. 'Not at all, Captain. How can I help?'

Slowing his pace to help the silver-haired doctor compose himself, Michael thought about how he was going to word the question he was itching to ask.

'Well, it's just strange...,' Michael said, scouring the land in search of something. 'Let me know if I sound stupid, Doctor, but how come the planet doesn't turn?'

The podgy man raised one of his dark eyebrows and replied respectfully and as simply as possible. 'That's not stupid at all, captain. In fact, a lot of the crew probably haven't figured that out yet. Many planets have different characteristics. Some are gas giants; some are essentially water worlds. Usually, the closer you get to the centre or the star of a galaxy, the dryer or barren the planet becomes. That is the usual set up of a galaxy. However, what makes this planet so wonderful is that it has a red dwarf star.'

Noticing that some sort of basic bridge formation lay ahead, Michael turned to Lieutenant Gemma Saunders, who was walking alongside the party. He signalled to a potential hazard on the route by using two spread fingers to point at his eyes, then closed them to point in the direction of the danger.

Lieutenant Saunders reacted without question and called up the extra security staff to accompany her. Moving at a pace faster than the expedition team's, she was determined to reach the hazard and gauge the potential danger to the crew. Roman, who had been watching along the opposite side, remained at his current pace, letting the lieutenant deal with trivial matters as bridges.

'Sorry, Dr Smith. You were saying?' Michael resumed his focus on the subject matter.

'It is fine... hmm... where was I? Oh yes, that's it. So, what makes this planet so different from the ones in our solar system is that the gravity here has such a dramatic effect on the speed of rotation. Meaning that it does turn, but at a much, much slower speed than the earth's. What I'm more curious about is the plant life.'

'What's weird about it?'

'Well, it's just strange. I mean, have you noticed that the light has a red tint to it? Well, that is because of the dwarf star. Plants should not be able to thrive in these conditions, not as well as they have, anyway. Fungi, however, would have no problem at all.'

'Not gonna lie, Doc. Most of that went over my head, but I thank you for trying to help me understand this place better.'

'Anytime, Captain.' Turning to face Michael, he hesitated but mustered the courage to ask, 'What are we going to do if we encounter intelligent life here, Captain?'

Michael, who was still moving forward, responded by turning his head slightly and giving the doctor a reassuring smile, followed by a child-like shrug. 'Who knows, Doc, who knows?'

Ahead, Lieutenant Saunders raised a clenched fist in the air, indicating a halt to the column of crew from the Aletheia.

With his eyes focused on the signal, Michael naturally and immediately called out, ‘Stop!’

All eyes were firmly focused on him as he switched his coms to the security dedicated channel, much to the parties’ dismay.

‘Report?’ Michael asked, hand still on his interface panel on his left wrist.

‘Ahh... you might wanna take a look at this, sir.’

The concern in Lieutenant Saunders’s voice was enough for Michael to turn to face the crew, rapidly seeking to meet Roman’s eyes.

‘Keep everyone here until I give the order to move, understood?’

Hesitating, Roman replied with a direct and underwhelming, ‘Yes, Captain.’

Satisfied that he at least got a response from the big guy, Michael turned towards the bridge and began to move towards Lieutenant Saunders. As he approached the formation, he could see her and the additional security guard crouched down, parallel to the bridge.

‘What’s up?’ Michael asked, startling the security guard.

‘The bridge,’ she said, pointing to the left-hand side where the segments of stone were protruding above the surface. ‘It looks unstable on that side.’

He followed her line of sight and could see the problem. Large sections of ancient stone had been fractured by strange looking vines and flowers. Although the flowers were beautiful and stunning violet bulbs, the roots had taken their toll on the stone.

After a quick inspection of the area, in hope of an alternative route, Michael knew that the party would struggle to traverse banks either side. The slopes next to the bridge looked like they would need climbing gear. So, he decided that the best course of action would be the basic, yet proven effective route technique.

‘Lieutenant, I want you to make sure that everyone gets across the right side of the bridge, in single file, *carefully and slowly*.’ The emphasis on the last part, he noticed, was well received by the lieutenant.

Following his orders, Lieutenant Saunders decided that the best way to check the instability of the bridge was to cross it herself first.

‘Understood, sir.’ Then, without hesitation or fear, she walked steadily and confidently across, sticking to the right-hand side.

Watching apprehensively, Michael felt as if every step was a potential landmine or that, at any second, he would have to move to reach her, and with the planet’s gravity, he would have to move fast. He relaxed only when she reached the other side and raised a thumbs up towards him.

Nodding, Michael was impressed with her audacity.

'Jesus Christ, Gemma, at least pretend that you were nervous.'

'What's wrong, sir? Worried that I've got bigger balls than you?' she replied sarcastically.

Smiling and tilting his head in a sign of agreement, he turned to face the crew and locked eyes with Roman. 'Roman?'

'Yes, Captain,' he replied in a monotone voice.

'I want you to move the party forward, in a single file, taking care to stay to the right while crossing the bridge. Understood?'

'Yes, Captain.'

I will make it a personal mission to turn you into a human, Michael thought, then raised his arm to wave the party forward.

Over the next ten minutes, most of the crew had crossed the bridge, overseen by the security team. Everything proceeded as planned, as they carefully walked across, making sure that every foot placement was intentional and controlled.

Michael filed in, close to the rear, behind Doctor Tang, who was muttering to herself about what sounded like a list of random medicinal compounds. Right then, a young man walking just behind Michael stopped, distracted by a flower that had begun to open its bulb and turn towards the direction the party was heading. Fascinated by this sudden and miraculous movement of plant life, he moved in for a closer look, crossing the central-line of the bridge. As he did so, the stone began to shift under his feet, resulting in the young man stumbling forward.

Under normal circumstances, reaching out to catch himself would have been the most normal and possibly successful reaction. However, the gravity of the planet meant that any downward force of his hand slapping against the side of the bridge was multiplied tenfold onto the stone. What he didn't realise was that the initial stumble had torn the bottom of his suit, just enough to cause an instability in its gravity resistive technology.

Michael turned at the sound of the tear, knowing the severity of the situation. Any damage to the suits in these conditions could be fatal. His concern grew when he saw a man lying face down on the floor.

'Medic!' he yelled, darting over to the man.

Taking care where he was placing each step, not to succumb to the same tragic fate as the man on the floor, Michael reached the man. Assessing him, he wanted to check the casualty's suit for damage. He knew if it was damaged, then time would be against them. Feeling around the suit to find the tear, he didn't realise Doctor Tang had approached him from behind.

‘Don’t move him!’ she said abruptly.

‘I wasn’t planning to,’ he calmly replied, trying to keep the situation under control. ‘I was looking for the... there!’

He could see that the gash was just above the boot on the injured man’s left foot – a jagged flap revealed a grey mesh fabric underneath. The interweaving material, a vital factor of the gravity stabilisation process, was exposed and turning a dark maroon colour.

‘Multiple fractures, and he’s struggling to breathe.’ The urgency in Doctor Tang’s voice was barely noticeable. She had years of experience working under pressure, giving her the tools required to focus on the patient rather than the chaos.

‘I know, Doc, I’m on it,’ Michael said, reaching into a side pouch.

He pulled out what looked like a modified silver aerosol can with a wider funnel, locked in place by a bright yellow safety pin. Pulling the pin with a click, Michael hovered the can above the area of damage to the suit. Then, with a sound that resembled a shaving foam can being operated, a thick cement like lather sprayed onto the tear. Within a fraction of a second, the substance began to solidify and seal the hole in the suit.

‘Captain, is the situation under control?’ Roman’s booming voice sounded over the secure channel.

'Wait for further instructions, Roman,' snapped Michael.

'Understood,' Roman replied. He then stopped the party, who had already crossed the bridge. There was something in Roman's voice that disturbed Michael; it almost sounded like... humour.

'Captain, look,' Doctor Tang interrupted his inner monologue, pointing at the man's back, which had begun to rise and fall naturally.

'Ok, Doc, I want you to take...' Realising that he didn't even know who the man was, Michael pressed on his interface strap on his wrist. After a couple of swipes, a tracer identified the man as Donald Bishop.

'I want you to take Donald back to the shuttle. I'll assign you a couple of people to help out.'

He turned and pointed at two of the scientists watching the situation, who had also the least amount of equipment, and waved them forward. 'You two, help Dr Tang with Don here. Watch your footing and take it slow, understood?'

Reaching into her rucksack, Doctor Tang pulled out what looked like a metal box, which was actually multiple folded sheets comprising collapsed sections made of a magnesium-based alloy – light as a feather, but as strong as titanium. She placed it on the ground next to the injured man, unfolded it and carefully shuffled Donald onto it, taking care to support the fractured areas.

'Wait!' she barked.

'What?'

'Take this.' She reached into Donald's utility pouch and pulled out his spare can of sealant and handed it to Michael, her eyes not leaving the can. 'Hopefully, you won't need to use the fast-tar again. But take it, just in case.'

Nodding, Michael placed the can in the empty side-pouch where his had been. As the two scientists were lifting Donald, he looked at Doctor Tang then at Donald.

'Will he be ok?'

'He'll be fine,' she said. 'I'm not sure if the field hospital on the shuttle will have the equipment that I need, but I'll keep you informed.'

Stirring on the stretcher, Donald began to incoherently mumble, trying to point at the flowers peeking from between the cracks of the bridge. Tilting her head, she looked at her scanner. 'We need to get him some pain relief fast. Captain, we've gotta go.'

'Ok.'

Michael switched to the security channel.

'Roman...' he said, looking at the party ahead, 'I want you to personally escort the doctor back to the shuttle, you know... just in case they need to swap out carrying Donald.'

A noticeable silence hung over the radio as Michael awaited a response. He could see Roman marching through the column ahead towards him. So, Michael raised his hand and tapped the side of his helmet with his finger.

'Understood, Captain,' Roman said begrudgingly.

You bet it is, asshole, Michael thought. He made a mental note to have a chat with the big guy about his somewhat lacking communication skills.

'Roman is going to escort you back, Doctor. Think of it as an extra pair of hands if you need them,' he said with a smile.

Lacking the same amusement that Michael had, Doctor Tang moved her head indignantly and walked alongside the injured man, towards the direction of the shuttle.

Catching up with the rest of the crew and letting Roman pass without a glance, Michael was approached by Lieutenant Saunders.

'Pissing contest?' she asked on a direct channel, nodding at Roman's direction.

'Yeah, something like that,' Michael answered, adjusting the straps on his side pouches.

'You know, you might wanna cut him some slack. I don't wanna speak out of line here, but he's your head of security. He's not supposed to be best friends with anyone.'

'Gemma, that's not what my issue is with the guy.' Michael stood there, looking back at the doctor and Roman walking away. 'It's... it's just that I've served alongside guys like him before, and when shit goes side-ways, he's the type to leave people behind. I just... I don't know. Something seems off.'

As she rested an arm over the top of her weapon, it could be seen that she wanted to add something but decided not to pursue the matter.

She straightened up. 'So, what now, Captain?'

Michael hesitated as he looked down the line of the expedition team and turned back to Lieutenant Saunders. 'Hell, we made it this far. Be a shame to turn back now.'

'Understood,' she agreed, switched to the open channel and announced to everyone. 'Ok, everyone. Move out.'

'But watch your goddamn feet,' Michael added in a tone stern and clear enough to get the point across.

The next half hour was thankfully uneventful. The accident on the bridge had left the moral of the crew somewhat tainted. Carefully selecting where they would place each step, they found themselves becoming increasingly apprehensive, about the planet's unforeseen dangers.

The scenery during the journey remained relatively the same, open patchy land stretching off into the distance, apart from the huge built-up structure that the party was approaching.

They were all walking through an area that resembled a massive, curved cobbled courtyard, spanning the width of the massive stone-cut structure. The centre of this, much to the crew's dismay, had collapsed in on itself due to centuries of harsh conditions and strong forces ferociously pulling at stress points.

'Ok, guys,' Michael said, raising his hands in the air and stopping the party. 'We don't have much time left down here, so do what you need to do fast. We leave in sixty minutes.'

Lieutenant Saunders took charge of organising the scientists into groups, designating areas where they could set up their workstations in the courtyard. The scientists immediately began to do what they did best. They took readings, pictures, soil samples and rock samples; anything that could be collected, they collected it. Michael moved closer to the centre of the structure where the entrance had been blocked by huge slabs of rock. A group of scientists were caught up in a heated disagreement.

'No, there is no point,' said one, pointing at the structure. 'There's nothing in there. I'm detecting no signals from behind there at all. Besides, the signal that brought us here has dissipated.'

‘What’s with the light, guys?’ Michael asked, interrupting the argument. He had to shield himself from the unbelievably purple glare bursting through the seams of the rubble.

The scientists started darting their heads back and forth, frantically trying to catch any flicker of illumination. Finally, bewildered and disappointed, one of them turned and asked him, ‘What light?’

Chapter 12

Out of the Woods

Commander Elizabeth Jenkins stood leaning over the communications console, on the bridge of the Aletheia, deep in concentration and trying to digest the rapid outpouring of information from Doctor Tang.

'I have examined the area of the injury. The patient has suffered quite a painful compound fracture, breaking his fibula and tibia. Also, because of the fall, it has protruded through the skin tissue. The facilities on the shuttle are inadequate to deal with the loss of blood.'

'I'll have the med bay ready for when you return, Doctor,' Elizabeth assured her, looking directly at the communications officer, who understood the signal. 'I will also pass on the update to the captain. You just focus on your patient. Is Roman still with you?'

A few seconds later, a short reply boomed through the radio. 'Yes, Commander.'

'Roman, you and the other two crew members may as well return aboard. It would be pointless to return to the landing party now. Just make sure the landing area is secure for when the shuttle returns to pick up the others.'

'I agree, Commander. We will secure the landing area and return to the ship.'

'Good, Aletheia out,' Elizabeth said, ending the communication.

The communications officer said, 'Commander, the med-bay crew are prepping as we speak, but they were saying something about checking if the patient was one of the emergency back-ups that were destroyed?'

Elizabeth was stumped about what they could mean. What would be the point of destroying blood back-ups?

'I'm not too sure what they are talking about, but I'm sure they have everything under control,' she said, not trying to think too much about it. 'Make sure that you send down a data packet to update the captain.'

'Yes, Commander,' the officer affirmed, turning back to his console.

Elizabeth found herself staring out the view glass, concerned about property being destroyed aboard her ship. She had not reached her position by ignoring the small details, and she was not going to start now.

'I'm going down to the med bay to personally check on the preparations,' she announced, hoping her curiosity was covered by her drive for due diligence.

The communications officer nodded. 'I'll keep you informed of any changes in situation, Commander.'

Just as she was about to leave, she stretched over the captain's chair and opened a ship-wide call. 'Janine Thomas, please report to the med bay ASAP. Thank you!'

Janine and Elizabeth had become close friends on the training base. Elizabeth felt that Janine matched her on an intellectual level, plus had the same dry humour. Numerous times, she had witnessed Janine's husband squirm under a feigned disagreement. It was always fun to watch when Janine would ask the dreaded question, 'How do I look?' Then, using her husband's rehearsed and complimentary answers, she would cause a fake argument. 'What do you mean I look great? I was fantastic yesterday.' Although this was not the most sophisticated humour, Elizabeth couldn't help but love the simplicity of Janine's technique.

Elizabeth began her long walk across the ship, striding past crewmembers along the way, much like a power-walker striding towards the finish line. Reaching the moving platform, she took a moment to collect herself and leaned her back against the handrail.

'First bloody planet,' she said to an empty room. Then, as if she were having a private conversation in her mind, she thought, we have not come all this way for him to get someone bloody injured, on the first bloody planet. He is a buffoon!

She of course was thinking about Michael, who she had her reservations about from the very start of the mission. She didn't doubt his ability to command, as unorthodox as it was, for it had proven amazingly effective throughout his career. Well, she amended in her head, the career that she had access to anyway.

It wasn't even a case of jealousy. Being second-in-command on a mission as historical as this may chip away at some people's pride. She, however, found that being in a secondary position gave her more space to manoeuvre the crew. Sometimes, crew members would be more comfortable making suggestions to her, without fear of embarrassment or harsh repercussions. She preferred it that way, and she thought she always would.

No, the doubts about him started to creep in the day she first saw him. She recalled the exact moment; it was at the training base in Nevada. Michael stood in a hallway, outside a meeting room, where he had just finished a briefing with Admiral Taylor. Elizabeth had been asked to attend as a kind of informal meet and greet. As she approached him from around the opposite side of the hallway, ready and eager to introduce herself, she hesitated. At that moment, she had seen a flicker of the man behind the grey-eyed, cool-as-a-cucumber charm.

He looked as if he had been frozen in time, motionless like a mannequin in a clothes shop. He stood in front of a picture that was hung on the wall, gazing intently. Chillingly, he gave off what can only be described as an aura of sorrow and stomach-churning rage. It was the type of feeling of being stuck in the middle of two rival gangs who had somehow ended up in the same bar: a sort of quiet before the storm.

He gripped the bottle of water he was holding so tightly that its contents had spewed out from the funnel and over his hand, leaving a growing puddle on the floor. Then, with a grunt, he spun away from the picture and abruptly headed towards the exit, slamming the door behind him.

She remembered being relieved that he had just turned and stormed off in the opposite direction, taking the oppressive atmosphere with him. Elizabeth could recall moving, no rushing over to inspect the picture that had caused such disdain, to see what on earth would cause a man to fill the hallway with such darkness. To this day, she still couldn't understand why he had reacted the way he did at the picture on the wall, which was of two cartoon animals. The header was accompanied by an American flag, which simply said 'we are all family'. Underneath was a picture of a big and smiling brown bear labelled Daddy-bear, and a tiny grey rabbit sat cuddled up in its fur with the words 'Hunnie-bunny' written underneath.

'Commander?'

Breaking out of her reverie and immediately tapping her wristwatch, Elizabeth replied, 'Go ahead.'

'Commander, Janine Thomas has arrived at the med bay and is waiting for further orders.'

'Good, I'm five minutes out. What's the ETA on the shuttle?'

After a brief pause, the communications expert stated, 'The shuttle has broken atmosphere and will dock in exactly seven minutes.'

'Thank you. Commander Jenkins out.'

Shortly after, Elizabeth reached the med bay. She was greeted by a bewildered Janine, who was trying to figure out why she was requested there.

'Hi, Janine,' Elizabeth said, slightly out of breath while approaching her.

'What happened?' Janine asked, moving towards her.

'There's been an accident down on the surface, and I might need your help.'

Still as confused, Janine delicately asked, 'Help with what?'

'I'll let you know in a couple of minutes.' Then, as she opened the door to the med bay, she lowered her voice and said, 'Hopefully, it's nothing.'

As they walked in, they were met by the soft white glow of the med bay. The lighting was the same as you would find in any hospital or treatment room. There were smooth tables designed in such a way that they could be thoroughly cleaned and sterilised, with as few edges as possible to avoid any build-up of dirt, removing the possibility of contamination.

The advancements in technology in recent years had dramatically changed the appearance of the standard hospital beds. The large, awkward and cumbersome beds surrounded by various bits of test equipment had been replaced by translucent pods. The sides of the pods were collapsible, capable of sliding up or down for patient access.

'Commander,' acknowledged one of the medical staff.

'Everything ready?' Elizabeth asked, straight to the point.

'Yes, Commander, and we've just been notified that the shuttle has docked and that the patient is on the way,' answered the curvaceous shaped, brown-skinned nurse.

The nurse was wearing the standard medical white uniform, with the med-bay logo displayed on her chest. She looked curiously past the commander's shoulder at Janine.

'She is here at my request,' stated Elizabeth, removing cause for concern. She then begun to look around at the members of staff. 'Who was in charge of the blood samples?'

The head nurse turned her head sharply towards one of her colleagues, resulting in her bun, packed with dark coarse hair, to wobble slightly.

'Umm I was... am,' said a shy, petit girl with a couple of freckles dotting under her worried brown eyes.

Elizabeth started to open her mouth when the med bay door opened, prompting her and Janine to quickly move aside.

Doctor Tang glanced at them both, but paid them no further attention as her focus needed to be on her unconscious patient.

Pushing the transport cart alongside the bed, the medical staff had already moved to position to treat the patient. After the patient was shifted on top of the bed, a nurse placed what looked like a gauntlet over his wrist. The strap moved of its own accord, automatically moving into a position for vein access.

'We need to get fluids into Mr Bishop, *now*!' Doctor Tang put emphasis on the last word. 'He has lost too much blood.'

Then, darting her head over to the young, freckled girl, Doctor Tang simply asked, 'Well?'

'No, Doctor, his wasn't destroyed,' the girl said, shaking her head as she moved to the head of bed. When she pressed a touch-sensitive button, a curved panel started to slide out from the wall, directly above the bed.

'Good,' Doctor Tang said, then turned to face the nurse. 'Karen, start the transfusion. Set him up with the IV drip and pain relief.'

The nurse replied with a focused, 'Yes, Doctor.'

Doctor Tang cut the rest of the clothing away from around the injured area. Previously, she had cut only enough for quick access to the lower part of his leg and arm. Now that she had the area cleared, she carefully removed the blood-soaked bandages that Roman had surprisingly helped secure. Although there was an exceptional amount of blood, she was relieved to discover that no arteries were severed in the incident. So, she continued to slowly remove more of the red cloth. Then she placed a small silver, almost a dinner tray like piece of equipment over his leg. The rest of the medical staff had finished their individual tasks and had taken a step back from the bed. Doctor Tang followed suit and did the same. The freckled nurse pushed a button on the wall, after which, with a faint hum, the side panels began to rise.

Once the panels were locked onto the shelf above the bed, Doctor Tang moved to the side of the bed where an interactive screen had appeared, showing the area of injury surrounded by various touch sensitive options.

'That's so cool,' whispered Janine, leaning towards Elizabeth. 'I was told about the med pods, but seeing one in action...'

Commander Jenkins stood patiently, arms folded and watching curiously. Then, she leaned back so that Janine could hear. 'It is an impressive machine.'

'No mumbling in my med bay, please,' Doctor Tang said, not looking away from her control panel. This caused Elizabeth to clear her throat and tighten her already-crossed arms.

The doctor had already started a sequence of procedures – first was sterilising and numbing the area of injury, done by spraying a fine mist from inside the table above his leg. Then, by selecting a filter option on the display, she was able to toggle through different scans. This enabled her to see bone, muscle, and even circulatory systems individually.

After flicking through the screens and checking Donald's vitals, she administered the anaesthetic and went straight into surgery. She started by selecting the bone structure filter, which highlighted every section of the injured bones, even the tiny splinters that had broken off during the incident. Selecting the bone fragments, she highlighted the segments on the screen. They turned a light green, contrasting against the pale background. When she was finished, she selected an option which said 'reconstruct'.

Without her having to do anything else, four small robotic arms came to life from inside the silver table, reaching directly into the wound and reassembling the bones back to their original placements, as if it were putting a jigsaw puzzle together.

As the small arms held the fragments in place, Doctor Tang pressed another button labelled 're-form'. This sent a signal to the medical table, placed over the leg, to release a small drop of gel in the box.

'Come on,' Doctor Tang said, concentrating intently on the screen.

Commander Jenkins turned her head to Janine, who returned the gesture by shrugging with a perplexed face.

'Come on... yes!'

Through the magnification of the screen and listening to the gleeful voice of the doctor, Elizabeth could see that the bone had been kind of, welded together.

'The reconstructive fastening gel or G583 is very experimental,' said Doctor Tang, who seemed slightly less tense than she was just a couple of seconds ago. 'It works like a glue, but also as a fast-acting wheeling paste.'

'Wheeling paste?' Elizabeth asked, trying her best not to come across as rude.

'Welding paste,' the head nurse interjected, with her large dark eyes cautiously darting towards Doctor Tang.

'So, Doctor, how does the G5... 8... 3 gel work?' Elizabeth asked. Janine, who had now moved closer to get a better view, also wanted to know about the process.

'Yes, yes. I will explain later.' That edge of frustration now returning. 'But for now, I need to finish the surgery.'

Reading between the lines as being told to shut up, Elizabeth just continued to watch the procedure.

Multiple functions now were sprawled all over the screen, but the doctor moved so quickly that Janine release a quiet breath in awe. The mechanical arms retracted on the viewing screen, followed closely by a transparent film placed over the wound. The screen then turned a light blue, and the doctor turned around to face the head nurse.

'Keep him under observation, and let me know when it has reached seventy-five percent.'

'Yes, Doctor,' the head nurse replied, nodding, then moved into position in front of the screen.

Pursing her lips at the anticlimactic end, Elizabeth moved beside the nurse now in control of the interactive screen. 'Is that it?'

Pulling off her gloves and shooting the commander an incredulous look, the doctor sighed. 'No. No, that is not it. The process will take several hours to complete, and that's just the muscular reconstruction.'

'I'm sorry,' Elizabeth said, holding her hands up a sign of surrender. 'I've just never seen anything like this before. Anyway, can I speak with you in private for a second?'

Doctor Tang raised her arm in the direction of a room, just off to the side of the treatment area. Elizabeth signalled Janine to follow. As they entered the room, the doctor started to remove her clothing. 'Could you close the door behind you please?'

'Of course,' Janine said, pushing it shut.

'I assume you have come to ask about the attempted murder?'

'Murder?' Elizabeth blurted out. 'What murder?'

Forcing her bloodstained clothes into the hazardous waste bin, she stood for a second, mirroring the commander's stance, wearing nothing but her tiny white underwear.

'As I said, attempted murder. In my eyes, intentionally destroying samples that could potentially save a patient's life constitutes attempted murder.'

Janine, who was standing by the door, behind Elizabeth, was relieved when she spotted some large antibacterial wipes box on top of a chest of draws.

'Here,' she said, passing the box to the doctor, immediately defusing the rather uncomfortable situation.

'Thank you.'

The doctor took the box, pulled out a large sheet and began to wipe it over her athletic body.

'Look, Doctor, I understand that you are mad. This is the last thing I would want aboard our ship, but we are not going to find any answers without help.' With that, Elizabeth looked directly at Janine.

'Ah... I was wondering when I'd find out why I was here,' Janine said. She turned to Doctor Tang. 'Can you let me access your terminal, please?'

The doctor hesitated at first, but reconsidered, seeing the mixture of confidence and slight arrogance in Janine's approach.

'Please, help yourself,' she said, pointing at her desk, then looked at the commander. 'But we have already been though the logs and found nothing.'

'Doctor, this is Janine Thomas, wife of Andrew Thomas.'

Noticing that the doctor had failed to see her point, Elizabeth continued.

'What a lot of people don't realise is that as much as the world has changed because of her husband, Janine is as equally renowned for her skills with data and pretty much anything to do with a computer chip.

So, if anyone can find out who has been in the network who shouldn't have been, it's her.'

Raising her eyebrows, the doctor turned her head towards Janine, just in time to see her crack her knuckles. Janine placed her hands on the console, smiling mischievously, 'Ok, let's see who's been naughty.'

Chapter 13

The Hand that Rocked the Cradle

'Ow!' Professor Thomas playfully yelled from his quarters. 'That hurt, you cheeky monkey.'

The professional drooler began to twitch and wriggle as his father ticked his stomach, releasing bursts of infectious giggles. As soon as he stopped, Billy restarted his assault on his daddy's ear but was distracted when he noticed a thread from the fabric on his father's shoulder.

Andrew stood in the centre of the room, gently bobbing Billy from side to side. Projected on the wall in front of him was a direct link, overseeing the engineering room. To the sides of the projection were a full range of technical data such as core reactor readings, exterior drive temperatures and compression values. Trying to stay ahead of any power surges, whilst looking after Billy, who was now chewing on his shoulder, proved to be challenging. That is, if challenging were trying to juggle whilst driving a bus full of explosives, he thought.

No, everything seemed normal and, dare he say it, calm. So, a five-minute break wouldn't hurt. Switching his screen over to his own personal research, he began to move into the kitchen. 'Let's get you something a bit yummier.'

Opening the fridge door, he was about to reach in a grab a premade bottle of milk, when he paused to look at the time on a small white time dial above him.

'Uh-oh... we're too early,' he said, as Billy reached towards the fridge, ecstatically looking at his dad.

'O...kay,' he said in an Elmer Fudd voice. 'But don't tell Mummy, because she will kick my bum.'

Noticing the extra big smile from that last bit of advice, he continued to playfully repeat the word bum twice more, squeezing Billy as he said it. Then, he retrieved the bottle, placed it in the pre-set warming machine that Janine's ogre of a mother had gotten her and waited for the ding.

As soon as it was ready, Billy began to clap. 'Yeay... there you go.' Passing the bottle to Billy was like that scene in Jurassic Park where the cow got lowered into the Velociraptor pen. He swooped it out of his dad's hands, foregoing grateful pleasantries, as babies usually do.

Just happy that Billy had stopped wriggling and was now cuddled up into his chest, Andrew walked back into the living area and shifted his focus to his work. Of all the projects he had done or participated in, for some reason, this irritated him the most.

Abort, hold off thee... what the hell does it mean?

He knew it was significant, because everything else that had been highlighted on the chalkboard in his lecture room had changed the course of humanity forever. But... he just couldn't see it.

'Is Daddy losing his mind?' He asked the room. His reply was a quiet sucking sound from his thirsty son.

Abort... what if that meant to abort a launch or something? Something big? No, that's ridiculous. Even if it were the case, why give us the means of travel then tell us to stay put.

Adjusting Billy in his arms to compensate for the fatigue setting in, he continued to equate, to determine, hell, to outright guess. Hold off thee...

Now to hold off something is the same as saying to repel, but it has no context.

He was just about to let out a sound of frustration when he noticed that Billy was kindly holding out the now empty bottle.

'Good boy!'

Squatting to place the bottle on a side table, he noticed the predictable tiring eyes of his well-fed son, so he said, 'Let's go for a walk.'

Andrew found it peculiar how he and his wife had recently discovered that the fastest way to get Billy to sleep was to take him for a walk around the halls of the ship. He picked up Billy's favourite blankie and did his best to drape it over him as they left the quarter.

The halls were thankfully quiet near the officers' quarters, with most of the ship's crew at their posts, compiling data sent from the planet nearby.

'A gentle breeze from Hushabye mountain

Softly blows on lullaby bay...'

Andrew sung Billy a lullaby. The acoustics were quite good as they were walking slowly through the red gloom, pillaring through the viewing ports of the ship. It reminded him of the time he had attempted to pick up black and white photo development using orthochromatic films. The red light used in a dark room was specifically used because it wouldn't interfere with the process of the print. As logical as he was, the gloom still gave him the heebie-jeebies.

'It fills the sails of boat that are waiting...,' he continued, to ward off any evil spirits brought forward by the creepy light. Then, he increased his pace, ever so slightly, towards the direction of normal LED lighting.

Composed and more relaxed in the comfort of a windowless section of the halls, Andrew turned when he heard footsteps approaching from behind him. Out of his view, the unknown person's heavy steps became louder and louder. Whoever it was clearly had no concept of trying to sooth a baby.

Then, from around the corner, like a medieval golem in the darkness, appeared an enormous hulk of a man. Stopping with military trained control, hands placed securely at his back, he regarded the professor and his stirring son for a moment.

'My apologies! I did not know you were there.'

'It's fine,' Andrew said whispering, taken aback by the Russian's stature. 'I don't think we've formally been introduced, I'm...'

'Professor Andrew J Thomas. I know who *you* are, Professor – the man who made the T-Drive, correct?'

Andrew was already starting to dislike the way the Russian was rolling the letter r in every single word. He thought it sounded like a rattlesnake, sending a warning.

'Yep, that's correct... well, kind of. You must be the lieutenant everyone's talking about.'

He reached out his spare hand, expecting him to return the gesture.

'Lieutenant Commander Roman Sokolov,' Roman said, keeping his hands in position and putting emphasis on his full correct title.

Returning his hand and adjusting Billy in the crevasse of his shoulder and chest, Andrew pursed his lips together and responded, 'Oh... sorry, Lieutenant Commander. To be honest, I'm still getting used to all the military ranks, and I don't think I'll ever get them right.'

'It is quite alright, Professor. Would you please excuse me.'

Turning to the side, Roman was clearly tired of the conversation; he started to walk away.

As he did, a small excitable voice chirped, 'Edd...'

Andrew jerked his head towards Billy, whose eyes, to his father's dismay, were wide open. He had pushed a little arm out of the blanket covering him and was pointing at Roman with a stubby cocktail sausage finger. 'Edd...'

Raising his head, Andrew looked at Roman, in a feeble attempt to figure out what Billy was trying to say. Roman also halted and, out of some sort of curiosity, looked at his attire for an answer. Raising his hands, the child spoke again, 'Edd... Edd...'

Looking in the direction of his son's finger, Andrew was then able to see what his son had been trying to point out. The clever boy had been trying to say the word 'red', not edd. However, the proud father moment quickly passed as he realised what his son was pointing at. 'Lieutenant, you have blood on your hands.'

There was a delay in the response of the big Russian, despite having no facial reaction. He took a moment to collect his thoughts by pausing to try and construct the correct words for his unexplained and outright suspicious appearance.

'Ah, there was an incident on the planet where a man was hurt, and I was assisting Dr Tang.'

'No way!' Andrew said, his tense demeanour replaced with concern. 'Are they ok?'

'I believe so. He was taken to the medical bay. Now, if you please excuse me. I need to go and clean myself.' Roman conveyed his point by holding out his hands, palms up, towards Andrew.

'Sure, no worries,' Andrew said, letting the man pass.

Watching Roman walk away left him feeling relieved; he couldn't help but think about a statistic he had heard once. You have about three seconds upon meeting someone to determine if you like them or not. He knew without any doubt that he absolutely hated that bastard.

Happy that he and Billy were alone again, Andrew continued to walk the halls, praying to the heavens that his son would drift off to sleep. Still looking over his shoulder, he couldn't shake off that feeling of unease. In fact, Billy must have picked up on this, as he picked that moment to scrunch his face with flushed cheeks.

'Thanks for that, Billy,' he said, feeling some heat radiating from his son's diaper. 'Come on then. Let's go back, and get ya changed.'

He rushed Billy to the changing room and carefully, holding his breath, disposed of the diaper. Luckily, the diapers were utilised in the same manner, just as all the human waste aboard the Aletheia, in the botany lab. Andrew remembered chuckling at a joke he had made in the pre-launch briefing. 'So, every time someone uses a restroom, we can all breathe a bit easier? Not if I go first....'

He also remembered that the joke didn't get the response he was hoping for as the professionals giving the brief just ignored him and proceeded. They passionately continued with how the system works similarly to a microbial energy production system, which grinds it up then digests it with the help of thousands of microbes, and he couldn't remember the rest. It was all very interesting, but just not the field of science to which he was drawn.

'There,' he whispered, having cleaned and replaced Billy's diaper with a fresh one. 'That's much better.'

Looking down at his son made him smile. As a parent, there are moments where you just stop and stare. It's a strange combination of love, pride and wonder. Obviously, these moments, Andrew had discovered, were in between nights of unsettled sleep, the constant fear of them getting hurt and, of course, the mind-numbing pain when accidently setting onto one of their toy blocks.

Billy was fast asleep, sucking on his thumb; his short little tufts of blond hair lay softly on his head.

You are going to be a heartbreaker when you're older, kid, Andrew thought. Then, he realised where they were. The probability that he would grow up and meet girls, like a normal kid, was unlikely. Andrew stopped smiling at that thought and gently picked Billy up off the changing table.

'Let's get you to bed,' he whispered to Billy when the latter stirred.

Carrying his son from the restroom, he moved into the larger of the two bedrooms and laid him down in his crib. Leaning over the guard rail, Andrew moved a stuffed toy to Billy's side. After switching on a soothing night-light, he left the room cautiously.

Releasing a sigh of relief as he crossed the living room, Andrew moved into the kitchen and made himself a nice and warm cup of English tea. He also had a secret stash of biscuits hidden at the very back of the food cupboard. Being careful not to disturb any of the containers in front of them, he reached in and grabbed a handful. A couple wouldn't hurt, he thought, licking his lips.

Holding his cup of tea and his sinful but delicious sugar-filled biscuits, he took a seat on the sofa and opened the projection screen.

Switching back to the direct link to the engine room, he could see from the readings that nothing was out of the ordinary. From the live feed camera of the projection, he could see Irish Chris was up to no good. Chris was standing behind Big Bob and sneakily dropping what looked like nuts into his tool belt. Pressing a button on his wrist strap and swiping a couple of times, Andrew remotely activated a buzzer behind Bob. This caused Bob to turn around and catch Irish Chris in the act, then swiftly slap him round the head whilst mouthing profanities that could make a monkey blush.

Laughing a guttural laugh, Andrew dropped one of the biscuit treats on the floor. Even scientists follow the five-second rule, he told himself, reaching down to save it. It had stopped near one of Billy's toy bricks, which had escaped the clean-up earlier. Leaving the block where it lay and making a mental note to pick it up in a little while, the professor sank back into the couch.

He selected his personal research tab on the projection screen and began to study it intensely. His mind, however, drifted back to the encounter in the corridor earlier. His son almost said his first word, the colour red. Alright, granted it sounded like 'edd', but he was going be clever.

Then the picture of the lieutenant's hands came to the forefront of his thoughts, bloodstained and unsettling. Whoever was hurt, he hoped that they were... he stopped, mid thought, as if he had been struck by a bolt of electricity. Putting his tea and biscuits down with a clunk, he moved to the edge of his seat. Then he looked back to the projection where the riddle of the beam was visible in bold, large writing.

Abort, hold off thee.

It's not a message or a warning, he thought, his mind racing at a million miles per hour. It's so simple. Why didn't I see it?

The light in the lecture room that had given him the concept of the T-Drive had come in through the window blinds erratically. It hadn't put the calculations in order; he had. What if the words weren't in order either? What if the letters were jumbled too!

Abort, hold off thee. He remembered the word 'blood' again. 'Blood...,' he said to an empty room. 'That fits!'

His mind raced through every combination that he could think of that the letters could form into, but one phrase kept leaping out at him, like some voice subconsciously shouting at him that it was the right answer.

Blood of the father! That's it! That's the answer.

'Blood of the father!' He found himself proclaiming to an empty room, now on his feet, ecstatically smiling from ear to ear. He had figured it out. However, he quickly stopped, for even though he had solved it, he still didn't know what it meant.

Chapter 14

Fallen Kingdom

'What do you mean you can't see it? It's right there!' Michael said impatiently, pointing in the direction of the rubble.

'Captain, with all due respect...' the scientist began in a condescending voice, 'there are a number of us here, and not a single one of us can see this... light that you speak of.'

As the group went about conducting their speedy tests, shadows had begun to creep out around the planet's red-tinted landscape. Some had gathered enough samples and were cataloguing the data for further examination aboard the Aletheia, while several more had already moved towards the rendezvous point, ready to depart.

'Look,' Michael said, breathing out a sigh of frustration. 'I don't know why you are doing this. Being such a pain in the ass, I mean. Or, if this is a weird little prank that you science people like to pull... and honestly, I couldn't give a damn... but I'm telling you that there is a light coming from right there, and that is where you will focus your investigation. Are we understood?'

Recoiling slightly, the scientist reluctantly nodded and muttered something not nice under his breath as he turned.

Michael readied to make an announcement. 'All stations, if you have finished your jobs and have your samples secured, please join the rest of the team at the base of the ruins, over and out.'

A short while after that, more and more hands were available to start moving the rubble. At first, it seemed like a pointless task, with many of the group wondering if shifting the rubble was going against protocol, fearing it was too dangerous. That is, until one of the scientists hastily walked over to Michael. Slabs of stone were moved out of the way to reveal more and more of what seemed to be a passage.

'Sir... umm... Captain, we have moved the boulders blocking an entrance,' an excited young Indian man said eagerly.

Michael looked at him, smiled and moved up towards the hole where the rubble sat. However, his joy was short lived as that feeling of unease had returned. Intently glancing down the long dusty corridor, he hesitated for a moment, pushed his feelings down and proceeded inside.

He walked into a dirt-coated empty room and looked around in amazement. Areas were sporadically lit up by the crew's torches from their bodysuits, as they flooded in behind him to investigate the wonder. Michael was at a loss for words, except for four that slowly rolled off his lips, 'Son of a bitch!'

The curvature of the walls created a dome like structure, spread wide and built in such a fashion that it would support an extreme amount of weight pushing down from above it. The celling was covered in fragmented symbols and drawings that had long since been obscured by dust and time.

As Michael moved further inside, with the others following suit, the dazzling purple light that had drawn his attention faded, until it was nothing but a single flickering cat's eye in the centre of the darkness.

'Captain?' A quaky voice yelped from behind him. 'Captain?'

Michael turned, only to discover that it was the cocky scientist who had told him that investigating the area was a waste of time.

'Shoot,' Michael said, still looking around in amazement.

'Captain... I think I owe you an apology. If it weren't for you—'

Michael stopped him. 'Forget about it,' he said with a smile. 'Water under the bridge. Just make sure you get as many pictures and samples as you can from this place.'

'Yes, Captain.' The scientist brought his feet together and performed a swift about-turn. Ex-military, Michael noted, there wasn't any need for that, but he appreciated the respectful gesture anyway.

He turned back around to where the light was emitting and saw nothing but darkness, with the occasional flicker of torchlight from the crew. Whatever was or wasn't casting that purple light, he wanted to see it for himself. The crew around him had begun setting up portable light stands, and some had started to take photographs of the walls, floor and ceiling to document the strange symbols. Software aboard would then render and reconstruct the photos, which would help them understand the pictures more clearly. Michael could see two people sealing dirt samples in vials and then placing them in cylindrical metal tubes for protection.

The sound level of the room had grown quite loud, with the crew excitedly speaking through the open channels of their suits, through gleeful laughter and technical phrases, most which sounded like 'What a beauty' or 'Look at that'.

In the very centre of the chamber stood a small column, looking like a hybrid of carved stone and some root-like plant. At its peak sat a spherical object concealed in dust, resembling an ostrich egg. At the base of the orb, immediately catching Michael's attention, was a small glint of a black crystal material, peering through the dirt underneath.

Moving forward towards the beckoning object, he could feel the crack and snap of something beneath his feet, which, under a closer inspection, made Michael's skin crawl. Slowly, carefully lifting one foot, he could see what he was walking on: the skeletal remnants of what must have been the last living being on the planet.

'Umm, guys?' he called through the com-channel.

Two members of the landing party approached him, as he stood to the side of the column.

'I think you might want to take a look at this guy.'

The expressions on both scientist's faces cycled quickly from horrified shock to a combination of curiosity and awe.

'Oh, and this thing over here. I'm not sure what it is but...' Michael placed his hand on the sphere.

Just as he did so, the room rumbled.

The two crew members standing next to Michael recoiled several steps in absolute fear, hands shaking to their sides, as though they were expecting to be attacked. Many of the party, frozen to the spot, could do nothing but dart their eyes around the chamber in desperation to seek out the source of the violent vibrations they were feeling.

However, Michael looked unnervingly calm. He was staring ahead with eyes wide open but not really focusing, a cathartic look appearing on his face. It was as if his body stood there with his hand on the sphere, but his mind had travelled far away.

'Shit, Captain!' they yelled, 'What should we do?'

They turned to face him when there was no response. 'Captain! Captain...?'

The sphere that Michael had placed his hand on began to emit a brilliant purple light, now visible to everyone in the chamber. The light somehow began to flow down the stem of the column the sphere was sitting on. Stunned onlookers could see the glow feeding down what looked like veins, reaching out through the floor and miraculously climbing up the tall walls.

Realising that Michael could be in danger, Doctor Ryan Smith began to move towards him as quickly as his age would permit. Pushing past crew members who had started to make for the exit, Doctor Smith got to Michael's side. Then, just as he hesitantly reached out a hand to shake him, Michael shook his head and pulled back his hand.

'Are you alright?' Doctor Smith asked, withdrawing his arm.

'What the... what the fuck was that?' Michael asked, rubbing his wrist, feeling slightly disorientated.

'I can honestly say that I don't have clue,' Doctor Smith answered, heaving a sigh of relief. 'But take a look at what happened.'

He turned to the side and, like a lobby host of a luxurious hotel, opened his arms to the wonder of the room. The walls were pulsing with the neon purple glow, highlighting lines and symbols underneath centuries of dust and dirt. More so, the light had now displayed pictures and star charts that appeared to be moving in a closed loop.

'Did you do that?' Doctor Smith asked uncomfortably.

'Do what?' Michael shot back. 'I just touched this thing and... and... ah, shit, I don't think I did?'

Regaining himself, he quickly opened a channel to everyone in his vicinity. 'Ok, guys, I want you to record everything. We don't have much time left down here, so get to it.'

Noticing Michael was more direct than usual in giving his orders, Doctor Smith looked at him with concern.

'I'm fine, Doc, just a bit shaken is all.'

For the next thirty minutes, the chamber was full of life and cautious energy. To think not only had they found existence of intelligent life but also the sheer concept that these lifeforms had and the type of technology was mind blowing, if not overwhelming.

The walls were mesmerising, displaying a story much like a tapestry, dedicated to keeping the history of its people alive and safe within the confines of this room. The area that seemed to get the most attention was a sizeable and detailed star chart, full of galaxies further away than ever dreamed of. The Milky Way and the Andromeda galaxies looked so small in comparison to the other massive super clusters.

Beautifully, the display scrolled though segments of galaxies, held in their groups by margins, resembling large petals on a flower. Just like a flower, all the petals led back to a central point, where the pistil sat. The segments were highlighted by the purple light, then slowly enlarged. Then the light would fade, and the process would repeat for the next section. The central part of the flower map was too dim and slightly blurry, to the scientists' dismay, resulting in no further data to be ascertained.

The extra light now covering the chamber also highlighted a bookcase, spanning the base of the walls. It had appeared to be a mound of dirt because of the way it blended in with the floor. Apparently, the rubble at the entrance did not block all the weather elements from seeping inside.

The scientists took especial care in removing the documents, mainly scrolls, from their weathered shelves and placing them in moderately sized silver boxes. Several of the crew repeatedly approached the captain in a hopeful effort to obtain larger storage containers. They were swiftly disgruntled as Michael had to remind them that this was not their primary mission and that they could take only whatever they could carry.

As the land outside had begun to be enveloped by darkness, most of the crew had more than their fill of samples, recordings and such. The last few of them were collecting bone fragments in the area that Michael had unknowingly stepped on. Extreme care was taken with these samples, as the importance of knowing what creature they came from could be the biggest breakthrough in history, second only to Professor Thomas's T-Drive.

'Ok, guys, lets wrap it up,' Michael said, rotating his finger in the air. This prompted the rest of the crew to begin the removal of the standing lights, staggered throughout the area.

Doctor Smith struggled to carry some of the equipment towards the exit and was looking over his shoulder for the chance that someone could help, only to see Michael waving at him.

'Need a hand?' Doctor Smith offered begrudgingly.

'Yeah... sorry. I'll help you out, but I need your help with this first.' Michael stared at the orb at the centre of the room. 'Have you got a cloth or something?'

Reaching into his side pouches, Doctor Smith eventually pulled out a small rag and handed it to Michael.

'Are you sure that's a good idea?' he asked, moving closer the Michael.

Michael was lost in the orb's dark wonder, which was glinting due to the purple neon light bouncing off its reflective smooth surface. He couldn't explain it, but he knew that he had to take it with him. It felt like it was his... like it had always been his, like it had been waiting here for him in this dark room, on this lonely dying planet.

'Michael?' Doctor Smith asked after intentionally clearing his throat loudly.

'Just keep an eye on me, ok.'

Carefully and with impressive speed and precision, Michael placed the rag down on top of the orb with one hand, then deftly scooped it from its perch with his other. As he did, the purple neon glow of the room pulsed, then slowly faded back into darkness. Adjusting his grip in the strange sphere, to compensate for the gravity's pull, Michael slowly turned towards the hesitant man. Then he jerked his head in the direction of a small storage box, close to where the elderly man stood. Delighted that Michael could place the orb in the box himself, without any setbacks, Doctor Smith closed the box and breathed a sigh of relief.

'What shall we to do with it?'

Michael looked at him and nonchalantly shrugged. 'Don't know. Find out what makes it tick? But we need to make sure no one else touches the thing, that's for sure.'

Tapping his wrist strap, Michael opened a channel to all the crew on the planet. 'Right, everyone, as much as I want to stay down here and party some more, we have a mission to achieve. So, form up, and prepare to move. Quade out.'

Taking one more look around the chamber, Michael realised he felt unusual, as though leaving the place was like leaving somewhere familiar. Who the hell were these people, he wondered.

He turned towards the exit and slowly walked out with his head down, leaving the wonder behind.

The journey back to the Aletheia was as routine and normal as such a new transport could be. The expedition team stayed well clear of the landing area, to avoid and dust or stone being kicked up at them. The shuttle landed closer this time, having learnt that the bridge structure they used to get there was not worth the risk of being crossed again. Samples were loaded and secured, lighting kits and power banks were placed back in their boxes and the crew boarded and strapped themselves into their seats. Everything was smooth except for one moment, when a woman struggled to lift a container onto the loading platform of the shuttle and Michael moved in closer to assist her.

She jolted her arm away from him, dropping the box she held. She was terrified of him touching her, fearing that whatever magic he had used to cause the room to come alive, he would do it to her somehow.

He stepped back to give her space, and she managed to heave the box up. After strapping it down, she quickly moved to her seat, keeping her head down.

Michael realised to his dismay that most of the crew now had the same look in their eyes as that woman did: a horrible mixture of distrust and fear. He realised that this wasn't good.

Far away from the planet where Michael and his team were, a blue light started to pulse in a room under a canvas of darkness, a room that had been quiet for a very long time. The light bounced off two ginormous metal statues, menacingly standing to either side of a strange control panel, which sat prominent in the centre of the room. The huge muscle-bound warriors had a look of terrifying strength, and due to a lack of lighting, cast a looming presence of power.

A small hum began to fill the room as the light pulsed constantly. The hum increased in volume, echoing through the room, and an electrical buzz joined in unison. The source of the sound came from jolts of electricity, rapidly arching from underneath the console, jumping to the ground below.

With a rumble and a screech, a door opened directly opposite the control panel, casting a candlelit rectangle on the ground. Plumes of dust rained from the hinges, cracks and crevasses onto the floor beneath. Stretching out, the light stopped just short of the diamond panelled floor, which curved all around the centre of the room. Then, a silhouette emerged in the doorway and began to move towards the console, almost hovering off the ground.

The hooded creature reached the console, moving its hands swiftly across the dials, activating several via rehearsed actions. Then it waited for what looked like an answer to a question. Blue light began to bleed into the ground, push to the sides and up the walls. Only then could the actual size of the room be seen in its entirety. The chamber was vast and reached as high as the eye could see.

The air above the command panel, where the strange being was waiting patiently, started to change, creating a heat mirage. It gave the illusion of a tremendous, localised temperature, manifesting without any device or apparent source. Then, the area began to change again. A small light came into fruition, followed by another, then another. Shortly after, the lights which hovered above the ground, sorted themselves into lines and symbols.

The hooded figure waved his hand, which made the holographic star map focus closer in on the single purple light. Using another command, the stranger zoomed in closer, and the purple light changed into a clear three-dimensional picture of a planet.

The stranger reached out his hand towards another dial but hesitated. Withdrawing his pale white fingers into a shaking fist, the creature paused and withdrew his hand to his side.

He stepped back from the control panel and started to pace back and forth, never taking his gaze off the planet.

Stopping abruptly, as if he had made a decision, he moved up to the panel, reached for the dial and pressed down with intent. Heat became light. Light became a star map. The star map became a planet, and the planet became... a picture of a man with grey eyes.

Chapter 15

Unlikely Allies

Roman stood in front of the bathroom mirror, leaning down and staring at the emotional void that was himself. Having already taken off his bloodstained clothing, he now had the last task of removing Donald Bishop's blood off his hands.

Blocking part of the light from the roof, he cast shadows on his physique, highlighting his well-defined torso and the veins on his bulging arms.

The shadows of his face lent him a cold and sinister appearance, emphasising every battle scar and old war wound on the pale skinned man. One scar sat directly above the ridge of his right eye, and another, barely visible, stretched like a surgical line, close to his hairline. The menacing look of the man had been a strong factor in achieving the position he now held. People would often find themselves uncontrollably shaking when Roman stood over them. No other rival could dominate the room as he did.

He positioned a giant red stained hand against the tap symbol built into the wall, then rotated his hand to activate it. The water started to pour out of the rectangular faucet, and he placed his hands underneath. He repeated the mundane process of washing his hands with soap until the blood started to fade.

During one of his cleaning cycles, a deep buzz followed by a quick two-toned beep came from his wristband, placed on a shelf to his left.

'Answer,' he commanded the device to activate the hands-free function.

'Lieutenant Commander, it's Eric... Eric Rosiak. I was assigned to your security team last month.'

'I know who you are, Eric,' Roman said simply, leaving enough of a pause that he could hear the Lithuanian boy swallowing on the line. 'What is the problem?'

'Umm, I was ordered to let you know when the shuttle returned... and...' Eric stopped, and the line went quiet.

'And what?' Roman demanded, impatiently raising his voice.

'... and Commander Elizabeth Jenkins said I needed to report to you in person... to gain more experience?'

'Ahhh... so, it was her who ordered you to disturb me,' he said, with contempt in his voice, wiping his hands vigorously with a towel. 'Very well, come to my quarters in... five minutes.'

'But, sir...'

'FIVE minutes!' Roman said, then ended the call. Smirking and taking great pleasure at giving an impossible task to such a young boy, he took his time getting dressed into a clean pressed uniform. Then, he waited like a gargoyle, just outside his quarters.

In exactly four minutes and fifty-five seconds, Eric came into view, running around the corner at the end of the corridor, pushing against the wall to slow himself. Roman stood forearm raised, taking note of the time.

'You are late,' lied Roman in a disapproving tone.

Out of breath and leaning forward with his hands on his knees, Eric regretfully looked up at Roman. 'I'm... sorry, sir... won't happen... again.'

'Make sure it does not. Now come.' Roman set off down the empty corridor at a fast pace, without any hesitation. Eric, who was trying his best to catch his breath back, followed immediately.

'Why are you here?'

'Sorry, sir?' the boy asked, doing his best to catch up and stay in step with his lieutenant commander.

'I asked, why are you here?'

'Umm, I wanted to be part of history, sir....' His breath was now levelling out. 'And to make my family proud that I was going to be flying through the stars and...'

'No,' Roman interrupted, irritably glancing through the corner of his eye. 'Why are you here, in my security team? You do not look like you have had any experience in security at all.'

'Well, no, I don't... not really anyway. But I am good with cyber security. I was in America for years, working with organisations such as the FBI and the FDA,' he said, emphasising the last, hoping that it would win Roman's favour.

'Ohh, cyber security...,' Roman drawled mockingly. 'We will need that when aliens call us and ask for our credit card details.'

Eric went quiet, still following behind like a good pet, while Roman chuckled hoarsely to himself. 'I tell joke, you are to... what they say, lighten up.'

'Oh... sorry,' Eric said, his morale increasing slightly. 'I also asked to work with you specifically.'

'Oh, and why is that?' he asked, looking down at the fair-headed boy who, in his eyes, looked no older than eighteen.

'Well, before I was born, my father, Urik Rosiak, fought alongside you in the twenty seventy-two St Petersburg riots. He told me that you stayed in contact and that when he spoke to last, you talked about me joining the team. He said that you would... help me out?'

Roman stopped abruptly, stoic like a bear standing over a buck. He turned to look down at the chatty boy, wearing an expression that was a weak imitation of a smile.

Roman placed his hand on the boy's shoulder.

'I told your father that I would help you, and I will,' he said, patting the skinny lad on the head before moving again. 'Now come.'

As they walked through the vast maze-like corridors of the ship, an augment could be heard in the distance. The back-and-forth volley of insults seemed to be coming from the botany lab, situated in a middle modular section of the ship.

Turning a corner a few feet from the open door, Roman flung his arm out, preventing Eric from walking any further. As he did so, a metal clipboard struck the opposite side of the hallway with a crash that made Eric jump.

'Oh yes, that's really mature of you!' a man shouted in a strong Nepalese accent.

'You asshole!' a woman's voice fired back, 'How dare you call me immature.'

Roman lowered his arm and proceeded to walk into their line of view and stood tall in the doorway. 'What is going on here?'

'Great,' the man said, throwing his hands up in the air. 'Just, perfect. Now, because of you, we have security breathing down our necks.'

Slapping his pointed finger away, the dark-tanned woman with nothing but contempt in her eyes yelled again, 'Because of me? Because of me?!'

Reaching a boiling point, she launched herself at him, only to be interrupted by Roman, who had swiftly placed himself in between the arguing couple.

'Enough!' Roman bellowed, immediately stifling both scientists. He then pointed at the man. 'We will go to your office and have a talk.'

Turning to face the woman, whose hands were squeezed tightly like talons on her hips, he said, pointing to Eric, 'You will speak to him.'

Over the next ten minutes, Roman and Eric were forced to listen to how Satkar had put his name on the research samples that Karen had brought from the earth. According to Karen, it was highly inappropriate and unprofessional of him.

Satkar, on the other hand, claimed that he was the lead researcher, and Karen, who technically worked under him, had no right to add her name to the documentation. All of this was made worse by the fact that Satkar and Karen had been married for fifteen years now and the novelty had worn off an awfully long time ago.

'But you have to understand that I didn't mean to upset her... I just didn't think,' Satkar said, fingers rubbing his forehead.

He sat in a chair behind a cluttered table, filled with documents, coffee-stained name tags and two computer tablets. Behind him were shelves filled with pots of vibrant coloured plants, some of which Roman had never seen before.

'Do you and your wife argue often?' he asked, indifferently.

'Not really...,' Satkar began, then continued without noticing that Roman had filtered his voice out of his focus.

Roman slowly walked alongside the pots, getting a closer view and reading the labels underneath, whilst feigning interest in the feeble man behind his desk. Underneath the various pots were description tags – plant names, followed by their more common names: Pothos, also known as devil's ivy, a green plant that hung down from the pot with soft and reflective leaves.

'... But she thought, it was me who left the towel on the floor...,' Satkar murmured in the background.

Tillandsia, also known as the air plant, was a pale green plant with long furry leaves. Spathiphyllum, better known as the peace lily, was a long-stemmed plant with beautiful white petals, standing tall.

Moving slowly along the shelf, Roman stopped to admire a plant that was relatively smaller. A little blue bulb was protruding out of the dark green foliage. Ipomoea learii, also known as...

'Lieutenant Commander?' Eric interrupted at the door.

'Yes?' Roman replied, turning and taking note that Doctor Satkar Gurung had thankfully stopped talking.

'I have Karen here, who would like to say something.'

Alongside Eric stood Mrs Gurung, red faced and puffy. Strands of jet-black hair had come lose and were sporadically covering her face and shoulders, giving her a manic look. Roman gestured her to proceed, and she walked into the small office, brushing her hair back quickly and lifting her head high, trying her best to regain some dignity.

'I wanted to apologise for my actions earlier. It was unacceptable behaviour aboard this ship, and it will not happen again,' she said, with the last bit while looking back and forth between Satkar and Roman.

Satkar stood up from behind his desk and moved around to the front, embracing her in a sorrowful hug. 'And I am sorry. I promise we can look through the samples together, as partners, ok?'

A pneumatic release of air came from just outside the office, causing Roman to shift his focus from the pathetic demonstration of love to whatever caused the sound.

'It's quite alright,' Satkar said, letting his wife go and walking over to the office window. 'It's just the air filtration system.'

Roman gave him a look of indifference, mistaken by the man as confusion.

'I will show you!' Satkar said, with excitement in his voice, then left the room before Roman had a chance to protest.

Suddenly, the head of security and his trainee found themselves on a spontaneous tour of the botany and environmental control lab's work area. It consisted of various plants placed on overlapping trays, segmented and divided by specific lighting and moisture-controlled over-heads; the trays were stacked from floor to ceiling. Robotic arms fixed to horizontal conveyor belts, were constantly in motion, controlling the cleanliness and growth of the plants.

Satkar went into great and relentless detail, explaining that all the plants were providing oxygen to the ship's crew. They did this by constantly topping up the reserve tanks. The carbon dioxide and other gases were being filtered and carefully divided in two categories, useful renewable fuel or wastage for disposal.

'Over here is where the oxygen is extracted from their containment unit...,' Satkar continued, pointing at a vast collection of pipes, while Roman and Eric stood listening and watching. 'Each unit is completely self-contained and protected from contaminants...'

'Doctor?' Eric spoke up, interrupting Satkar.

'Yes, go ahead.'

‘Doctor, how many of these plants are there?’

‘Good question.’ Satkar smiled at Eric. ‘In this section, we have ten thousand. But we also have four other sections. That might not seem enough to adequately provide for the oxygen requirements of the ship, but fortunately for us, we have my wife to thank for that.’

He offered his hand to Karen, who took it to stand by his side; they seemed vastly different than the snarling couple from before.

‘It’s not all thanks to me. It was mostly the cell biologists in the University of Natural Resources and Life Sciences in Vienna. I just gave them a nudge in the right direction. You see, these are not exactly normal plants. Not like any plants you have ever seen anyway.’

Karen moved next to the viewing glass of the plants, while the automated arms did their work, whizzing from left to right in the background.

‘You see these plants have been genetically modified and carefully designed to produce more oxygen, not only from the atmosphere but also from the saturation deposited in the soil.’

Karen’s excitement was reciprocated by Eric, who genuinely looked interested, moving forward to investigate through the glass. Roman, however, stood arms crossed, uninterested and repeatedly looking at his wrist strap time display.

'Well, I think that's awesome,' Eric said, turning to Roman. 'Don't you think?'

'Yes, yes, it is all very impressive.' He turned towards the exit. 'We will leave now.'

Before he started to move, he arched his head back at the couple, not directly looking at them, and added, 'Do not let me hear of you two fighting again. I will not be so calm next time.'

The severity in his voice made the couple cower slightly, moving closer to each other. Then Roman left the room with Eric in tow, closing the door behind them.

Immediately, while walking down the corridor, Roman noticed that Eric was having difficulty with his intimidating methods.

'You handled yourself well in there,' Roman said, almost painfully.

'Thanks,' Eric replied dejectedly.

Still moving forward, trying to ignore the spoilt child, Roman thought that if Eric were a dog, then the situation would be so much simpler. He would walk the dirty annoying puppy straight to an airlock, tempt the animal in with a treat and simply launch it into the darkness of space. How unfortunate, he thought.

'What is wrong?' Roman asked, getting annoyed at the mouse like squirming and grunts coming from behind him.

Eric contemplated for a while, before answering. Trying his best not to overstep his position, nor insult a man who could crush him, he said, 'With all due respect, sir... you are nothing like what my father described to me. He said that the only thing that was as big and strong as you was your compassion for people in need.'

Trying to hold back a snigger, Roman put on the best pained face he could muster. 'That was a long time ago, little Eric.' He stopped abruptly, turning and displaying his sorrow. 'A lot has happened since then, my friend.'

Falling for the wounded soldier performance, Eric looked taken aback and responded, like any naive little teenager, 'Ah shit! I'm sorry.'

'Do not worry, Eric,' Roman said, his pained face vanishing in an instant, returning straight back to the previous emotionless void. 'I may seem different to you, but I assure you, I am not. Besides, I mean to honour your father's wishes and teach you everything I know.'

'Thank you, sir,' Eric said, wide-eyed and hopeful.

'Call me Roman, and when we get back to the earth, we will celebrate with your father and drink together, telling him tales of our adventures in space.' Roman walked on ahead, chuckling to himself with a guttural laugh.

Following behind, Eric kept his eyes on the back of Roman's head, confused by what he had just heard. He was grateful and somewhat relieved by Roman's offer to take him under his wing, but something else he said deeply worried him. He was especially confused by the last thing that he had just heard, because it sounded like Roman had forgotten that a month before they left the earth, he had sent a message to Eric's home.

The message was a personal condolence letter to his mother, following the death of Eric's father. So why did he think they could all drink together? It must have been a mistake, Eric thought. Then, like a good dog, he shook his head and followed his master.

Chapter 16

Bright Lights

The transport shuttle landed in its designated spot within the landing bay. After the signal changed from red to green, the pilot gave the all-clear signal to disembark, with the room refilled with breathable air.

The atmosphere was tense between the passengers as they had their heads down, wearing sombre expressions. Considering that they had just witnessed concrete evidence of extra-terrestrial life, not one crew member spoke a word.

To Michael's dismay, he had the feeling that he might be the reason for the tense mood on the shuttle. What happened on the planet and specifically in that chamber had left an irreversible scar on their minds. Michael hung back, while the others filtered out through the exit of the shuttle. Staring into space, he was lost in his own thoughts. If only he had left the goddamn thing alone, then everyone would have been celebrating instead of staring at their feet. Thinking further on it, it dawned on him that if he hadn't put his hand on the sphere, then all the star-charts, pictures and light-show shit wouldn't have even happened.

A hand grasped his shoulder, and he jerked in his seat, his head snapping around to see Doctor Ryan Smith. The doctor recoiled quickly, reacting like he had just burnt his hand on an open flame.

'Shit, Ryan, I'm sorry,' Michael said, kicking himself for being so edgy.

'It's ok,' Ryan said, letting out a breath. 'I should have made a sound or something... Anyway, I'll take the box to my lab and keep it locked.'

Ryan tapped on the hardened silver container that he was holding up in front of him, prompting Michael to look at it with wondering eyes. Realising how much of a paranoid fool he was being, he quickly moved his focus to Ryan's lined face.

'Nah, don't lock it up,' he said, getting to his feet. 'I think you guys should see what makes it tick.'

A cautious expression came over Ryan's face, 'But... what if it...'

Michael interrupted him, 'Yeah, I'm no scientist, but I think what happened down there was a fluke or something. Though, take precautions. You know, just in case.'

'Yeah, I agree. We'll keep it under strict test conditions, just to be safe.'

Ryan started moving towards the door, then turned around to ask, 'Are you alright?'

'Peachy. Just keep me updated, ok?'

'I sure will... and, for what it's worth, I think what you did was very cool, terrifying but cool.'

He smiled at Michael and left the shuttle.

Waving at Doctor Smith's back, Michael left the shuttle and immediately headed for the med bay. Ignoring the side looks that the crew were giving him and not so subtle whispers in the acoustic corridors, he activated his wristband.

'Captain?' Elizabeth's light voice answered.

'Commander, we've docked and I'm on my way to the med bay to check on Mr Bishop.'

'Actually, Captain, I'm already here,' Elizabeth said with a serious tone.

Michael stopped suddenly. Fearing the worst, he quickly shot back, 'What? Is he ok? What the hell happened?'

'No, no, it's not that, Captain,' she said, reassuring him. 'Donald's fine, it's just... well...'

'Well, what?' he barked, irritably.

'I'll explain when you get here, it's very sensitive, Captain.'

Picking up on the direct and professional tone, he could tell that she did not like the way he was speaking to her.

'Ok. I'll be there in five.'

Arriving at the med bay, he was pleasantly greeted outside by Janine, followed by a concerned look.

'Are you ok, hun?'

Her direct question and mothering tone immediately disarmed him.

However, his worries returned almost instantly when he realised where they were and, more importantly, because she was there.

'Are you ok?' he asked her.

'Yeah.'

She paused then quickly added, 'Oh, no, I'm fine. I'll let Lizzy explain. Sorry, Commander Jenkins.'

She pushed the release button to the door, leaving Michael relieved but still confused. Quickly, she grabbed his forearm, making him turn to face her.

'Get some rest, ok,' she said, then smiling warmly, changed to a playful tone. 'That's an order.'

Tapping her hand with his, his fatigue starting to show, Michael simply replied, 'Yes, ma'am.'

With a slight squeeze, Janine released her hold on him and walked away, towards the living quarters.

That moment of humanity was like a shot of clarity to him. He felt as though he had been walking across the ship under a haze of something, something dark and draining. His head started to ache, realising that it had been aching since he put his hand on...

'Captain Quade, how nice of you to visit,' Doctor Tang said, with a surprising hint of sarcasm.

'Doc,' he said, tilting his head and squinting slightly at the lights in the room. 'How's our patient?'

'Our patient is doing absolutely fine,' she said, glancing to her side, then pointed at something on a tablet that Nurse Karen was holding.

'He's conscious, if you wish to talk to him,' she added, casually.

'Oh, ok. Sure, if that's ok with you, Doc?'

'It's your ship. Follow me please.'

She started to move towards the recuperation area, then spun to face Michael with dramatic urgency.

'Are you clean?' Doctor Tang asked, taking a step back and looking him over.

'Yeah, all the expedition crew went through the decontamination shower when leaving the shuttle bay.'

To reiterate, Michael spread his arms wide and slowly turned around on the spot. 'See... safe.'

Still looking at him, Doctor Tang seemed like she was content, but far from satisfied. 'Humm... right this way.'

Again, and with disturbing speed, she turned and walked towards Mr Bishop, with Michael following.

He could see the outline of Donald through the glass side panel of the med-tube. Donald was lying down, one leg under a silver box, and the other bent at the knee.

'Don?' Michael called, stopping just short of the bed. 'It's Captain Quade.'

Donald Bishop arched his head forward, just visible through the glass panel. His thick red hair looked dishevelled, and his completion resembled that of a 1980s' vampire.

'Oh, Christ! It's good to see you,' Donald yelled in a strong Scottish accent.

'Ahem!' Doctor Tang said, giving Mr Bishop a stern look.

'Shite, sorry, Doctor. But I just wanted to thank the man who also saved my leg... Christ, he helped save me life.'

Michael couldn't help but notice that Doctor Tang winced slightly when Donald rolled his r-s. He wondered if perhaps the of it somehow went through her, like nails on a chalkboard.

He moved to the foot of the bed, placing his hands on the white end-rail, and said in jest, 'Saved your life? Wow, I thought you just stubbed your toe.'

The Scotsman burst into a fit laughter, slapping his good leg with his hand repeatedly, while his head shot back. 'Aye, and a bloody big rock it was.'

'But seriously, how are ya?' Michael asked, leaning his forearms on the rail and looking up at the ghost of a man.

'I'm alright, Captain, a wee bit weak, but I'll be fine,' he said, nodding at Michael, beaming with gratitude towards him.

'Captain, the patient needs to rest, and Commander Jenkins is waiting in *my* office.' Doctor Tang placed a nasty little emphasis on the word 'my'.

'Thank you, Doctor,' Michael said, standing up straight and starting to leave. Before he headed to the side office, he turned back to Donald. 'Take it easy now, you hear? I need your background in geology for a special project we've got for ya.'

'Sounds good, Captain.'

Then, just as Michael was about to leave, Donald spoke up again, 'Oh, Captain, do you know if anyone grabbed a sample of the flower that moved towards you?'

Michael was wondering what the man was talking about. He was also distracted by the growing pain that his headache was so kindly providing. He just shrugged.

'Probably. Those guys took a piece of everything down there.'

'I wasn't making it up, you know? I mentioned it to the doctor, and five seconds later, they had me hooked up to a bastard machine. They were checking if I had a bleed on me brain.' Donald gave a half a laugh with his eyes lowered, carrying a sullen look about him.

'I tell you what...,' Michael negotiated, 'If you rest up tonight, I'll look into it tomorrow for ya. Deal?'

The Scotsman raised his head and replied with a hearty, 'Deal!'

Then, he laid his head back on the headrest of the bed.

The lights in the room started to become uncomfortable for Michael as he moved towards the side office. Reluctant to seek help for his pain just then, he decided he would request some pain relief later, after he had spoken to Elizabeth.

'Captain?' Elizabeth greeted him, concern now showing. Understanding dawned on her as to why he was short with her over the com channel.

'Hey,' he said, moving into the slightly dimmer office, going past her. 'Would you mind if we keep this short?'

'Of course... pardon me for saying this, but you look awful,' she said, softly placing her hand on his shoulder.

'Ah, it's nothing. Just need some sleep.'

Stepping away from him and moving round the desk, she sat down and got straight to business. 'Then I'll get through this quickly. So, I was informed of our blood situation, shall we say. And it did not sit well with me. I mean, I wanted to find out why the blood was destroyed and, more importantly, who did it.'

Picking up a chair from the opposite side of the desk, Michael moved around and placed it to the right of Elizabeth, to see the viewing screen that she had activated.

'I asked Janine to help me with the tracking down. She left just before you came in.'

'Yeah. I saw her on the way out,' he said, leaning back in the chair and rubbing his temple.

'Oh, good. Anyway, she's like a goddess when it comes to computers and managed to find this.' Elizabeth pointed at a series of code highlighted in red, stacked one after the other on the screen.

Michael leaned forward, wishing that he had kept the pressure on his temple. Letting his hands go only pulled the pain sharply back. 'What am I looking at?'

'Ok, so bear with me on this, because Janine had to break it down for me too. Here is where person D remotely accessed the automation terminal and destroyed the blood.'

'Person D?' he asked, turning his head.

'Oh, D stands for Dick. Sorry, Janine kept saying it, and I guess it stuck with me.' Smiling, she carried on by switching tabs at the bottom of the screen.

Wanting to chuckle at the in-joke, Michael hesitated due to the headache. He just smiled and turned back to the screen. 'Person D, it is.'

'So, this part...,' she pointed at two lines of access code, 'got Janine really excited. To put it into her words, it gave her a lady boner.'

Laughing and clamping his jaw in place to stop himself, he giggled through his shoulders instead. 'That woman does have a way with words.'

'I love her. She's amazing. Anyway, she said that this code was one of the most complex ones she had ever seen, but she figured out that it had been uploaded prior to launch, but not activated until after.'

'So, how does that help us?'

'Well, being the badass that she is, Janine planted a code on top of this one. Essentially, it will let us know when and where it's being used.'

'So, a trap,' he said, resting his head on his fist, looking intrigued.

'Yes. Although we don't know who it was yet, we will soon, and she disguised it as normal background code, so they won't be able to tell it's being monitored.'

'Awesome, just let me know if it works. And good work,' Michael said, slowly standing to leave.

'Apart from Don in there, how did the expedition go?' she asked, noticing the extra strength he needed to muster just to get up from his chair.

'It was weird, but I'll fill you in tomorrow, ok?' he said, trudging round the desk.

'Ok, I'll sort the crew's shift patterns tonight. You go see the doctor on the way out. You need something to take the edge off.'

The look of compassion she gave him was heartfelt and sincere. Michael appreciated the concern, slowly nodded and gave her a thumbs up before leaving the office.

Doctor Tang stood, arms crossed, in the middle of the room, holding a cup of water in one hand and something else in the other.

'Honestly, Doc, there's no need to drug me. Just buy me a drink, and I'm yours.'

'Take these.' She held out her hand, dropping two capsules in his, ignoring the childish joke. 'And drink this.'

Taking the biodegradable cup from her, he took a sip, popped the tablets in his mouth and swallowed, washing them down with the rest of the drink. He crumpled the cup and threw it into the bio-bin.

'Thanks, Doc.'

'If the migraine persists, come back here at once for me to diagnose you further,' she added, then walked into her office, joining Commander Jenkins.

Accepting Doctor Tang's way of saying, to not bother her unless it was an emergency, Michael left and headed in the direction of his quarters.

The problem with most mid-level painkillers, he thought, was that they take so goddamn long to start working. In fact, by the time he finally reached the door to his quarters, he had just enough energy left to send one recorded voice message.

'Commander Jenkins, I just wanted to say thanks for taking the reins tonight. We will carry on with the mission tomorrow. Quade out.'

He entered the room and winced, like a vampire stepping into daylight for the first time. Reaching for the sensor on the wall, he immediately turned the brightness level down. Then, not bothering with decorum, he pulled the sealant tape from his ankles, feeling every Velcro sounding tear as he did, kicked his boots off his tired feet, got undressed and left his clothes where they lay.

The body suits were designed to handle all types of terrain and negate a small percentage of planetary exploration, such as gravitational pull. Also, with the suits' own environmental control systems, they had the capability of handling warm or cold environments, to a certain degree. However, what was unusual in this case was just how much Michael was perspiring. He made a mental note to reach out to the tech guys in the morning and have them do a thorough search of his suit's internal wiring.

Looking like a gymnast, drenched in sweat, after a vigorous training session, he moved to his bed and climbed into the fresh chilled covers. Removing his wristband, not before setting an alarm for a total of six hours sleep, he placed it on the table stand and laid his heavy head down. One of the advantages of sleeping on a spaceship was the silence. The only sound he could hear was the sound of his heartbeat, which, due to his migraine, was pulsating irritably above his temples.

Finally, after what seemed like an eternity of teeth-clenching minutes, he at last loosened his jaw muscles and relaxed his breathing, then drifted off into a deep sleep.

Chapter 17

Distant Echoes

Michael awoke suddenly, sitting up in bed feeling unsettled and disorientated. His eyes darted around the room. He had a strange sensation that he couldn't explain, like something wasn't quite right. The feeling that a soldier got, just before shit hit the fan. Trying to calmly rationalise, he thought that he had surely just closed his eyes for a minute or two, but something felt different... something was amiss... Then, he saw it.

The room started to separate, as if it were made entirely of segmented panes and plasterboard panels, moving in opposite directions into the dark nothingness of space. He reached for his wrist strap and missed it, only to realise that the bedside table was now probably about seven feet away, creeping further from him. With a grumbling sound, his bed, along with the sheets and pillows, also started to move from under him. He saw all of this unfold apprehensively from above. His bed, and the ground of his quarters, became smaller and smaller as it sank into sheer darkness, leaving him inexplicably hanging in mid-air with no idea of any bearings or sign of land.

'What the fu...?'

Then, with the strength and beauty of a sunrise, a powerful blue beam materialised out of the corner of his eye, causing him to turn his body to face it head on. Along the side of the all too familiar beam was the Aletheia, the ship that he was supposed to be sleeping on, the ship that he was now outside of.

Controlling his emotions, he managed to stay calm and collected in the surreal experience. His body moved sideways, in parallel with the ship, as if he were being pulled alongside at the same speed, powerless to stop it.

He could see all the port side sections of the ship, gun-metal grey and shaped like the whale-shark hybrid that he remembered. The shadows of the small crevasses and indentations gave the exterior a scale like texture. Small and dim lights twinkled from the windows, resembling distant stars in the shadow of the beam. Edging closer to the ship, he could now see small ant-like people, going about their daily duties, unaware of Michael, the captain of the Aletheia, watching them from outside.

From the mid-section, Michael could see the weaponised defence structure that he was secretly briefed about. Four support beams straddled two large cylindrical poles, joined together by three large insulation rings. The beams moved in unison with the poles, as the structure grew, then locked in place.

Trying his best to remember the device, Michael racked his brain to remember what it was called. He could remember only one protocol linked to this: the Omega protocol.

He recalled what the admiral had said verbatim: 'In the infinitesimal chance that the ship, crew or any property thereof, is to come under attack by any foreign or superior force, this protocol can be activated.'

Designed as a last line of defence, Michael, or whoever holds the captain's chair, would have the security clearance to initiate the highly classified defence system.

The head of the ship looked like a glowing snowplough as it radiated with white light, cast by something glowing in the same direction the Aletheia was heading. He slowly turned his head and raised his hand to shield himself against the light.

Stunned, he could see that what the light was dominating, even the shine of the beam, was a vibrant white flower. When Michael's eyes adjusted to the light, he could see it contained all the solar systems they had seen on the walls of the chamber, displaying what must have been hundreds of galaxies on each massive unravelling petal. The largest of the petals highlighted a collection of three neighbouring systems, close to the centre of this cosmic wonder.

All the surrounding darkness looked like it was being pulled into the white bloom, resulting in wisps of space warping and changing into tendrils of light. Celestial in its grandeur, something was terrifyingly familiar about it, and the ship and all its crew were headed straight for the centre.

Michael, who had drifted within arm‘s reach of the ship, couldn't help but wonder if this was the most lucid dream he had ever had. He would sometimes dream vividly about his childhood, how he used to love laying on the floor of the family room, watching reruns of eighties TV shows like Star Trek or Mork and Mindy. His mom would go about doing the housework, occasionally sitting down on the mustard-coloured frilly armchair, just behind him. He could tell that sometimes she was watching him, watching how he would kick his legs back and forth when he got excited at something onscreen. He didn't mind her watching; something was warm about his mom looking over him.

The dream would always turn darker though, turning and growing more claustrophobic somehow when his supposed 'on the wagon' father would clumsily open the front door.

'Sandra?' His father used to loudly slur.

This was prompted by the door handle slamming repeatedly against the battered wall in the hallway. Michael always remembered the look of dread on his mom's face as she headed straight out to welcome her intoxicated husband.

He couldn't recall all the conversation, but he could remember most of it, especially the louder parts.

'Joe, your gonna hurt yourself,' Michael's mom would plead, desperate concern evident in her voice.

'Not gonna hurt me... I paid for it, so I can goddamn dra... drink it woman!' His father shot back.

Michael remembered one time when they were arguing in the kitchen, where he used to sneak up to the doorframe and carefully peek round to see them. His father was hunched over the cheap, rusty table appearing to have passed out, holding a half-empty bottle of poor man's bourbon. This was a regular occurrence in that house, but Michael remembered that day more than any. His mom was trying her best to remain quiet, attempting to remove the bottle from his father's grasp.

Joe woke up and kicked his chair back as he stumbled to his feet and leered at Michael's mom. If only Michael had walked in then, maybe it would have been enough of a distraction to stop it. He should have at least tried something, instead of squeezing the doorframe and trying not to move in terror.

Joe looked at Sandra as she moaned and attempted to cower. His bloodshot eyes darted to the bottle in his hand, and then, he slowly lifted his head to face her, with a look of sheer menace. She began to explain herself, and that was when his arm rounded on her face with such force that the bottle disintegrated. Shards of glass, bourbon and splashes of blood spread over the floor of where she dropped. She lay there unconscious.

Michael could still remember that first time and the stomach-turning feeling of fear, fear that his mom had just been killed by his father, and the panic of realising that his father was looking straight at him, standing by the doorframe.

'Get in here, boy!' Joe demanded, pointing his finger to the floor by his feet.

'Is Mom ok?' Michael asked, tiptoeing around her, shoulders hunched and head down.

'What?'

'Ss... sorry. Is Mom ok, sir?'

'She's fine,' he said, still smiling menacingly. Michael hated that goddamn smile.

'She just fell over is all. Clean it up, boy. I'm gonna have a shower.'

Michael had been just over eight years old when he had first cleaned up the destructive mess left in the wake of his father. It was only when he was seventeen that everything changed.

As a seventeen-year-old who was physically fit, with dark hair and grey eyes, Michael was extremely popular in high school, particularly with the ladies. His fame and hormone fuelled groupies who followed him everywhere, which made him forgo the moralistic upbringing that his mom had tried to instil in him. Arrogant and fearless, he was on track to be your stereotypical high school jock. Without ambition, he was focussed on only when he was going to kick the next field goal and deciding which woman's underwear he would he be taking off with his teeth that night.

He often dreamed about the time when Heather Lee Barts, the head cheerleader at the time, sat distraught on his front porch, waiting for him. Although practice had finished over an hour before Michael had gotten home, Heather still wore her cheerleader outfit, bright red with a tiger's face printed on the front. She was a perfect blue-eyed blond-haired girl, with silky smooth skin and a toned physique. Being the same age as Michael, she thought they were perfect for each other. The problem was, so did Lindsey Heart, who was her best friend, and the girl Michael was with before he returned home.

He couldn't remember the entire conversation, but he could recall the argument being about him not being faithful, and her typical and completely justifiable comments: 'you douchebag' or 'asshole'. He remembered Heather beginning to hit him, pounding on his upper torso to try and release her anger on him. The next moment, he twisted his body, using his weight to push her away. The lapse of control in that half a second, resulted in Heather falling down the steps of the porch.

The look on her face was of saddened horror as she got up and limped down the long suburban sidewalk. Frustrated, he went inside where he was greeted by his mom in the family room. She must have seen the altercation that had happened on the doorstep, because she had been standing there, waiting for him. Surprisingly, she was not angry but wearing a look of concern on her bruised face.

'What happened?' she asked quietly.

'Nothing,' Michael replied, throwing his backpack down by the side of the door. 'It was an accident.'

'You should never treat a woman like that, Michael Quade.' Her voice was stern but shaky, as if she were trying not to cry.

'Why?' he said defiantly. 'Dad treats you worse, and you're ok.'

He regretted saying those words every single day after that. The fact that it plagued his dreams did not seem enough of a punishment. His mom, heartbroken and with a sense of failure, didn't utter a single word to him after that. Then, the next night, when his father was drowning his wages at the local bar as usual and he was being entertained by Lyndsey Heart at a local make-out spot, Sandra Quade wrote a letter, got into a warm bath and slashed her wrists.

That was the first time Michael had ever seen a deceased body, made more visceral and painful as it was his own mom. He had discovered her only after noticing that a single knife was missing from the rack, which had never happened. She couldn't control her life, but she made a damn good job of controlling the cleanliness of their home. The alarms started to ring louder in his head when she didn't respond when he called out to her from outside the bathroom. He remembered kicking the door so hard that the force almost took the wooden doorframe with it. His voice cracked painfully as he yelled at his motionless mom, but she didn't answer back, and it slowly dawned on him that she never would again.

Frantically, he called 911 and had to wait for the police to arrive, along with the paramedics. Michael watched, with tears flowing down his face, his mom being get carried away. A friendly female officer stayed with him for a while, consoling him with an arm across his broad shoulders. She moved outside when she noticed other officers dealing with Michael's father, as he attempted to walk up the pathway, laughing at his own hiccups. A short time after, Michael had to wait alone in the quiet house with his thoughts, while the police forced his father to drink water outside.

When everything settled down, Joseph Quade made it into the house, ignored his grieving son and passed out on the couch. Michael went upstairs to his room, shooting a look of pure hatred towards his father – it should have been you was his only thought.

Curling into a ball on his bed and pulling his pillows into him, he felt a piece of paper carefully placed in the lining. Pulling it out and delicately unfolding the letter, he instantly recognised the writing. It was his mom's. What was written in it was so profound that it changed him forever.

'Michael, my beautiful boy. Please don't turn into your father. You can be so much better than him. I love you with all my heart. Forgive me, I'm sorry.'

Those huge moments had such an intense impact on him as he grew up, particularly in terms of his treatment of and respect for women. From the moment he lost his mother and read the note she had left him, he never treated a girl disrespectfully ever again.

Waking as if from a dream within a dream, Michael was shocked at the amount of detail he could remember about those days in his childhood, even the details that he had forgotten. He reached out to steady himself on the ship, and he could feel the cold hard metal alloy of the exterior beneath his hand. Trying to understand the situation, he asked himself why he was revisiting these dreams now.

Then his mind wandered again.

There were more frequent dreams during his adult years, mostly of his time in the military. Normally, his dreams were filled with replays of his time in conflict areas and situations he thought he would never make it out alive. The most persistent and disturbing dream was of him watching helplessly as his squad was being picked apart by a highly effective sniper, while he was pinned down by a very aggressive Palestinian tank. Michael had never forgotten that day; every detail was burned into his subconscious, from the feel of the hot dusty wind clashing against his skin, to the smell of freshly detonated ordinance that surrounded them.

It was the worst misunderstanding of troops on the ground he had ever witnessed. The term blue on blue didn't technically fit the situation, as not one of Michael's squad members were technically killed by the allied tank. However, the resulting action of the tank commander's blunder, plus the lack of clear communication, meant that neither Michael and nor his men could get to effective cover – they were sitting ducks.

Up until that point, Michael had never believed in God or any such unforeseen powers, but that day, and what had happened there, couldn't be as easily explained by probability. Remembering what seemed like an eternity of delayed cracks and snaps from the sniper, and thunderous explosions of brick and mortar caused by the relentless shelling of the tank, Michael recalled every time one of his guys got hit, knowing that the man would not get back up from it.

After holding a couple of his dying comrades, as the light and warmth slipped out of them, Michael had undergone quite a drastic change in mindset. His beliefs had changed drastically, from the lack of faith in any religious superior being to welcoming the determined and unwavering fact that he was being followed by Death himself. There was no other explanation for it. Death had trailed him for years, reaching out and taking close friends and family members, who only tried to live their lives peacefully. The metaphorical grim reaper would play with him, keeping him alive to watch as people surrounding Michael would simply die. Michael sometimes felt as if he was present in the world but also absent from it at the same time, as if everyone reacted slower or made the wrong decisions that led to their deaths, every goddamn time.

Reminiscing physically took a toll on Michael in this waking dream. Shaking his head back and forth, while holding onto the ship, he turned his head away from the glare of the flower and gasped at what he saw. He could see his shadow stretched and being cast along the side of the ship, but another shape was closing in on him. He immediately let go, jerking his body to spin to face the strange object. Against the vast black canvas of space, he could see nothing but distant stars.

Focusing intently, he tried to see any shape or mass obscuring the wavering twinkle of lights. Unexpectedly, he began to pick up a familiar scent.

Then, it hit him. The smell was of... something, someone... Abby!

The moment he turned to see her was the exact moment a hand touched his shoulder.

'Captain?' a voice cried in a panicked concern.

Elizabeth stood over his bed with Doctor Tang. Lieutenant Gemma Saunders stood guard in the hallway by his open door.

'Captain, it's me, Elizabeth. Do you know where you are?'

'Abby?' he asked, still dazed and more than a little confused.

'No, Captain,' she said, looking over to Doctor Tang. 'Abby's not here.'

As the doctor moved closer towards him, Michael regained his composure and got out of bed.

'I don't think that's a good idea, Captain,' the doctor said, placing a sensor strap on his arm as he stood up. Sweat dripped and rolled down his scared body, and his soaked underwear did not leave much to the imagination.

'What the hell happened?' Michael asked, looking directly at Elizabeth.

'What happened?' She eyed him up and down before continuing. 'What happened is that you have been out of contact for three hours after you sent me this.'

She reached for her wrist strap, swiped and pressed down, turning on the loudspeaker function on in the room.

'Commander Jenkins, I just wanted to say thanks for taking the reins tonight.'

Michael recognised his voice and the message he had sent earlier.

'What's wrong with that?'

Doctor Tang slowly moved away but gave Michael a peculiar look, the sort of look a child gets when they finally have the toy from an arcade claw machine. She then quickly gave Elizabeth the universal hand gesture of 'He's ok'.

Elizabeth frowned at the doctor, expecting that she would have found something wrong with him. Then, turning back to Michael, she exhaled. 'Michael, can you not hear what is wrong with that message?'

'For Christ's sake, NO! Tell me what's wrong?!' Struggling to keep calm, he waited for her to answer.

She hesitated for a moment, trying to find the best way to word what she had to tell him. She placed a hand on his arm for comfort. 'Michael, apart from my name... none of what you said is in a language we have ever heard before.'

Chapter 18

Metamorphosis

Michael quietly sat by his desk in his quarters, wearing his loose but comfortable grey civilian clothes.

'Again,' he demanded, doing his best not to show his frustration.

Elizabeth sat across from him, starting to show signs of fatigue on her elegantly lined face. 'I just don't think you can hear it.'

She turned to Doctor Tang, who was focused on the sensor strap on the captain, in order to check his vitals.

'Is it possible that something is affecting his hearing?'

'Unlikely,' the doctor said, raising her head and looking straight at Michael. 'If that were the case, then his responses would likely be loud and inconsistent.'

'Hey, I'm sitting right here. Don't talk about me as if I'm not.'

Elizabeth quietened into concerned deep thought and played the recording one more time, in the hope that this time, he would be able to hear the difference for himself. He didn't.

Leaning back in his chair to stretch out his back, he incredulously interlocked his fingers behind his head and looked straight up at the light fittings. Something was... different.

He was trying to recall his dream, which had left him in a wet sweaty puddle, a short time ago. No matter how hard he tried, the memory just felt slightly out of reach. Same as the language in the message too. Why couldn't he hear it?

'What about this bit?' Elizabeth asked, holding a single finger up. 'It sounds like a mixture of what could be Arabic and Navajo.'

Michael leaned forward, fingers still interlocked and listened intently, then raised his hands in a defeated manner. 'Nope.'

'We should go down to the med bay and run further tests,' the doctor interjected. 'And I'll call if I find anything.'

The doctor was strangely calm, given the unusual circumstances. She looked like a puppy waiting to be let out, her metaphorical tail wagging, obviously eager to leave the room with the captain.

Elizabeth looked at her for a moment, trying to work out what was making the doctor act in such a peculiar fashion. Then, hesitantly, she raised her hands in defeat. 'Fine... but may I suggest the ship remain in the planet's orbit until we have more answers?'

'Yep, good idea.'

Michael stood up from his desk at a speed that startled the women in the room. Even Lieutenant Gemma Saunders, who had been guarding the doorway quietly, braced herself for the unexpected. 'Let the crew have a rest and give them some time with the samples they collected. Oh, and, Liz, let's also keep this under wraps for now. Don't want the crew losing their shit over this.'

'Yes, Captain,' Elizabeth agreed, somewhat surprised that she actually liked him calling her Liz. She rose from her chair and softly added, 'Also, Captain?'

'Yeah?' he answered with a sigh, moving around the desk.

'Who is Abby? You asked for her as you woke.'

Michael stopped moving, halfway around his desk, shocked and embarrassed. 'I asked for her?'

Frowning with intrigue, Elizabeth realised at that moment that she had no idea who Michael Quade was. She was about to delve further, but felt Doctor Tang's hand cautiously grab her arm. Turning to face her, she saw a soft face staring back, shaking her head ever so slightly and indicating that it was a sensitive subject.

'I'm...sorry, Captain,' she said, turning back to Michael. 'I didn't mean to...'

'No... it's ok.' His voice suddenly matched the awkward silence in the room. He spoke very quietly and painfully, 'Abby was my wife...'

Realising what the doctor was trying to warn her about, Elizabeth softly said, 'I'm so sorry. Look, I'll sort the crew out. You just get checked out, ok?'

As he nodded, in a repressed excited voice, Doctor Tang said, 'So, Mr Quade, shall we get going?'

Smiling that she had just referred to him as Mr Quade, Michael put his own wristband on and gestured towards the door.

The door automatically closed behind them as they left the room. Then they made their way down the luminescent hallway. Crew members passed, ignoring the fact that the party were dressed in uniform, apart from the captain, who looked like he was out fresh from the gym.

Reaching a T-junction, Commander Jenkins squeezed Michael's arm, gave him a kind sympathetic glance and proceeded onto the bridge.

'You good from here?' Gemma asked.

Michael opened his mouth. He was about to speak but was interrupted hastily by Doctor Tang, 'Yes, we will be fine. Thank you.'

Nodding at Gemma, Michael looked at the doctor, who had started to walk towards the conveyor belt walkway. He tried to figure out why she was in such a rush, but then, ever since he had met her, she had been a bit… well, weird.

'Thanks, Gem,' he said over his shoulder. She smiled politely, which emphasised the lines at the corner of her dark eyes, then continued down the hallway.

Michael managed to catch up with Doctor Tang and noticed she was wearing a cute smile, profiling her cheekbones.

'You, ok? You're acting a bit… weird,' he asked, joining her on the walkway.

Leaning against the handrail, the doctor turned to face him. Her medical lab coat was open, revealing her medical ID lanyard hanging loosely from her neck and sitting snug on top of her chest.

She began to form a word, then quickly looked down at the portable vitality reader that she held in her hand. Still smiling, she looked back up at Michael.

'Do you know that I studied at Peking University in Beijing?' she asked casually, crossing her legs.

Positioning himself opposite her, he mirrored her posture and placed his elbows on the handrail.

'Really? That's cool,' he replied, not having a clue if the university was a good one but trying to be polite.

'It's ok,' she said, sending him a playfully sceptical look. 'I wouldn't expect you to know it.'

Tilting her head, she gazed out at the planet that they were orbiting and continued as if she were reminiscing the old days.

'It is known as one of the most prestigious medical universities in the world. Thousands of students apply to it, but only the best get selected. I have always been at the top because I worked hard to get there. I liked learning; it was like I couldn't get enough, you know?'

'Uh-huh,' Michael replied. 'The learning part, I don't get as much, but the drive to better yourself, I have some experience with. We all gotta better ourselves, right?'

'Exactly,' she said smiling at him, slightly squinting her jade green eyes. 'Better ourselves. That's why, when I studied there, I didn't just specialise in clinical medicine, I also studied biomedical engineering, which—given the volume of the course content for both—was very difficult.'

'So, you kind of did two courses at once?'

'Yes, that's exactly what I did. I, how do you say it, graduated with the best scores that they had ever seen.'

She turned to him then and, with a supressed excitement, continued, 'I have worked on all types of projects, and I have seen samples of almost every type of biological specimen on the planet. I once discovered an entirely new species, completely by accident, at the bottom of an excavation site where my father worked. I was extremely happy that day.'

'I bet that's a big deal, right?' Michael asked curiously.

'Yes.' She laughed. 'It is a big deal and a great moment for the scientific community and my family. It will go down in history somewhere. But you know what... I don't care anymore.'

Confused, Michael just stared at her, not sure what to say and wondering why she was telling him all this.

'I don't care because I have found something truly and wonderfully unique. I don't think anyone has ever seen it before,' she said with determined passion.

'That's great,' he replied incredulously. 'But, what does that have to do with...'

'It's you,' the doctor said, moving to stand beside him, bringing up the small device.

'What?'

'Just look at this.' She indicated to her tablet for him to see what she meant. 'This is an example of your first blood sample, prior to coming to the ship. Everything normal, right? Well, yes and no. You see, your blood cells look and act exactly like a normal person's would, except...'

She used her thumb and forefinger to zoom in further to the sample.

'Here, you can see that your cells are amazingly special, even before the mission. Your red cells have developed a way of compressing even more oxygen for your body to use, and that's not even the best part. I used a small sample of your backup blood donation, to test a theory I had regarding your white blood cells. And you know what I found?'

She asked as if she were a host on a game show. Michael just shrugged, trying his best not to get lost in all the medical mumbo jumbo.

'Your white blood cells...' she quickly looked around to make sure they were not being overheard, 'completely destroyed every foreign body sample I tested them against.'

Again, Michael found himself struggling to understand what she meant by all this but knew it must be important by the look of glee all over her face.

'Sooo...?' He urged her to elucidate further.

'So?' She seemed disappointed for a moment, then returned her little smile. 'So, I looked at your entire medical background and found that you only ever once had a medical appointment, which was regarding your eyes. Michael, you have never been sick. Not once.'

'So what? I've known lots of guys who have always been fit and healthy.'

She gave him a patient look before responding in an almost condescending tone.

'I guarantee that your friends, at least once, have had influenza or chickenpox at some point. You, on the other hand, have never had anything affect you because you are naturally immune. I think it was never picked up because you never had your blood taken. Even then, they wouldn't have known what to look for.'

'Hold up,' he said, thinking back for a second, 'What about when I was recovering in the hospital? They must have known my blood type. Or, what about when I was overseas and they gave me vaccinations?'

'First, I looked at your time in the hospital, and they only hooked you up to an intravenous drip to build your fluids back up. And second, as far as I'm concerned, any vaccine you have ever had in your entire life has been a complete waste of time.'

He stood there, looking perplexed for a moment, trying his best to remember the past, for any point in his childhood, for any occasion, where he felt ill. He tried to remember any time his mom had had to nurse him back to health from some ailment. He couldn't recall any illnesses at all.

'So, why tell me now?' he asked, discomfort in his voice.

'Because I checked your blood in your quarters as you were waking and...,' she said, swiping her finger across the pane of the device, 'your cell structure has changed.'

She held out the device, with a mixture of excitement and nervousness. Michael put his hand underneath to help reduce the shaking screen. He could see that his cells were strangely different from the other slide. In the last picture, the red blood cells were like little discs with indents on the top and bottom. In the slide he was looking at now, a single cell comprised five or six layers, all connected and resembling tyres stacked on top of each other.

'What the fu...,' he muttered.

'I have a theory,' she interrupted him. 'A theory that no one has been able to conclusively prove, yet.'

She zoomed in closer to a single cell, displaying what could now been seen as multiple sections within each ring.

'My theory is that we harness an individual cell and somehow change it into a storage container of sorts. Then, we will be able to store a phenomenal amount of data in the human body. Just imagine, generations of knowledge passed on down a family line. It was totally theoretical until just now, in your quarters.'

Turning his back and leaning towards the handrail, Michael looked out of the viewing port. The combination of the red light from one side of the ship, mirrored by to blue light of the opposite side, would have been overwhelming if not for the overpowering florescent lights from above.

'Will I die from it?' he asked, fearing the worst, but always preferring to be ready for anything.

She looked at him, folding away the screen and slotting it into a wide pouch in her uniform. 'Honestly... I have no idea.'

He remained quiet, dwelling on the fact that he could be some kind of goddamn computer or something.

'Hey,' the doctor said abruptly, snapping him out of it. 'This is a good thing.'

'Easy for you to say, Doc. You're not the one who's just found out they're a giant memory stick.'

As the walkway came to an end, they stepped off and continued to the med bay, hardly looking at or saying a word to each other. Doctor Tang stopped in the corridor, a couple of feet away from the med bay doors. Michael turned and noticed that she had her head down, and her hands were clasped together, like an apologetic schoolgirl.

'You, ok?'

'I am sorry,' she said in a quiet, innocent voice. 'I didn't think for a second how you would react to this information.'

'It's not that,' he calmly replied, moving closer to her. 'It's just... I have a lot of questions, you know?'

Nodding, Doctor Tang moved towards the doors, causing them to slide open automatically, then proceeded to walk into the room ahead of Michael. The med bay was quiet with only two nurses on duty, going about their work. All the beds were empty and perfectly folded in the manner of military hospital premises.

Donald Bishop was sitting, stroking his chin, in a comfortable chair positioned outwards, in the recovery area. He was surrounded by art sculptures of soft shapes and pictures of abstract brush strokes of vibrant colours. The recovery room was more like a children's play area, created to make the patient feel relaxed in a safe space. Donald seemed enthralled with something he was studying on his tablet, then raised his head when he realised someone was coming.

'Ahh, Captain!' He smiled, lowering his tablet. 'Have you got a sec? I need to show you something.'

Turning to Doctor Tang, who tipped her head towards Donald, Michael asked begrudgingly, 'Will it be quick? I'm kinda in the middle of something.'

'Aye, sir. It won't take longer than a minute. It's just important, sir.' Donald reached out with the tablet towards Michael.

'I'll just be in the examination area,' Doctor Tang said quietly, then walked away.

Michael took the tablet from Donald and sat in the chair next to him. 'Ok, Don, what am I looking at?'

'I managed to get the body-cam footage off the lad that was walking behind me on the expedition. Just you wait until you see this.'

Leaning over his chair, conscious of his injury and trying his best not to move too quickly, Donald pressed play on the recording.

Michael watched as the member of the expedition team walked behind Donald. Although the camera spun around with no regard for the people watching the recording afterwards, the four times ultra-definition footage was clear as crystal. After a while, just as Michael was about to give up, unable to see the point of Donald's miniature movie night, he saw something he almost refused to believe. As if the night couldn't get any weirder, Michael sat in amazement as he could see movement near to himself on the footage. The inexplicable thing was that flowers leading up to and scaling the weathered and dusty walls of the bridge were all writhing and stretching towards him.

'You see, sir,' Donald said, 'I wasn't losing my marbles, after all.'

Stunned by what he was witnessing, Michael just sat quietly, trying to think of an explanation. With nothing coming to mind, he returned to the same question, over and over. What the hell is going on?

Chapter 19

Respite

The mess hall was relatively empty apart from Roman and his security team, who sat around a large silver table like pack animals waiting to feast. The open plan layout was a combination of polished silver and blemish-free whites. The room curved in such a way that it almost compelled a person to sit and gaze out at the universe, while having a meal or drink. To the right of the seating area, the sophisticated kitchen area with the latest designed cooking machinery was fully stocked with vacuum packed meals, lunches and fruit. One device was for correctly dispensing food and drink, which could be selected from an extensive touchscreen list. The large column resembling a vending machine measured and dispensed plastic trays, along with cups to crew members. At the end of every function, a three-note melody signalled that it was ok to take the meal from the large flap in the midsection.

The odd crew member came and went quickly, taking their food to go, after the order to stand down, came through from Commander Jenkins. Many of them resorted to filling their pockets to carry as many food packets as they could, eagerly anticipating long days of uninterrupted research. Some, however, just left the hall after vowing to do the looting another time, as the security department were present and would not look too kindly on excessive binging.

Roman's group, were all intently listening to a story, being told by a smirking, youthful straw-haired man.

'So, I just walked over, slapped her ass and gave the manager the finger on the way out!'

Erupting in fits of laughter, the group filled the empty hall with enough volume that the sound echoed into some sort of reverberated roaring mess.

'I bet her guy just stood there, pissing his pants,' a tan, dark-featured man blurted out, repeatedly slamming his hairy fist on the fixed silver table.

'I didn't give a fuck,' the blond man declared arrogantly, who wore his red uniform shirt open to expose his pale, well-defined chest. 'That little bitch wouldn't have lasted two seconds against me. He would have kicked your ass though, Gorman.'

The young man added that last bit with a maniacal smile in a provocative tone.

Rolling his eyes then nudging the trainee's boot under the table opposite him, Gorman gave a menacing grin through his jet-black whiskers, 'There he goes again. He knows I'm the strongest guy here, but Burk keeps forgetting.'

Gorman continued, leaning forward and facing his rival, 'I seem to remember wining the last two sparing matches outa the both of us. Or did you forget?'

'Bullshit, you wanna go again now? Cos I won't take it easy on you,' Burk said, sitting up in his chair.

'I'm ready when you are, pointbreak.'

They both shot up, ready to engage in battle, causing Eric Rosiak to shuffle uncomfortably in his chair. Eric quickly darted his eyes over to Roman, who sat emotionless, reading something intently on his tablet.

Grabbing a hold of each other from across the table, the two security team members became more aggressive, tugging and pulling at each other. Burk was just about to throw the first punch when they both stopped suddenly, for Gorman had inadvertently tipped over his drink, spilling it across the table. They both watched in horror as the liquid trailed passed Gorman and painstakingly headed in the direction of Roman. Frozen with fear, all the men could do was trace the stream of liquid and prey it stopped before it reached its target.

Eric, pre-empting the disaster and assuming that Roman was unaware of the mishap, reached an arm out to block the path. He hesitated when he realised that Roman was looking directly over his tablet and staring at him. He slowly switched his gaze towards the two men, who looked like they were holding their breath as the liquid slowed its pace. Then, it finally stopped at the very edge of the table where Roman sat.

Even though the crisis was over, both Burk and Gorman still found themselves waiting for any sort of reaction from Roman. After some excruciatingly long couple of seconds, Roman slowly looked down at the table, frowned and looked back at the men.

'You know, a long time ago, in a place called Mesopotamia, it was common practice to flay or peel the skin off humans as a punishment. Did you know this?'

The men immediately released each other and lowered their heads, demonstrating that the point had been understood. In the following silence, one man retrieved a cloth to clear up the spillage, while another reset the cups and plates on the table.

The vacuum of sound was interrupted, like a hammer on an anvil, as the door to the mess hall flew open.

'Ah, Lieutenant Saunders. How nice of you to join us for the morning briefing,' Roman announced in a casually sarcastic tone.

'I'm sorry, sir, by the time I...'

'By the time you finished doing something last night, with Commander Jenkins, Doctor Tang and Captain Quade, you must have been quite tired.'

He delivered the statement in such an implicating tone that it made Gemma feel uncomfortable, putting her on the defensive.

'I was requested by Commander Jenkins to accompany her and Doctor Tang to the captain's quarters.'

'Is that so?'

'Yes, sir,' she shot back with venom, understanding that this was turning into an interrogation disguised as a conversation.

'And what exactly happened in the captain's quarters, Lieutenant?' Roman said, leaning forward to judge her response.

Shocked by the question, she was conflicted between answering a question from a superior officer or sticking to her guns. She decided to reply in a monotone voice akin to reciting the core values of the mission. 'I am not at liberty to say, sir.'

Roman's eyes widened at the response. Then, precisely placing his tablet down on the now dried table, he asked again in a cold, almost whispering tone, 'Lieutenant, what... happened... in the captain's quarters?'

Another moment of silence ensued where Gemma frowned at Roman, who was regarding her with unwavering expectancy. Suddenly, Burk accidentally dropped a plastic cup, making Eric physically jump in his seat.

Noticing this in his peripheral vision, Roman broke eye contact, placed his hand on the kid's shoulder, drew back his lips back to reveal an uncomfortable smile and said, 'Do not worry, little one. It is only a cup.'

Eric relaxed his shoulders and shook his head in embarrassment.

'Lieutenant, would you please sit with us. I would like to brief you all at the same time,' Roman said, gesturing towards a space on the table.

Gemma's posture also relaxed, but she responded with a very firm, 'Yes, sir.'

Roman waited for the others to return to the table, having disposed the paper rags. Then, he addressed the unit with the aid of his tablet.

'So far, there have been few security problems. The usual arguments between man and wife, which I dealt with personally. I want you all to... as you say, keep your eyes open for changes in the crew's behaviour.'

Spotting that some of the team were confused by this statement, Roman clarified. 'It is all too common for people to start... over-reacting to situations out of their control. Like when a thorn in the side becomes more annoying over time.'

'A thorn?' Gorman asked, confused.

'Yes. A thorn. It starts as a small problem but becomes bigger problem in the end. Understand?'

All heads surrounding the table nodded, prompting Roman to swipe up on his tablet and continue.

'Now, onto serious problems. There have been two critical matters that I have been concerned about. One is the extremely dangerous injury, sustained by Donald Bishop. The other is the disappearance of the blood donations from the med bay.'

Roman placed his tablet down on the table and addressed the group left to right. 'Any suggestions on how this could have been avoided?'

Gorman, who sat to Roman's immediate left, spoke up. 'Well, first, I think a proper recon should have happened. You know, when I was in the Army down in Mexico, we always followed ruta probada... the proven route.'

'Yeah, he also used to follow the cocaina too,' Burk added in a ridiculous Mexican accent, earning him a piercing glance from Roman.

'Continue,' Roman said plainly, turning back to Gorman.

'Well, urmm, if that had happened, then we would have spotted the hazard on the bridge earlier.'

'It was done!' Eric blurted out like a disobedient child. 'I'm sorry. At least, I think it was; the planet was scanned, right?'

'Look, kid, no matter how much a planet is scanned, you can never beat good old-fashioned line of sight,' Gorman shot back.

'Oh... ok.'

Eric hung his head, looking dejected.

Realising that he might have come across a bit too strong, Gorman continued, 'But you are right, Ese, the money spent on these top-of-the-range scanners should have picked something up.'

Roman nodded, and Eric lifted his head, a little grateful to have been taken seriously.

'As for the other thing, who the fuck would steal blood? Are we sure they didn't just fucking leave the shit behind?'

'I'm with him on that one,' Burk said. 'Either that, or we got a fucking vampire on board. In which case, we are all fucked.'

Eric and Gemma both chuckled at the thought.

'Oh, you liked that, did ya?' Burk teased. 'I bet that would float your boat, you dirty lil perv.'

Eric couldn't help but burst into laughter.

'Ok, ok,' Roman said, 'I agree. It does sound unlikely that blood should suddenly disappear, and I very much doubt that it was a creature of the night...'

'Aah...,' Burk said, feigning disappointment.

'But we still have to investigate it as a serious crime. Dr Tang has been...mmm... very determined to find who did it. So, I want two teams. Burk and Gorman, you will take statements from the medical staff. Lieutenant Saunders, Eric and I will investigate the digital records. Understood?'

Both the men nodded along with no reservations. Gemma, on the other hand, raised her hand slightly.

'Yes?' Roman asked casually.

'Well, sir, it's just... well, I'm not very good with computers. And I was thinking maybe I should swap with...'

'The teams will remain the same,' he said, shutting her suggestion down.

He looked at Gemma directly, with an expression void of emotion, 'Any other questions?'

The table remained quiet, and Gemma reluctantly accepted her orders.

'Good. Now, starting from today, we will all, at some point, go to the med bay and donate blood, to replenish what has been lost. So, keep hydrated and keep to your exercise schedule. I will have no room for people without discipline on my team. Dismissed.'

The party disbanded, leaving the table with high-pitched squeals from shifting their chairs back. Roman moved towards the window and looked out with his hands behind his back.

Eric, who was the last of the security team to stand, waited apprehensively, after Gemma shot up from the table and stormed out of the room.

Alex Burk and Enrique Gorman left like two mischievous children, barging into each other to be the first ones out of the doors.

Eric slowly got to his feet, then carefully positioned all the chairs back under the table, dwelling on whether he made the right decision by joining this mission.

Then, he remembered the last conversation he had had with Roman, and it still bothered him, such that if he didn't get to the bottom of it, he knew that it would become a problem.

'Sir?' Eric asked, cautiously walking over to the window area.

Roman, who looked like he was galaxies away, deep in thought, slowly turned his head to the left.

'What is it, Eric?'

'Sorry, but I've got to ask...,' Eric took a moment to carefully construct the question that he knew would have to be asked delicately. 'I wanted to ask you, if I ever thanked you for helping me out here?'

Turning his head back to the window, Roman answered in a monotone voice, 'It is, as they say, my pleasure.'

Now that the conversation had started, Eric continued, still taking care with how he constructed his words. 'Ever since I was young, I wanted to make something of myself. To make my family proud.'

'That is very noble of you, young Eric.'

'Thank you. I especially wanted to make my farther proud, even after what happened to him...'

Eric let that statement hang in the air for a moment, hoping to see Roman's reaction, maybe even get closer to an explanation as to why he thought his father was still alive.

To Eric's dismay, Roman restrained his movements to that of a simple nod, again, leaving no clue to his thoughts and feelings.

Maybe he was wrong, Eric thought. Maybe he was reading into something which was too difficult to think about, let alone talk. Roman must have served with hundreds of soldiers in the past, and the way the world had changed; he must have lost so many of his close friends. That must be it. Roman has lost too many friends that he doesn't believe that they are gone.

'Let us not dwell on the past, little Eric,' Roman said. 'Let us focus on the mission and, more importantly for you, your training.'

Eric stood beside him, mirroring position. 'Yes, sir, where do we start?'

'We will start with your physical training; it is important that your body is just a strong as your mind. But what I want to know is...,' Roman turned, leaning over Eric with a menacing smile on his face and a somewhat challenging tone, 'just exactly how good are you with cyber security?'

Chapter 20

Reflex

After the revelations that came from Doctor Tang and Donald Bishop, Michael kept quiet for the remaining time he spent in the med bay. He talked only when answering a direct question and tried his best to remain calm, when his mind wanted him to scream with confusion.

He went through the series of tests that the good doctor had carefully administered herself. Bloodwork, skin tissue samples, blood pressure, CAT scans, MRI scans and several other scans that Michael gave up caring enough about to remember what they were for.

He talked a little more with Donald, who was recuperating in the rest area, the conversation ending with a friendly secrecy agreement, prohibiting Donald from telling the other crew members and, in his words, freaking everyone out.

Knowing that his blood was different than everyone else's, plus the fact that plants now practically chase after him, Michael just wanted to leave and blow off some steam. His one consistent outlet in life was the gym, the place where he was able to fully thrash his anger and stress. It was the one area where he didn't have to worry about what he said, how he looked or what goddamn blood he had inside him.

He reached the on-board gymnasium to find that a few crew members were already training, as per their daily routine. Although the effects of body degradation were reduced in the artificial atmosphere on the Aletheia, sedentary work still took its toll. Michael remembered from the countless pre-mission briefings that it was important to keep on top of muscle density and cardio, regardless of the fitness levels on the ship. As his old high school coach used to say, doing something is always better than nothing.

'Good morning, sir,' Ensign Josh Thomas said in a staggered breath, pushing hard on an exercise bike.

'Morning, Josh, you reach Kansas yet?' Michael jested, referring to the bike's digital projection of a sunny open road, which resembled an area near Penn Valley Park.

'Not... yet, sir. But I'll say hi to Dorothy... when I get there.'

Michael chuckled, then passed him. He went over to his locker, where a few crew members had stored their gear. Retrieving a small rucksack, Michael moved over to the multifunctioning training area. He unclipped the clasps on the bag and pulled out a set of speed gloves and a worn pair of red hand wraps.

He was lost in his thoughts for a moment as he started to wrap his hands, autopilot kicking in as he went through the motions of over and under, over and under, keeping the fabric tight against his hands, but not so much that it affected his ability to make a fist.

All that had happened in the past twenty-four hours was pressing on his mind. He felt like a ship in a stormy sea, ready for the last wave to hit before he capsized.

Stopping himself from dwelling on the uncontrollable factors of his life, he began to loosen his arms by swinging them across his body, back and forth, over and under.

In normal circumstances, Michael would have warmed up with about fifteen minutes of skipping rope drills. Normally, he would alternate between steady and fast speeds, every three minutes or so, but today was not the day to warm up. No, today was the day to repeatedly hit something as fast as he could. So, he began to strike the heavy bag, slowly at first to get his form, oblivious to the fact that he had left his gloves on top of his bag on the floor.

Then, picking up his pace and power, he hit with his straight left, then a straight left, followed by a straight right. He began to settle into his rhythm, repeating the process over and over, occasionally throwing in a solid hook. Michael found his mind was drifting away with every strike.

The thud sounds of his hands striking the bag started to increase in volume and the time between each strike reduced. He was so relaxed and comfortable in the moment that Michael didn't notice Josh approach the training area. Josh stood a couple of feet away, wiping the sweat off his neck with a white towel. When he saw Michael, Josh could only look on in awe.

To Michael, his hands were moving fast but not too fast that he would lose form or would exhaust him quickly. To Josh, who was quite a boxing fan for a while, Michael had speed and technique that he had never seen in his life. It was as if someone had unintentionally pressed fast forward on the fastest middleweight he had ever seen. It looked like the bag just hung there, hunched over at the point where Michael was hitting the bag. He could only guess its position because Michael was just so goddamn fast.

'Holy shit!' Josh said, breathless just looking at him.

There was no response. Michael just continued, emotionless and even more bizarrely, with no sign of sweat or fatigue at all. Moving round to the side to be in view of Michael's line of sight, Josh cautiously attempted to get the attention of the machine that was his Captain.

'Are you ok, sir?'

Thinking back to when he was a young boy, Josh recalled watching an 8K version of Bruce Lee's *Game of Death*, a movie where Bruce Lee showed just a small percentage of his speed on camera as his character categorically fought off his foes.

Michael stopped abruptly, causing the heavy bag to drop from the raised position with a loud girding clunk of the carabineer against the securing hook.

'Sorry, Josh,' Michael said nonchalantly. 'I didn't see you there.'

'That was insane!' Josh said, still bewildered by what he had just witnessed. 'Where the hell did you train?'

Confused, Michael looked at him for a moment, wondering what the hell he was talking about. Then, from the corner of his eye, Michael could see the markings that he had left on the punching bag. That's impossible, he thought.

The bag, which had a slight swing, had changed dramatically. When Michael had entered the area, the bag was fresh and relatively brand new; the leather on the black finished surface was crease free, and untarnished, and the seams were neat and intact, interlacing threads showing no signs of wear. It was in good condition.

'What the fu...,' Michael said as he looked at the bag, horrified by what he saw.

The bag from the back looked just as it did as before. However, the front and most of the sides in the exact areas that Michael had been working it, looked like it had aged by a few decades. Massive sections were worn, cracked, and showing signs of tearing. The leather had fractures on it that resembled forks of lightning, spreading in an outward pattern. Michael, still gathering the unbelievable evidence, noticed that down by his feet, just at the base of the bag, was a small pile of black flakes, which probably came from the same source.

Reaching out slowly with his hand, Michael began to gently feel the wear on the bag. Curiosity compelled him to touch the damage, but for him, it was also to test if he was still dreaming somehow.

'I have never seen anyone move that fast, sir,' Josh said, eyes widening as he regarded the damage himself.

'It was only five minutes...' Michael said, under his breath, looking at his torn and tattered wraps.

'Oh my God!' Josh exclaimed, sounding astonished. He eyes darted from the bag to Michael, then back to the bag again. 'That's crazy!'

As if snapping back to a fractured sort of reality, Michael tried to play down what had happened. 'Oops. Guess I went a bit hard there, huh?'

'Hard?' Josh replied in jest. 'It looks like it's been hit by a fricking train!'

Michael laughed awkwardly, then put his hand on the boy's shoulder. 'Look, Josh, can we keep this between us?'

'Really? Sir, this is awesome. Some people will lose their shit if...'

'And that's the exact reason why. It can't go any further.'

Michael placed his hands on his hips and stated in a thick playful Texan accent, 'Don wan the good people of this town to go all crazy now.'

As soon as Josh was about to reply, the gymnasium doors opened.

Doctor Tang walked straight in, without bothering to check if anyone else was in the room. She walked straight up to the captain, glanced at Josh and continued, with a controlled panic in her voice.

'We have a problem.'

Michael looked at Josh, who gave him a professional nod, turned and started to leave, but quickly stopped and said, 'Oh, sir? That thing that you said before. Yeah, it's staying in this room.'

Michael gave him a wink and a thumbs up as the boy left. Good kid, he thought.

'What's up now?' Michael asked, turning to the doctor, with a hint of annoyance in his voice.

'First, ouch,' she said sarcastically. 'Second, our chief engineer is in the med bay with a headache.'

'Big Bob? He's a big boy. He'll be ok.'

'It's not just him. Several other crew members are experiencing the same symptoms. Headaches, dizziness, increased perspiration. I ran a few tests and came to two conclusions.'

Michael, who was now taking the matter seriously, intently listened as she continued.

'First, the patients with these similar symptoms, all came from the vicinity of the ship's engine room. Some from the adjacent quarters running alongside of it. Secondly, after several tests, I have diagnosed the issue as a mild form of hypoglycaemia.'

Michael thought for a moment before quickly raising his head, 'That's low blood sugar, right?'

'Yes, and if it's not treated quickly, it could lead to fainting, or seizures and... well you get the point. I do not want to wait that long.'

Nodding, Michael decided to put his own concerns to one side and focus on the safety of his crew.

'Where's Bob now?' he asked.

'Still in the med bay,' she said with a sigh. 'I wanted to make sure his vitals were good before releasing him, but...'

He picked up on her reservations and frowned as he shrugged.

'Oh, he's just so loud. And I swear, I can feel his eyes on my ass from across the room.'

Michael frowned at the last part, but before he had a chance to respond, she continued.

'I tell you one thing,' she shot back, pointing her finger at him. 'The next time he makes a stupid innuendo or looks at my ass, I promise you, I will medically castrate the pervert. There are ways.'

'Jesus Christ! Okay! I get it.'

'Good,' she said firmly. 'And I'm still waiting on some of your test results too.'

Michael walked on ahead, glancing back at the punching bag, deciding to revisit that later.

Down the end of the corridor, a small figure followed by a giant dressed in gym gear walked toward Michael.

'Roman,' Michael acknowledged with a courteous nod, walking towards him. 'Everything running smoothly?'

'Ah, Captain,' he replied, disdainfully returning the gesture. 'All is, as you say, running smoothly. In fact, I was just about to teach little Eric some fighting techniques. Would you like to join? I very much would like to see what skills you possess.'

Not reacting to the maniacal smile creeping on Roman's face, Michael looked at Eric, who looked like he was lost, and gave him a wink.

'Well, you see, the thing is that my skills aren't exactly teaching friendly, and I wouldn't want to... you know, embarrass anyone now. So, I'm going to have to ask for a rain check.'

'Another time then,' Roman shot back, proceeding to walk towards the gym, with Eric meekly in tow.

Michael opened his mouth and was just about to explain that a rain check is the same as saying another time, but he decided it wasn't worth it. Shaking his head, Michael and the doctor headed towards the med bay.

'What was that all about?'

'Ah, it's nothing. Just a friendly competition.'

'Friendly competition?' she asked doubtfully. 'If that was friendly competition, then I'm a chicken farmer.'

Michael stopped and turned to her, frowning with confused smile. 'Chicken farmer?'

'Oh, I don't know! It was the first thing I could think of. Anyway, shall we?'

She gestured to move on down the corridor in a mocking tone, Michael nodded.

'Yeah, sure, Doc. Let's go before you lay an egg or something.'

They walked down the twists and turns of the ship's corridors with an occasional jesting 'cluck, cluck' from Michael. The sounds of giggles and laughter reverberated off the walls, faded as they moved further away.

Roman stood a still as a marble statue in the centre of the sparring ring. His mind seemed distant, as if trying to rationalise something of great importance. Eric placed a set of speed gloves on a bench, just outside the ring. Then, turning to face Roman, who looked captivated by the heavy punching bag, began to wrap the fabric around his hand.

'You will not need that,' Roman said dryly, facing Eric.

'But... I thought we...'

'There are many things that you have been taught about war. Most of what you have learned is incorrect.'

Roman began pacing back and forth in the ring, as a personal trainer would in front of unsuspecting clients.

'You see, war is not what the movies have shown. It is not about honour or about strategy.'

Eric left the wraps on top of his gear and cautiously entered the ring. As he did, Roman moved without any indication or sound and swiftly held a curved blade to Eric's throat. Frozen to the spot and wondering where Roman had had the knife concealed, Eric just slowly looked up at Roman, resembling an animal caught in a trap.

'I will tell you the true secret of war,' Roman continued, releasing Eric and taking two steps back. 'To win in any conflict is simple. Kill the enemy before they kill you.'

Deftly spinning the blade in his one hand, then moving his hand to indicate that Eric should stand front and centre of him, Roman lowered his body and stood in a solid fighting stance.

'Eric, I will teach you how to fight. I will teach you how to use a blade. By the time I am finished with you, you will be able to cut so precisely that you will be able to cut the wings from a fly's back.'

Eric widened his eyes at the mere concept of him being able to do that, but what he found most surprising of all was the fact that he truly believed Roman was capable of such a feat. However, this did not impress him; in fact, it filled him with a stomach-turning realisation that Roman was nothing like the honourable patriotic man his father had described. No, he was far from it. In fact, the closest word that he would use to describe Roman would be monster.

'Now, little Eric... let me see what you've got!'

Chapter 21

Limitations

A young girl's voice could be heard singing loudly from the med bay, accompanied by music from the speaker system.

'Do you like peanuts and lager? And getting caught in the rain!'

'Are you fooking kidding me?' Bob growled, repulsed by what he was hearing.

He sat in a treatment chair, in the mid-section of the room, cradling his head with one hand and resting the other inside a treatment tube.

'Excuse me?' the cute and angry nurse asked.

'Ok, firstly, it's Pina colada. If you didn't know that, then shame on you and your parents for not bringing you up right. Secondly, I'm over here with my arm in this thing, which is fooking freezing by the way, and my head feels like it's in a meat grinder. So please, if you would be so kind, sing the right words!'

The nurse turned down the volume on her wristband, then with her lips pursed, moved over to where Robert was sitting. Leaning over with her hands placed on her knees, intentionally exaggerating her cleavage, she smiled. 'You're a bit of a prick, aren't ya?'

As if he was given a shot of adrenaline, Bob dropped his hand from his head, looked at the girl and exploded with joy.

'Holy shit! You're a Scot? I mean, I saw the red hair but just thought it was a dye job.'

Standing and turning with a huff, the nurse did not dignify the man with a response, but carried on with the other patients suffering from similar symptoms.

'Bob?' Michael called out, standing in the doorway. He stopped as Robert held his hand up, indicating to the captain to wait for a bit.

Michael traced Bob's line of sight and was not surprised to discover that it was on the peach-shaped backside of the nurse who, just a moment ago, was about two seconds away from clocking the guy.

'Bob,' Michael repeated, more forcefully, and moved in front of the supposed ailing man's eye-line.

'Oh, Captain, the things I would do to...'

He was interrupted by Doctor Tang, who coughed not so subtly while walking past, giving Michael a threatening and knowing look.

'Cut the shit, Bob. I've been hearing some complaints and...'

'Yep, I knew that was coming,' he said, scratching his chin through his beard. 'I was only having a laugh, and fook's sake, just look at them, they look like catwalk models.'

'I don't care if they look like early-years Dolly Parton. You can't keep doing this shit.' Michael made sure that he kept a commanding tone to his voice.

'Ok, I'll tone it down,' Rob replied.

Michael stood back in a more relaxed posture and relaxed his commanding gaze.

'Shit! I think that's the first time I've seen you become... you know, official like.'

'Yeah, well, I lost my calm about twelve hours ago, so I'm a bit on edge,' replied Michael.

'No, I like it. It's about time someone had some balls round here,' Bob said. He then saw for himself how tired Michael looked and continued to take a bite of his half-eaten, synthetic peanut and chocolate protein bar.

'So, what do they think it is?' Michael asked, pulling a chair from a side table and taking a seat.

'Fook knows. But I do think it's a bit of a coincidence...'

'What?'

'That all of them and me start getting symptoms after our first big jump? The timing is just too convenient.'

Leaning back in his chair, Michael tried to calculate the repercussions of that possibility. What would that mean? Would they have to put a hold the mission and just stay orbiting the planet? How long would that take?

'Well, I think you should message Andy, just in case. I'm sure the professor can tell us if it's possible or not.'

'Aye, will do, boss.'

There was a tap at the doorway, followed by Doctor Tang beckoning Michael with a wave.

'That's my cue,' Michael said, standing up and placing the chair back. 'Let me know what Andy says, and you take it easy now.'

'I will... oh, and about before, I'm sorry, mate,' Bob said, giving Michael an embarrassed but sincere look.

'Don't sweat it. You're just a horny old-timer,' Michael replied, giving him a side grin.

He then left the room, ignoring Bob's guttural laugh.

Doctor Tang waited outside the door apprehensively, arms crossed and a frown on her face.

'It's dealt with, Doc. He won't be hitting on you or the girls anymore.'

She shot him a doubtful glance that let Michael know she didn't exactly share the same faith in Bob, as he had for the man. If Michael were truly being honest with himself, he knew that this probably wouldn't be the last time that he would have to reign Bob's urges in.

Michael quickly changed the subject. 'So, Bob does have a good theory for the headaches.'

'Oh, does he?' she asked, sceptically. 'And what is Mr Humphries' theory?'

Rubbing the back of his neck awkwardly, Michael remembered the first time he had met the doctor. On the transport shuttle, she seemed so sweet and shy. Now, look at her. She had a way of letting others know she must be listened to and an inner silence that well... gave him the creeps.

'He thinks that there could be a connection between everyone here and the long-distance skimming of the ship. Is that possible?'

Contemplating on that, she looked like she was computing an equation. Then, with a huff, she turned back to face Michael.

'As a hypothetical cause to the afflicted personnel, it could very well be possible stimuli...'

'Normal speak please, Doc.'

'Yes, Michael, it could be the cause,' she replied, then turned and headed towards the main treatment area, with Michael following close behind.

She pulled a monitor towards her, which was attached to an extendible arm on the wall. After a few swift commands, she displayed various test results.

'Yes, and this proves it.' She pointed at the screen to explain to Michael. 'The bloodwork obtained after the test phase of the T-Drive showed no abnormalities. But, looking at this, I can see that the furthest point the prototype ships went was only 384,873 kilometres. The route they travelled was... yes, there it is, Earth to test base thirty-two, just past our moon. We have travelled farther than that, so no wonder we missed it.'

'I've asked Bob to get a hold of Professor Thomas,' Michael said, with an element of concern in his voice. 'I want him to give us his take on this.'

He couldn't help but feel like if they didn't get ahead of this problem, then it could spiral out of control, very quickly, ending the mission before it ever truly could begin.

'I'll ask the professor to come see you after I've spoken with him. But first, I need to go to my quarters and get a change of clothes. Can't exactly walk about the ship in my sweatpants all day.'

Doctor Tang didn't even acknowledge what he said, consumed by the copious amounts of medical details displayed on the screen in front of her.

He left her to it, deciding that he was going to stop at the mess hall on the way back to his quarters, to pick up a bite to eat.

Walking straight to the canteen area and waving down salutes from a couple of eager crew members, he opened a freshly stocked cupboard filled with silver packages of varying sizes. Each small package had a different stripe of colour across it and a description of the contents in bold writing.

Peanut-butter and jelly, he read. Don't mind if I do. Then he tore the wrapper away with the grace of a caveman, and leaning against the work surface, faced the quiet empty room.

As he was trying to understand all the unsettling issues that had arisen in the past twenty-four hours, he came to the conclusion that whatever happens, happens. It wouldn't do anyone no good if he started to lose his shit over what had happened. Instead, he would take the bad news, as it came.

Surprisingly, he felt full. In fact, he felt as if he'd been to his hometown's legendary 'Buffalo Bills' all-you-can-eat buffet. Looking down at the small bar of compressed nutrients in his hand, he saw that he had taken only one underwhelming bite.

'Damn it.' He regretfully dropped the almost full bar into the food compressor.

Leaving the mess hall, Michael thought that with everything happening, no wonder he had lost his appetite. Just then, the motion censored doors opened, and Commander Elizabeth Jenkins stood in the hallway, arms crossed with a furious look in her eyes.

'Commander Jenkins. How's the ship doing?'

'The ship?' She shot back, not budging an inch. 'Are you serious?'

'You look pissed...'

'Of course, I'm pissed! You are the captain of this ship, and even though it's my duty to step in when you can't, a little bit of professional courtesy would be nice!'

Michael looked around to check if any innocent bystanders would get caught up in this, but there were none. So, he decided the best solution was to let her get it all out.

'And another thing, not only am I kept in the dark about what's going on with you, but you obviously don't give a damn about what's going on around you. Some of the crew members are going down with migraines, and the scientists are freaking out about what they discovered down on the planet. We can't go back to the site because the chamber collapsed a few hours ago. Oh yeah, and we have a hacker on board, who probably incinerated all the blood samples!'

By the time she had finished, Elizabeth looked flustered and red in the face.

'You done?' Michael asked calmly.

Taking a breath, she let her shoulders relax and corrected her posture. 'Yes, sir,' she said formally. 'Yes, I am.'

'You...,' he began saying, pretending to be stern and commanding, 'Commander Elizabeth Jenkins, are my second on this ship, and you are....' He moved closer to her, relaxed his aggressive front and placed his hand on her shoulder, solemnly saying, 'Absolutely right.'

She began to open her mouth, ready to stand her ground, but stopped when she realised that he had just agreed with her.

'Wait, what?' she asked, taken aback.

'You're right. I've been an asshole,' he said, lowering his arm.

'Well, I don't think I called you an asshole,' she replied, holding back a laugh. 'But, if the boot fits...'

Michael rescinded to her judgement.

'Look, I'm sorry. The way you stepped in for me, though all this shit, well, has been amazing. To be honest, I'm still taking it all in myself. It's been one thing after goddamn other. So, all I can say is thank you for helping me out, and I'm ready to get back on the horse.'

'Thank you,' she said quietly, 'but that's not what made me angry. Sure, it was annoying having to deal with all the other, as you said it "shit" alone. But what really got to me was you didn't even let me know how you were doing? The last time I saw you was in your quarters, and well, you were...'

'Speaking a different language in my underwear?' he said jokingly, trying to lighten the concerned look on her face.

He didn't realise until that point that he really felt uncomfortable knowing that she was upset. Even more so because he was the cause.

'Yeah,' she said, with a bashful smile. 'That was a sight that's burned in my brain now.'

She pointed to her head, with her index finder. As she did, they began to walk down the hallway, in the direction of his quarters and the bridge.

'I'm finding this all a bit strange, you know,' Michael said, with a touch of sadness in his voice.

'We are walking on a spaceship, next to a planet that's not in our solar system... I think it's ok to feel a bit weirded out.'

'Yeah,' Michael agreed with a snigger, 'It's all the other crap, I guess. Honestly, I don't know why the admiral gave me this role. He knew I'm a better fighter than a leader.'

Elizabeth stopped, shot him an incredulous look, then continued next to him.

'That's bullshit,' she said sternly.

Michael was surprised and amused by the way she cursed. Her English accent gave it an almost royal tone.

'I have seen some of your mission reports... well, the ones that I was cleared to read anyway, and...,' she stopped talking, physically covering her mouth to prevent further embarrassment.

Then, working out what she wanted to say and muttering 'screw it' under her breath, Elizabeth continued, 'You are a hero.'

'I appreciate what you're trying to do, Liz, but that's one thing I definitely am not.'

'Yes, you are. Your decisions have saved literally hundreds of lives. So, whether you like to admit it, you are a genuine, one hundred percent, all-American hero.'

'Shit, you make me sound like I'm a goddamn superhero.'

'I'm not finished,' she said, cutting him off. 'You are also the most frustrating man I have ever met. I'm normally a good judge of character and can figure someone out pretty accurately. But you... you, I have no idea what you are going to do from one moment to the next. But do you want to know what I think you should do?'

'Sure?' he asked cautiously.

'I think you should get you head outta your ass!' Elizabeth put on her best Southern American accent for the last part.

Cringing at possibly the worst attempt at an accent he had ever heard, Michael couldn't help but burst into laughter.

After a short while, they had reached the steps leading up to the bridge. There, Michael smiled as he thanked her, then headed to his quarters, where he showered, shaved and changed into his uniform.

Just as he was about to leave, he hesitated. Walking back over to the mirror, above the hand basin, he wanted to check if he was half presentable, compared to the dishevelled look he had been portraying earlier.

His niggling headache had vanished, and his vision was clear again. No, his vision wasn't just clear, it was better, it was... improved somehow.

Looking at his own reflection, he focused on a random area of his face. Without warning, his eyes adapted almost instantaneously, and the area became larger, then larger with amazing clarity.

Whilst keeping his focus, he was able to see so much more, so much more than he ever had in his life. He could see hair strands as big as pencils protruding from his facial hair follicles. He could see the intricate, intertwining weavings of skin tissue. He believed that if he continued, maybe, just maybe, he would be able to magnify to a level only seen in a microscope.

As he pulled away in sheer disbelief and rubbed his eyes with his thumb and index finger, the picture zoomed out, then quickly returned to normal, surprisingly, with no discomfort whatsoever. It was as if that moment of biological wonder had just been another action that the body did as casually as breathing. Well shit, that's new, he thought.

Although this had never happened before to him and, as far as he was aware, was impossible for a human to even do, it felt ok somehow. It should have been impossible, but a lot of that was going around lately. Deciding what to do with this new trick, he chose to put his new skills to the test later. For now, he simply turned, looked at his wrist strap and left for the bridge.

Chapter 22

Non Solum

Three weeks had passed since the discovery of the weathered ruins of the long-abandoned civilisation. The dying planet now labelled Red Thirteen, after a suggestion from a crew member and fan of the popular game franchise Final Fantasy. It started off as a passing joke, but gained favour, as names tend to do in small communities.

Although the crew hadn't planned to orbit the planet for a long duration, they capitalised on the opportunity by gathering data for the system that they were in. When they weren't looking outward at the stars, they focused inward on the extensive materials they had collected from Red Thirteen.

The results were breath-taking. The crew had concluded that there was evidence of two distinctive races. Using one of the most advanced scanning techniques, the archaeologists aboard were able to sample and capture most of the imprinted sections of the scrolls, often kicking themselves at how close they were to missing them, under all that thick mound of dirt.

The scrolls carried a kind of transcript with a symbolic language very similar to Egyptian hieroglyphs, only far more complex. The sporadic sketches drawn with fading black ink displayed evidence of a small race of people who were essentially lighthouse or literal light-keepers. This was depicted by a picture which had faded over time, but the small indentations of the parchment were enough to get picked up on the scanners.

Doctor Ryuki Kazama, the lead researcher on the materials found on the planet, provided a cumulative and visual presentation to the crew through a shared video feed.

'As you can see from the rendered image, the people are surrounding the light at the centre of the chamber. This signifies two key factors. First, the orb that has remained dormant since Red Thirteen was fully operational and used by the caretakers.'

'Caretakers?' Donald asked.

'Caretaker is the term that we have decided to call the group of people who made the documents. It helps us differentiate between the races. The second point that we have all agreed on is that the caretakers, whilst intelligent, are definitely not the manufactures of the light source or the technology surrounding the chamber. This has been proven by the evidence provided in the brief notes that I have sent out across the ship.'

A few audible clicks could be heard over the videocall, making it apparent that some had not read the text that had been sent out several hours beforehand.

'Doctor Kazama?' A light voice asked, backed by the murmur of a small child in the background.

'Umm, yes?' he answered, uncertain of who had just spoken.

'Doctor, it's Janine Thomas. I have a question.'

'Hello, Mrs Thomas, please go ahead.'

'Thank you. Doctor, with all the physical evidence and samples that you and your team have collected, have you been able to establish how long ago the people were there?'

'You are welcome, Mrs Thomas, and that's an excellent question.' Doctor Kazama smiled reassuringly though a wrinkled friendly face.

'Using the samples that we have brought from the planet, which, in most cases, were extremely fragile I might add, we were able to estimate an age.'

Doctor Kazama paused for a while, looking as if he could hardly believe what he was reading himself. Then, with a quick intake of air, he continued.

'The results of our simplistic radiocarbon dating have concluded that the samples, along with the genetic samples of the human remains, all stem from a period from around about 1650 BC on our world.'

The revelation came as a shock to most of the viewers, followed by gasps and murmurs of several members. Not only did they now have conclusive evidence that life existed on other planets, but they were also presented with the knowledge that they existed thousands of years ago, possibly further; it was overwhelming.

'But, Doctor, if that is the case, then surely the bones would have... you know, turned to dust?'

'In most cases, yes, that would be the way. However, within the genetic samples, we have discovered a high volume and rather dense pockets of collagen and calcium. You see, without the right enzymes and environmental factors, bone remains are very difficult to break down. Luckily for us, the chamber worked as a large, vacuumed sarcophagus of sort, resulting in the prolonged preservation.'

'Ask him,' a voice urged. 'Go on. Ask him.'

'Doctor, it's Janine Thomas again. My husband...,' she shot him a stern look off-screen and slowly turned back towards the camera.

'My husband and I would like to know about the others. The other race? Do you have any insights?'

'Mrs Thomas and erm... Professor Thomas, at this moment, we can honestly say that we know little about them. The only hypothesis we have is that they are responsible for the superior technology. There has been no mention of them in the transcripts, scrolls or illustrations, which implies that little interaction existed between the races. Currently, they remain a mystery, but we are hopeful that we will find something.'

All the attendees were silent, deep in worrisome contemplation. With the presentation coming to an end and the atmosphere was changing to one of wariness, Doctor Kazama was about to wrap it up. However, a particular sound spilled over the speakers, coming from one of the attendees.

One of the participants on the invite list had a little speaker icon, which was pulsing and picking up sound. Strangely, no one could be seen on the viewing screen.

Realisation slowly hit everyone that the sound resembling pouring water was that of someone relieving themselves of bodily fluid, bringing floods of much needed laughter and giggles from others.

Then, as if nothing had happened, Chris O'Conner dropped into the vacant seat, and casually placed his headphones back over his ears.

Some people began laughing even louder, reacting to the dumbfounded look on his face. He had the type of look that you would expect from someone who had fallen asleep at a house party, only to wake up with a face covered in crude drawings.

'Umm, Chris O'Conner?' Doctor Kazama said, wiping a tear from his eye and trying his best to remain collected. 'Would you mind turning your microphone off next time, please?'

It still took Chris a few seconds to digest what had happened, then his eyes widened. He looked in the direction of the restroom, then back to the screen and through the list of people, only caring about one name that he didn't want to see on the list.

'Fook my life,' he said, after seeing the name.

A message came through on his wristband. 'Chris, your mic is on. We can hear everything (smiley face emoji).'

'Jesus Christ,' he muttered. 'Now you tell me!'

Dying with embarrassment and with a face that resembled a tomato, Chris O'Conner's feed went dead, along with his working microphone.

'Well, I think that's enough excitement for today,' Doctor Kazama said. 'I would like to thank you all for attending. I also want to reassure you that we will give you all the details as they develop. Hopefully, by the next instalment of these weekly updates, we will have more information on the power device, found by our good captain. Thank you.'

A chorus of goodbyes followed, as the crew logged out of the presentation. Chris just sat at his desk with head buried in his hands for a while. He looked at his wristband and thought, if anyone else heard him take a piss, he wouldn't have given a shit. But why did she have to hear him?

He was referring to Lieutenant Gemma Saunders, of course.

Two weeks had passed since the incident in the mess hall, where Tweedledee and Tweedledum, also known as Enrique Gorman and Alex Burk, were being absolute asshats.

Chris watched the schoolyard situation develop from a table adjacent to theirs. Gemma sat at one end of the table, while Burk and Gorman sat opposite, failing at an attempt of having a subtle conversation.

Chris could remember they were talking about all the hoes that they had been with, including detailed descriptions of what they did to college girls, when they were younger. 'Peaky Pussies' was the term they used while talking about them.

The hyenas continued to yapper on, until they moved onto the subject of Gemma, passively asking such questions such as, 'What do you think she's got down there?' and 'Do you think she's got both?'.

Chris, at this point, had lost his appetite and was now boiling with anger at the two dumb-fucks who didn't have any idea what Gemma had gone through or who she was. He looked down the table at Gemma and saw that she had overheard the conversation and was physically uncomfortable, but she let it go.

Chris knew that she was a strong woman who wouldn't give the satisfaction of a rise to assholes such as them, but it still felt wrong to him.

Burk and Gorman continued talking crap, with every statement about Gemma becoming viler; then, one of them said something that finally tipped Chris over the edge.

'What the fuck did you just say?' Chris growled.

Both Gorman and Alex jerked their heads towards him, displaying a look of disregard.

'I said... what the fuck... did you just say?' Chris made sure to slow down the question, implying that they were so dumb that he needed to do so.

Instead of giving Chris a response to his question, they gave him a smirk and turned back to each other, just continuing their conversation.

Chris got up from his seat, walked around the head of his table and stood right beside the two large security guys.

Gemma had stopped eating and was watching the situation unfold, bewildered by Chris defending her for some reason.

Lowering his voice so that only the guys could hear, Chris asked, 'Which one of you fuck-faces said you would fuck her so hard that she would turn back into a dude?'

Glancing over at Gemma, he ascertained that she was concerned but couldn't hear anything. He quickly turned back to the douchebags.

They carried on chuckling until Burk confidently said, with a wide snake-like smile, 'And she'd love it too.'

Chris didn't remember too much about what happened next, but Gemma filled him in on the details from the other side of a holding cell, where he woke up.

She told him that she could see that they were having a conversation and definitely not a friendly one because she could see Chris's hands were clenched and shaking at his sides. Then, either Burk or Gorman said something to him, to which he must have firmly disagreed with, to put it mildly. This was evident because Chris launched such a precise and fast left hook that Burk was on deck, with his feet up in the air.

Then Gorman realised what had happened because he swore in his native tongue and lunged at Chris, tackling him to the ground. Following this, Gorman proceeded to hit Chris with a series of unrelenting punches to the face. Then finally, Gorman sprang up in a quick motion, whist turning Chris, putting him in a vice-like sleeper hold. Then it was lights out for him. All this had happened within about fifteen seconds, she told him.

For a couple of days, Chris sat in the holding cell, which wasn't had bad, considering it was just as large as a storage cupboard with a bed and wash facilities. Compared to where he had grown up, which, in his own words, was a 'shithole', the cell was a palace.

A quick but formal investigation was launched to find out exactly what had happened, as Alex, embarrassed as he was, surprisingly didn't want to press charges. Even more surprising was that his perfect and lady-killer smile now displayed an obvious chipped tooth, right in the centre of his top row.

Apparently, when Roman took charge of the investigation, he had a quiet word with Alex in the security office, alone. Five minutes later, Roman emerged from the office, unfazed, cautiously followed by a hunched over and clearly distraught Alex.

Roman's decree was that Alex be let go with a cautionary note. Gemma had hoped that when Roman found out the whole truth, it would disgust him. However, it was more likely that the investigation irritated him, so he just dropped it for a quick resolution.

Two things happened after Chris was released from his temporary incarceration. First, he realised that he had growing feelings for Gemma, but for the first time in his life, he nervously kept a lid on it, because he didn't want to ruin the developing friendship they had. Second, Big Bob was strangely nice to him, which

Chris, who liked the usual fatherly banter, absolutely hated.

'Hey, Chrisy-boy,' he remembered Bob saying, whilst patting him on the back. 'You ok, son?'

He thought that the only and quickest way to make things go back to normal was to nip that in the bud straight away.

He looked at Bob with a cheeky grin, 'Yeah, I'm fine, but you look like shite, old man.'

After a moment of shock, Bob took the hint, flashed a smile before returning to his hard bravado. He replied elegantly, 'You cheeky little shit, get back to fooking work.'

From that point on, things seemed to return to normal, apart from the added tension in the mess hall that is. Burk and Gorman continued their deep intellectual conversations, only now, they did it with a bit more discretion.

One aspect that did pleasantly change was that Gemma had stopped sitting alone at the tail-end of the security table, except for briefings, and now sat right next to Chris.

So, for the past few days before Doctor Kazama gave his video presentation, both Chris and Gemma had been growing closer in their friendship. Chris would tell her the less embarrassing stories of his younger days in Ireland, and surprisingly, both found that they were huge fans of Bruce Willis movies. This prompted a playful but heated debate on what his best movies were and random throwing of movie quotes at each other.

Asking himself if it would be weird if he apologised for taking a piss, live on camera, and then asking her out on date, Chris decided to sit up in his chair and go for it anyway.

Before he could ask, suddenly, there was a flicker of the lights, followed closely by all the electrical equipment in his room switching on and off intermittently.

'What the fu...?'

He got up and went to his door, but nothing happened when he pressed the button. After a couple of failed attempts, the door hissed and finally opened.

Peeking out, he could see that the hallways were experiencing the same strange power surge, creating an eerie flashing effect akin to that from paparazzi cameras. His wrist buzzed with an emergency message that had been sent out, ordering everyone to report to their posts.

Swiping the message away, he quickly texted Gemma, 'What's happening?'

He waited, then finally got a response. 'It's the bridge. They said the beam is changing??? I've got to go.'

Thinking about what Gemma had just said, Chris sprang out of his room and, with the door closing behind him, darted down the hallway as quick as his legs could move.

In hindsight, Chris wished that he that he asked her out sooner, before all the chaos and heartache began.

Chapter 23

New Course

The bridge was exceptionally loud and active, with everyone scurrying around to find out what the hell was happening.

Michael had made a conscious decision a few weeks back, regarding his vision abilities. He decided not to tell the doctor that he had this 'gift'. She had already reached a point where she no longer had answers and was pushing more and more for further testing. Michael did attend some of the appointments, but sometimes declined, using the excuse that he was too busy with his duties. He also promised himself that he wouldn't attempt to play with his gifts anymore. This was a decision he made not only because something could go wrong but also because it made him feel uncomfortable, as if he were tempting fate. Besides, if he lost control and accidentally started to see through people's clothes that would make things slightly awkward.

'And you're sure everyone has eaten?' Michael asked on a conversation over the coms channel with the med bay.

'Yes, all crew members have confirmed. Even the parents of the fifteen children who are too young to acknowledge,' a small and formal voice said.

'Thank you, Doctor. Get ready to jump in forty minutes.'

Michael moved the viewscreen to the left. He stood up and was proud for a moment, watching as everyone carried on their last-minute checks. Commander Elizabeth Jenkins moved from station to station, checking that all systems were working and ready. Then she turned, gave him a thumbs up and moved closer to him.

'All green across the board, Captain. Just waiting on system to complete the pre-checks in twenty minutes. Fingers crossed that this time, the extra sugar in everyone's diet will prevent a repeat of last time.'

'Yep, I don't think the nurses can handle another visit from Bob,' He smiled at her, and nodding, she returned one back.

Although he was joking, he himself wasn't sure if it would work. Or if they would perform another skim at a medium speed, only this time, all the crew would become ill. Nope, it would work, he steeled himself.

He turned and moved towards his chair, planning to check if there were any last-minute issues.

'Look.'

'What?' Michael asked, turning back around.

Elizabeth, who was leaning over the navigation desk next to Josh, spun around with a blank expression.

'Captain?' she asked politely.

'Did you just say something?' he asked, doubtfully.

Perplexed, she pursed her lips and shook her head. Then she looked around to see if anyone else was looking at the captain. No one was.

'Weird... never mind,' he said, frowning. 'Must have been my—'

'Loook.'

There it was again, only this time, it seemed louder. What was unnerving was that Michael knew the voice definitely did not come from anyone on the bridge. He also had a weird gut feeling that it didn't even come from the ship. It was at that point that his gaze moved slowly towards the beam. His eyes widened, as he slowly mouthed the words, 'Oh my God.'

When humans are concerned, a lot can be said about their complacency. So many people have lost their lives, knowing there's a danger close to them but growing so accustomed to it that it almost becomes irrelevant. It is like a zookeeper feeding a deadly pride of lions, forgetting that the only real protection they have is the thin steel meshed fence between them. Then, one day, should the zookeeper forget to check the fence, it becomes dangerous for the zookeeper, but a great opportunity for the hungry lions, licking their deadly teeth.

Elizabeth could only look at Michael with growing concern as he seemed motionless, staring directly out of the heavily reinforced viewing ports. Then, just as she could swear his eyes were starting to unbelievably glow, he yelled.

'Get everyone to their stations, NOW!'

Elizabeth jumped at this, like a child who had just experienced a Jack-in-the-box, for the very first time.

Michael, who had sprung forward towards the viewing port, as if to reaffirm something, placed his hands on each side of the window. He looked closely, then darted over to Ensign Josh Thomas.

'I need you to move us further away from the beam,' Michael barked.

'Sir?' Josh asked, confused. Then, ashamed that he had even asked, he quickly added, 'Yes, sir.'

The ship slowly began to move away from the ever-powerful beam, but still on its course in parallel.

'What's happening?' Elizabeth asked, now standing at his side.

'Have you sent out the order,' he fired at her.

'Yes, but...'

'Good,' he said, resuming his tense stance and staring ahead.

Elizabeth didn't like the urgency in his voice, and she herself looked at the beam but spotted no signs of change. It looked exactly as it did the first day it had appeared.

'Captain?' she asked. No response. 'Captain?'

'Captain, something is happening,' Josh yelled, leaning forward, closer to his viewing screen.

As Elizabeth started to move, all the electronics on the bridge began to flash and flicker rapidly. Michael opened a ship-wide channel on his wrist strap.

'All personnel, this is your captain speaking. I need y'all to point all our scanning equipment at the beam now. This is not a drill, I repeat, this is not a drill.'

Then, with almost unfathomable speed, a small and impossible tentacle of pure light shot out from the beam and pierced the Aletheia.

'Brace yourselves,' Michael shouted and opened his stance. But, to everyone's surprise, nothing happened.

There was a moment where all crew members on the bridge were holding onto something, anything in preparation for a huge impact, with expectations of a huge shunt or at least, violent shaking caused by the substantial breach. It was only when Elizabeth talked again that they started to ease their grip on their terminals or whatever they were holding onto.

'Report?' she asked, sharply.

'Umm, nothing, Commander,' a shaky officer said. 'No impacts or beaches detected.'

'What?' she said incredulously, moving over to her own display screen.

'That's... that's impossible.'

Confused, Elizabeth could only look at Michael, who expectantly looked back at her.

'The ship is fine?' As she said the words, she could hear the doubt in her own voice.

Everyone knew that the earth had sent probes into the beam, time and time again. All had been destroyed instantly, whether they had broken up or vaporised by the sheer focused strength of pure light; the result was always the same.

'Where is the impact point?' Michael asked apprehensively.

Elizabeth quickly looked through the exterior cameras of the ship to gauge where the strange light sat, but stopped when she noticed Michael receiving a call.

'Donald?' Michael asked, answering the call.

'Aye, Captain, I... I think you need to get down here,' Donald Bishop croaked, sounding terrified.

'I'll be right there, Don,' Michael said in a deep calming voice, ending the call.

As if to confirm Donald Bishop's story, Elizabeth mouthed 'research' at Michael, as she didn't want the crew to panic any more than necessary.

'Commander, you've got the bridge.' Then, without hesitation or delay, Michael left and headed towards the research deck as fast as he could.

Three very fast minutes later, Michael approached the entrance to the scientific and research laboratories. He was greeted by a small crowd of lab coat wearing people, all whispering and peering through the wide-open double doors, where the all too familiar blue glow was radiating from. Michael edged his way past the white wall of spectators and made his way inside. He stopped to take in the surreal scene.

Donald Bishop and Ryan Smith stood close to the doors; arms spread in a desperate attempt to keep others out at all costs. Behind them was what could only be described as wonderfully terrifying: a large tentacle-like arm, like that of a squid, appeared to be penetrating the bulkhead wall without any sign of physical damage. Even more bizarre, it moved like it was a living creature, as it reached across the room.

The arm seemed to be slowly moving back and forth. In other circumstances, a person would even consider the scene to be quite hypnotic and relaxing, but this was not one of those scenarios. It impossibly channelled through every physical object, as if they were of no form.

The arm had inadvertently trapped two scientists against two storage containers, cornering them with no obvious means of escape. Michael instantly assessed the situation and gestured to the scientists that he would handle it.

'Anyone who doesn't need to be here can respectfully get the hell out,' Michael said, over his shoulder, at the group outside the door.

Taking the hint and quickly avoiding eye contact, the scientists started to dissipate down the corridors. With the onlookers fading away, Donald lowered his arms and turned, facing the entity. He tried his best to remain calm, but that was proving very difficult. This was made obvious by the pearls of sweat trickling down his face and by how shaky his voice had become.

'I didn't have time,' Don said, regretfully.

Michael walked slowly along the arm, squinting ever so slightly at the light coming from it. He found his eyes adapted to the light far better than the others, who had to raise their hands in front of their faces to block the glare.

He could see where it had passed through a chair, table and desktop, leaving no damage or sign of displacement. It reached all the way to the test chamber, on the other side of the lab, ending on, none other than the strange sphere Michael had found.

'What's it doing?' Michael asked, frowning and pointing at the sphere.

'Honestly, we don't know,' Don whispered, as if it could hear him.

Donald moved over to where they had the sphere in some sort of an apparatus, connected to a small probe, which was then connected directly to a computer.

'One second, we were trying to put a charge into the orb, only a couple of milliamps, just to see if we could get any data from it. Then, that... that light-thing came through the wall and made contact with it.'

He turned to Michael and, in his strong Scottish accent, sounded angry.

'It came through the bloody wall!'

Michael started to move towards the test chamber that housed the sphere. He could see the monitors connected to the test equipment, rapidly flickering between multiple pages, then switching to very strange coding and images. Donald, who had no idea that this could happen, still felt an overwhelming sense of guilt.

For now, Michael decided to put that to one side and focus on the two guys pinned in the corner.

He looked at their faces and remembered who they were from the personnel records. 'James and Dillan, right?'

They quickly nodded, keeping their backs to the storage unit and desperately trying to stay away from the moving arm of light.

'I'm gonna get you out of here, ok? You just need to stay calm and do exactly as I say.'

They were terrified, but understood. Michael knew that he had to move fast. The positions that they were in, they could not be held for much long, and he didn't want them to start panicking. He was worried that if they touched the thing, they would... well, he didn't know what would happen, but he didn't want to wait and find out.

He started by looking around the area. The only possible point of exit, which he could see, would be to go underneath the arm. Unfortunately, a desk and chair annoyingly obstructed the way. Doing his best not to get too close to the light, Michael took a knee near the desk. Placing his hands at the base of the desk, and with surprising ease, he managed to yank it from underneath the light. Once he had cleared the strange tentacle, he stood and dragged the desk over to Donald. Michael checked the area again. There was just enough room for one person to safely crawl under.

'Ok, Dillan? You first. I want you to slowly slide down, onto your ass. Then roll onto your gut, and crawl on through. Got it?'

'Ye... Yes, sir,' Dillan affirmed, with his voice croaking and tears welling in his eyes.

He began the manoeuvre slowly and cautiously, following Michael's instructions exactly. He wriggled his way under until he was within reaching distance of Michael. Then, not wasting any time, Michael grabbed Dillan by the collar and pulled him out. When he was fully clear, Dillan jumped up to his feet and exhaled deeply.

'Ok James, same as Dillan. On your ass, down onto your gut and get on through.'

James nodded, then proceeded to follow suit. He landed on his bottom with a thud, then awkwardly folded himself onto his stomach. He began to lumber forward, when he felt a tug on his lab coat. Sensibly, he didn't panic and kept low, turning onto his side. He tried pulling it slightly to release it, but it wouldn't budge.

'James, you ok?' Michael asked, crouched down and peering under the arm.

'Umm... yeah. Just a sec.'

Then, James yanked on the fabric with a panicked strength, tugging and tugging.

'JAMES WAIT! STO—' Michael screamed.

James ripped the coat free. Horrifyingly, as he did, it forced his arms to both fly upwards from the rapid release.

Michael helplessly watched as James screamed in agony. As soon as the scientist's hands contacted the light, it was just like dipping a joint of beef into a smelter. James's hands were engulfed in a brief flurry of red fire. So hot was the temperature that the blood, all the way up his forearms started to boil. Lesions appeared quickly on the remainder of his arms, then violently burst, staining his lab coat in a crimson red.

Michael sprang into action by dropping to his stomach, quicker than any soldier had ever preformed a burpee. Then, he reached through as far as he could, just about reaching James.

'Donald, get my feet!' Michael shouted.

Donald darted over with Ryan in tow. They each grabbed a foot and pulled as hard as they could, franticly trying to save the bellowing man in excruciating pain.

Although it took them a couple of seconds to pull him out, James had gone worryingly quiet.

'James..., James, stay with me man,' Michael pleaded.

James glanced up and met Michael's eyes, and with a look of exhausted acceptance, turned away and was gone.

'SSSHITTT!' Michael growled through his teeth, thumping the floor, which echoed through the room.

Donald and Ryan stood in silence after letting go of Michael's feet. Ryan, overcome with sorrow, had tears flowing down his round face. Realisation sunk its cruel teeth into him as he understood that he had just lost a man he considered a good friend.

Michael got to his feet and saw the true extent of James's wounds. His hands were completely gone, leaving two molten stumps for arms. His upper arms? Well, they looked as if they were burnt from the inside out. Michael remembered seeing something similar in the past, after seeing pictures of the poor victims involved in the Russian Chernobyl disaster. He also knew that even though the limbs were cauterised, the heat that travelled through him was insane, causing his veins to bulge over his entire body and all over his face; no one could have survived that.

'Get back, Captain!' Donald suddenly yelled.

As he did, the tentacle pulsed with light and started to withdraw through the solid objects, disappearing back from where it came.

So many times in his life, Michael had said the exact same word to himself and subconsciously to the universe, 'Why?'

His wrist buzzed. At first, Michael didn't care, but after the fifth time it rumbled on his arm, he answered.

'Captain?' Elizabeth's voice came through, which was comforting to Michael.

'Liz...,' he exhaled, then resumed after a brief pause. 'We lost someone.'

She reciprocated his pause, then quickly regained her composure. 'Look, I know it sounds awful, but we will have to deal with that later. We have a bigger problem.'

'What is it?'.

'The glowing arm has gone back to the beam, but…'

'Liz? What is it?' he asked hastily.

'We think it got into our navigation system. Don't ask me how. We haven't figured that out yet, but our course has been rerouted.'

Michael's head immediately turned towards the sphere that was sitting bathed in an eerie green glow, in the test chamber. Then, he looked at the computer it was attached to, then finally at Donald.

'Is that thing on our network?'

Donald, who was still trying to process what had happened to James, was now lying on the floor with Ryan, kneeling over him, his shoulders hunched as he mourned.

'Don!' Michael shouted to try and break his trance.

'W-what?' Donald croaked.

'Was the goddamn ball connected to our network?'

'Umm no, the system was set to read data only,' Donald said.

'Well, I think the beam just hacked us,' Michael turned back to his wrist.

'Liz? Where're we going?'

Michael could hear Elizabeth talking to someone in the background. She sounded panicked.

'It's taking us to a different solar system... what?' She was speaking to someone on the bridge. 'Oh shit, Michael... we are preparing to skim!'

Michael just looked at Donald, sharing his apprehension, and wondered what the hell was going to happen next.

Chapter 24

White Hat

Janine was sitting in her quarters, bouncing little Billy up and down on her knee, patiently trying to get him to rest, then hopefully sleep. Billy, however, resisted such calming techniques and proceeded to raise his hands above his head and clap whilst repeating the sound 'aka-awoo' over and over.

'Well, he's a ball of energy today,' Andrew said from the table behind her.

'Yeah, tell me something I don't know,' she said with a sigh. 'But at least, he's not Mr wriggle pants today.'

She leant forward, gave Billy a little squeeze and kissed the back of his head. Billy gave a little giggle and carried on with his baby chant.

Andrew had decided that he was going to give her a break soon. A real break, he thought. Not like 'oh honey, I'll change his diapers for you tonight, it's ok'. No, he wanted to take Billy for an evening and let Janine have a night to herself. She deserved it.

'Hey...,' Andrew said, 'How about I take Billy for a long walk later? So, you can have some time to yourself?'

She shuffled on the sofa so that she could turn her head and face him. When she did, she gave him a sceptical smile. 'Oh yeah? What are you after, mister?'

'Nothing, my love. I'll even put him to bed, no extra charge,' he said, sitting back in his chair and flexing his biceps. When he raised his arm to do this, he accidently bumped his elbow on the table, almost knocking over his mug of tea.

'You sexy man, you,' she said, stifling a laugh. 'Are you sure? I don't need to take all night.'

'I'm sure,' he said, rubbing his elbow.

'Well, even though you said don't want anything in return, I might still spend a little time sprucing myself up for ya.'

'Oooh, I think how you like.' He frowned, laughed and quickly corrected himself. 'I like how you think!'

As she bit her lip and playfully smiled at him, she was interrupted by a ping sound from her laptop, which was sitting on her armrest. Billy stopped clapping and inquisitively looked over at what had made such a weird noise.

'It's ok, baby. It's just Mummy's laptop.'

After a few keystrokes, her eyes widened. 'Umm, baby? Would you mind taking Billy now? I've got to go speak with Lizzy.'

'Commander Jenkins?' he asked curiously.

'Yeah... I know you are in the middle of your work, but I really, really need to speak with her.'

Nodding, he looked down at his work and realised that he was getting nowhere anyway, his mind still fixated on the riddle that the beam gave him. 'Blood of the father' still went round and round in his brain, distracting him from his work. Now was a good time as any to take a break anyway, he thought.

'You know what? As you are my wife, and I love you, aaand you have a nice heinie, you go and enjoy yourself.' He added a wink and a playful smile.

Placing Billy on the sofa next to her, Janine gave him a quick tickle and said in a high-pitched baby voice, 'Is Daddy a suck-up? Yes, he is, but we love him anyway, don't we!'

She stood and walked around the sofa, holding the laptop in her hand. Billy had already rolled onto his belly, wiggled down onto the floor and was making his way over towards the coloured bricks in the toybox.

'Sorry, baby, I know it's a bit earlier than planned,' she said, moving up close to him and running her finger through his hair. 'But I promise, I'll make it up to you.'

Staring at her, he looked at her warm smile and her kind eyes, thinking to himself that she could ask him to walk into an active volcano, and he would not only do it without question, but do so with a wave and a smile.

'It's fine, babe, you go do what you need to do.'

'I love you, Mr Thomas.' She leaned in to give him a quick kiss.

'Love you too, wifey.'

She turned and headed towards the door, then turned to face Billy, who had deftly gotten two bricks out of the toybox and was holding them. She noticed that he was looking up at her with growing concern as she was leaving.

'Ahh, its ok. Mummy is just popping out for a minute; you be good for Daddy, ok? Love you, my little Casper, bye!' She gave a quick wave and a smile and left.

Billy turned around to see his father hadn't also disappeared and was peering over the sofa at him, wearing a warm smile. Billy just casually turned back to his bricks and carried on nibbling the ends.

'Little Casper,' Andrew muttered to himself, 'I'll show her.'

Janine moved along the corridors, oblivious to what was going on around her. A couple of times, crewmembers had to quickly move to the side to let her through. She approached a junction where one direction led to the elevator for the lower decks, and the other to the officers' quarters and the bridge.

A fold-out maintenance table, designed to hold portable equipment, was on the wall, in line with the junction. So, Janine decided to use it for her laptop while she made a call to Elizabeth.

Before she did so, she typed in a few commands as if to confirm something. Looking around to check that she was alone, she began her test.

While she waited for the results, she used her wrist strap to send a message to her friend, simply stating, 'The fish took the bait, will find out who in just a sec. Drinks on you, Fizzy Lizzy x'.

As she sent the message, the lights in the corridor dimmed and flickered, just briefly, but she didn't notice; her focus was entirely on her laptop. However, she did notice that her state-of-the-art laptop was having issues with connecting to the ship's wireless network. Luckily, she knew that every level of the ship had a small cargo docking room. The rooms had a hardwired connection point that she could plug into. Quickly looking around, she was relieved that she was just a few feet away from one. That's lucky, she thought.

Then, laptop in hand, she walked and pressed the release button on the door.

The room itself had only two doors, one to the ship where she just walked through, and the other was to the exterior of the ship. It was designed to alleviate traffic during the construction of the Aletheia. There was a single terminal at the side of the room, used to check and log the cargo being loaded on or off the ship.

Janine pulled out a support tray and placed her laptop down. She always did prefer the foldable laptops over the current roll out ones even though the rollouts didn't break half as much as the solid ones – she was a bit old fashioned that way. She reached around the back of the terminal, fixed at chest height to the wall, disconnected the data cable from the back and plugged it into her device.

After a second, the laptop flicked on and had already connected with the network. She started the test again, only this time, she knew it would only take a few seconds. While she waited, she took in her environment. The room felt small and cold, giving her the feeling that the walls could close in on her at any moment.

Shivering at the thought, she looked at the open door to a quiet, empty corridor, until she was interrupted by a ping from her laptop. She turned back, and what she saw caused an overwhelming sense of horror to rush over her. The person responsible for not only destroying all the blood stores but had been lying to everyone from the start was...

Suddenly, the door to the room closed.

Startled by the sound, Janine physically jumped, gasping with her hands over her mouth. She stood facing the closed door, trying to calm herself. Then she walked over and pressed the release button.

No response.

Goddamn wiring, she thought and pressed it again. The second time she tried, she pressed harder and held it for longer.

Nothing happened. She could hear her own breathing, echoing in the room. Trying to remain calm, she told herself, 'It's fine, it's just a faulty circuit.'

The lights from both sides of the door began to flicker again, causing an unsettling strobe effect. Her wrist buzzed, then a ship wide announcement came from the captain. The message urged everyone to return to their posts immediately.

'I'm trying,' she yelled out loud to the eerie room.

She continued to frantically tap the release button door and began to panic when her wrist strap and laptop became unresponsive to commands. If only she could send a message or call someone, but something was stopping her.

Emotions were building and building inside her. An uncontrollable sense of claustrophobia started to bear down on her. Janine could only keep pressing the button and peer desperately through the port hole, pleading that someone, anyone let her out.

She pointlessly began banging her fists on the reinforced door. When she had been a child, her older brother had once locked her in a pantry. It was dark and terrifying, much like the room she was in now. He had held the handle from the outside, laughing at her as she screamed with all her might, until her mother came and rescued her from the darkness.

For some reason, she thought about Andrew and her two sons, Billy and Josh. Her panicked mind pushed her to the question: what would happen if the universe decided to take her? Would they be ok? Would they know that she loved them with every essence of her being?

She stopped fruitlessly thumping her sore fists against the door and returned to her laptop. Then, as if she were a woman possessed, she began typing. For about five minutes straight she typed without looking away from her monitor. Focus and determination replaced fear and concern on her face. As she was overcome with emotion, tears began to run down her cheeks.

'There,' she said, standing back, rubbing the tears from her face and raising her head. 'Please, God, if something does happen, please let them see this.'

The flashing light that had been pulsing in the room, like lightning flashes from an angry sky, abruptly stopped. The room went dark, except for the glow from her laptop and the ominous red light from the planet they orbited.

Someone is outside, she thought in desperation, then spun to face the door with hopeful speed. She couldn't quite make out who was blocking the porthole, so she darted over there and froze in terror when she saw who it was.

'Can you let me out, please?' she asked diplomatically, mouthing the words carefully to be understood.

Again, she found herself just standing there, with no response from the door. At this point, she could hear her own heartbeat and the quiver in her voice as she spoke.

'L-look, whatever you have done, we can work it out. Just let me out... please.'

Trying to plead to any form of humanity, she tried her best attempt at reasoning with the person who was essentially was holding her captive.

'I have my children on board, please don't...'

A red warning light started to flash in the top right hand corner of the room, above the message 'WARNING: ROOM PRESSURISATION'.

Her stomach dropped like someone on top a rollercoaster. The room that she was in was redirecting the air supply. They were trying to kill her, but they had to have been doing it manually, because of the system failures.

She immediately ripped the panel to her left that housed a small pneumatic crank handle, but it wouldn't budge. She knew that if she didn't wind the handle anti-clockwise, the room would continue to vent, and it would be goodnight, Janine Thomas. Digging deep, with all the strength that she could muster, and screaming a last attempt war cry, she pushed as hard as she could on the handle. It moved! But only a grand total of half an inch; the bastard must have been holding it from the other side, just like her brother.

Her eyes were glazed from the tears streaming down her red face. Her face was full of sadness and regret. She wished that she had gotten to hold her baby one last time. She thought of giving Josh one last cuddle. She prayed that Andrew would find her message, and she felt sad that he would have to continue the journey alone.

The room was growing darker to her, and the sounds from outside grew more and more distant. Her field of vison started to reduce, as if someone were drawing the curtains from either side.

In her last moments, she wanted to proclaim her love for her family, but she couldn't. No breath and no more oxygen reaching her lungs, she jolted as she gasped for air, then collapsed and fell to the floor. Her last thought was of waving at her husband and her beautiful little baby, then she drifted away.

The red flashing light stopped after a minute or so, turning green to indicate that the room had been pressurised, having been stripped of all oxygen. A short time later, the room was refilled with oxygen and the door opened without any hesitation.

A person, obscured by the darkness, casually stepped over Janine's lifeless body and stopped at the laptop. The message on the screen simply said 'SENT'. Physically squeezing the sides in anger, the person tore the laptop away from the cable, snapped the lid close and left without looking back.

Chapter 25

Life

The ship's T-Drive pushed its output to a shocking 80% in getting to its unknown destination, far surpassing its first two skimming manoeuvres. Big Bob and Chris barely had enough time to engage the several safety features before the ship disappeared from its previous position and reappeared in a completely new dark, beam-less solar system. Again, the crew members found themselves feeling slightly nauseous. Doctor Tang confirmed the diagnosis. The further the distance, the more glucose the crew needed in their bodies to counteract the deficiencies left by the immense journey.

Andrew Thomas, carrying his three-year-old son Billy, had quickly made it to the engine room. His focused was divided after trying desperately and failing to get in contact with his wife Janine. He knew that the ship was experiencing communication problems. Under normal circumstances, he would have asked a neighbour to look after Billy while he went to work. However, given that the ship had decided to skim of its own accord, he decided to get to the engine as fast as he could.

Billy was unnervingly quiet, saddened face and tears welling in his eyes. Strangely, Andy felt the same. It was a feeling that couldn't shake off, completely unrelated to the ship performing a skim without warning. Something just wasn't right. As he bounced Billy in his one arm whilst running a few test simulations with the other, Andy's eyes grew wider with the results.

'That's not good,' he said, exhaling to the room. 'That's not good at all.'

Concerned onlookers Chris and Bob were standing close to Andrew. Oblivious to the situation, Billy had decided to reach for Bob's long wispy beard. Having spotted what Billy was up to, with a smile, Bob grabbed a handful of hair and pointed it towards him.

'We need to let Michael know,' Andy said grimly, looking over his shoulder. 'Can you hold him for a sec?'

Big Bob squinted with happiness at the question and simply held out his hands, waiting to see if Billy was comfortable with the idea. He was. Billy stretched out his arms, and Bob carefully removed him from his father's embrace. Chris, who was watching this from the other side of the professor, noticed how gentle Bob was with the kid. Spotting the silly look growing on his face, Bob gave him a frown, causing him to look away promptly.

'Michael?' Andy said, swiping his wrist.

'I'm here,' Michael said, voice slightly distorted by the noise of the frantic bridge in the background.

'Mike, I'm down in the engine room, and it's... bad.'

'Fire away,' Michael said, with urgency in his voice.

He took a breath and looked down at the readings, then walked over towards the still and powerless engine.

'The engine is dead, Mike. Bob and Chris had enough time to only save the basic propulsion units, but the quadcore modules and the singularity bridge have dissipated.'

'People words, man, people words,' Michael shot back quickly.

'Alright.' Andy sighed, scratching his head. He tried to explain again, 'Imagine a car engine, ok? Now imagine a car with only one super powerful spark plug, one that was designed to never fail and always perform correctly. Well, our spark plug has failed, and we are a long way from an auto repair shop.'

There was a pause for a short while, and just as Andy was about to check if Michael heard him, the captain spoke again.

'Is there any way of fixing it?'

Andrew looked around, mentally working out how to get his broken baby back up and running.

'We can do it,' Bob said reassuringly, determined.

Slowly nodding, Andrew let out a breath and answered Michael.

'It's possible to get it back, but we won't be going anywhere for months, without a huge surge of current straight to the quad cores.'

'It needs a jump start, gotcha. Well, whatever it takes. Just let me know what you need.'

'I will,' Andy said and swiped his arm. Then, he swiped once more to contact Janine. No answer. Frustrated, he looked at Bob and Chris.

'Right. Let's get to it.'

On the bridge, Commander Elizabeth Jenkins was moving from station to station, getting individual updates from the controlled but shaky officers.

'Check again?' she asked, leaning over the navigation officer.

After a few moments and keystrokes later, the officer pointed at the console in front of him and glanced up at the commander.

She immediately turned and walked over to the centre of the bridge, where Michael was performing his own detailed situation check.

'Good news or bad?' she asked, hands on her hips.

He gave her a look that said he wasn't in the mood to play, so she took a breath and decided to give it to him straight.

'Well, the good news is that all life support systems, propulsion and the artificial gravity modules are all running fine, including the modular protection for every section of the ship, which, I might add, is great. I don't fancy being sucked out of a three-inch hole because we can't isolate that part of the ship.'

'The bad news?' Michael asked, moving his display to one side and leaning forward in his chair.

'The bad news is that we are in a solar system that is not in any of the star charts that we have. The beam is so far away that we can't even equate the distance yet, and if Professor Thomas doesn't get the ship running again, we will have to find a planet in this system to set up shop.'

'Jesus Christ,' Michael uttered under his breath. 'Where the hell are we?'

Elizabeth opened her mouth to say something, but just shrugged instead.

'SIR!!!' screamed Josh Thomas, tentatively piloting the ship. 'Sir, you need to see this!'

Michael darted over to the console where Josh sat dumbfounded by what he was seeing.

'What am I looking at, kid?'

Just as the words came out of Michael's mouth, he saw it. The planet they were orbiting was a combination of tranquil blue and green colours. It had massive areas of thriving land and equally large volumes of oceans. The planet was about four times the size of the earth, but from a distance, it could have been an exact replica. There were, however, significant differences, mainly the black tar-like formations scattered all over the land.

Michael looked down at Josh, hoping with all his heart for some good news. 'Is it?'

'Yes, sir. Its atmosphere is breathable, and its gravity is weirdly the same as the earth's... What does it mean?'

Josh reached over the console and, with a flick of his finger, showed the details of the earth and this new strange world side by side.

'Ah... sir?' a wavering voice interrupted them from behind.

Michael turned to the officer pointing at his screen. 'Yeah?'

'Sir, there's... people down there.'

Michael and Elizabeth moved alongside the frail and visually shaking man, who proceeded to enlarge a picture, captured from the surface of the planet. When the picture re-focused, it showed a tiny city, backed up against a beautiful assortment of mountains. One of them had flowing meanders, leading all the way down to an ocean to the west. It was a beautiful contrast against the barren desert in the east.

Eerily, in centre of the desert, was what appeared to be a huge black crater, so dark that it reflected absolutely no light. Like a dark entity coming out from a lagoon of the unknown, vast and stretching with winding arms, reaching out towards the surrounding area.

Michael walked over to the viewing port and looked down at the gigantic wonder. He felt something that he could not explain. Some inner part of him felt like calling out directly at the planet, as if his mind wanted to randomly shout to whoever had beckoned him, 'Here I am. Now, what the hell do you want with me?'

Since the first and only time Michael had discovered his visual abilities, he decided to use his gift to see what the fifteen-million-dollar telescope might not be able to see.

Just like the last time, his eyes adapted immediately, as if commanded by sheer will alone. His sight gained focus and magnification, beyond any human capability. His eyes also adjusted to the wonderful colour spectrum, as he moved through the atmosphere. Misty pockets of violet, sunflower yellows and magnificent cerulean blue flurried through his field of vision. The colours eventually faded like a flight passing through a soft cloud, then disappeared when he reached what would have been a couple of hundred kilometres above the city.

Noticing the architecture was carefully constructed so that the main enormous temple stood proudly above the rest of the land, Michael was drawn to what was on top of the main spire. Although his eyes could not quite make out what it was, having finally reached their limit, he could see the outline of three blurry but distinctive figures, all holding the same, albeit much larger versions of the sphere that they found on the planet Red Thirteen.

Again, he found himself being pulled by the planet, like a voice in the back of his brain was saying over and over, 'Come. Come. Come.'

He turned to Elizabeth, who had been watching him inquisitively, and said in a decisive tone, 'We need to get down there.'

She noticed his shaded eyes had that tint of a glow again, but she put it down to a simple case of light trickery, some sort of coincidental refection off one of the many lit terminals on the bridge. Maybe.

'We will, but, Michael... we need to make sure that we have a ship to come back to.'

Looking yearningly at the planet, feeling its pull and feeling his whole-body pulse with apprehension, he tore his gaze away and turned back to Elizabeth. Exhaling, he slowly nodded. 'Ok, Let's get to work.'

She unexpectedly reached out and gently squeezed his arm, reassuring him though touch and her beautiful sympathetic face. Something in his face made her feel for him, as if he was emitting his emotions directly to her.

'Hey, we'll get there.'

He gave her a flicker of a smile in gratitude, and for a moment, he felt like for the first time, in a long, long while, he was not alone.

Across the Aletheia, in the ship's security office, Roman sat behind a large desk, staring directly at the door. Unflinching, he was like a gargoyle, waiting for the right moment to come to life and terrorise whoever shall disturb its slumber. Even when the door opened with its pneumatic hiss, his posture remained unchanged, and his piercing eyes remained locked on the target, unseen by any mortal man.

Boots slapped together as someone wanted to respectfully grab his attention.

'Sir,' a bruised but focused young Eric stood to attention, waiting for his superior's permission to relax.

Roman's eyes slowly travelled up, until they met Eric's, then hung there for a few seconds until finally he said, in his usual rock salt voice, 'Stand at ease, Eric.'

'Thank you, sir.'

'Take a seat.'

'I'm sorry, sir, I haven't finished sweeping the ship with the others. If you want, I can—'

'Don't worry about that for now. Sit,' Roman said, cutting Eric off, then gestured towards the chair opposite his own.

Although Eric knew that the ship and its crew were in chaos, he also knew better than to second guess Roman's orders. The bruises on his face and body were a constant and painful reminder of that.

'Eric, I have been teaching you for a while now, and you have shown great promise. You are not that little scared boy who came aboard this ship. You are a man.'

'Thank you, sir.' Eric smiled, genuinely surprised by the complement.

'I have changed you... no... improved you as a favour to you and your father. Do you agree?'

'Yes, sir, I do. I am very grateful.'

'Good. Which is why I ask for a favour. It is a very sensitive matter, so I am putting my trust in you. It is also an opportunity to honour yourself and your father.'

Eric noticed that Roman had leaned over his desk slightly, hands clasped together, displaying his white calloused knuckles. Doting on his love for his father and thinking on the undeniable truth that the man before him had been spending a lot of time on improving him, Eric did want to return the favour and show his respect, no matter what the task may be.

'How can I help?' Eric said, leaning in towards Roman, as if they were sharing a damning secret.

Roman's lips parted as he smiled, like a shark ready to tear into its prey.

'Good,' Roman said, pulling out an old-fashioned laptop from an open draw beside him. 'I want you to find out *everything* that was or is on this.'

Roman emphasised the word everything, as he handed a damaged laptop to Eric. Reaching out to take it from Roman, Eric realised that his lieutenant commander had not let go.

'Remember, little Eric, I trust that you can keep this... between us,' Roman said, losing his smile and releasing his hold.

Eric uncomfortably shifted in his seat. The look Roman just gave was more intense than that of a friend asking another for help; it did, however, carry an undertone of a threat. Eric nodded, cleared his throat and cautiously asked, 'Whose is it?'

Roman didn't answer at first; he simply leaned back in his chair, staring at Eric. Then, waving his hands dismissively, he answered, 'It was from a crew member who would have caused, how you say... anarchy on this ship. Now, take that directly to your quarters and go back to your post.'

Eric stood, holding the laptop under his arm. In one swift movement, he brought himself to attention and began to leave.

'And, Eric...,' Roman said, causing the young boy to turn by the open door. 'Your father would be proud of you.'

Eric gave a firm but grateful nod, and Roman waved him away. Then, after Eric had left the room, and the door had resealed, Roman used his fingers to rub his temples and the hemline of his scarred face. His finger brushed, just underneath his ear and felt wet to the touch. A thin line of blood appeared from a hidden scar, a scar that scaled carefully up through his hairline and continued out of sight, around the creases of his entire face.

He lowered his hand and smirked as he looked at the red-stained tip of his fore finger, chuckled from the back of his throat, then repeatedly tapped his thumb and forefinger together.

Epilogue

The walls vibrated as the large heavy doors opened for the second time in an eternity. Soot mounds danced about in the light, just like two little dust devils on an open plane. The vibrant glow of light shone inside the dark and silent chamber, casting a hallway of illumination leading to the centre of the room, towards an ancient altar.

The shape of the mysterious hooded figure began to hastily move towards the altar that was still emitting the faint neon-green glow from the last time the chamber was used. The entity waited quietly. Then, the console reacted to the presence of a user by steadily growing brighter.

Reaching out its hand, it activated the control panel. On the hand was a porcelain white gauntlet, segmented like a modern medieval glove. Above the altar, suspended in the air was the picture of Michael Quade's face as a holographic projection. Reacting to the command of the user, the display suddenly began to warp and change.

Green specks of light first came together to form a planet, larger than the one previously projected. Slowly, as if in response to the outward stretched hand rotating, the planet started to spin on an invisible axis. This continued until an object appeared in the orbit of the planet. The picture started to enlarge and render simultaneously, until a ship labelled the Aletheia came into view.

Two pluses of energy could be seen, flashing through the transparent shell of the ship. One came from a room surrounded with simple and archaic test equipment, the other came from the outline of a human who was standing in what seemed to be a control room.

Highlighting both energy sources simultaneously, the display began to relay information onto a separate display. The additional display was controlled by the hooded figure's other bare hand, which looked old, pale and fragile.

The data suddenly stopped, and suddenly, the whole room lit up with streams of ruby red, flowing up the curved walls. The display that had once been an emerald green, had drastically changed to bright crimson, emphasising the highlighted human, with a strong constant pulse.

The hooded figure pulled back with excitement, sharply turning and quickly headed straight for the exit, from which it had entered.

It was as if the chamber had come alive. The doors creeped close, leaving the red light trapped inside, which was still climbing and highlighting pictures along the walls, winding and turning inside a great flower. Finally, the red light scaled the wall, reaching a glowing... blood-red sphere.

Printed in Great Britain
by Amazon

55007314R00209